A PLUME BOOK

THE LOVER'S KNOT

CLARE O'DONOHUE is a freelance television writer/producer. She has worked worldwide on a variety of shows for the Food Network, the History Channel, and truTV, among others. An avid quilter, she also was a producer for HGTV's *Simply Quilts*.

The Lover's Knot

A SOMEDAY ✂ QUILTS MYSTERY

Clare O'Donohue

A PLUME BOOK

PLUME
Published by the Penguin Group
Penguin Group (USA) Inc., 375 Hudson Street, New York, New York 10014, U.S.A. • Penguin Group (Canada), 90 Eglinton Avenue East, Suite 700, Toronto, Ontario, Canada M4P 2Y3 (a division of Pearson Penguin Canada Inc.) • Penguin Books Ltd., 80 Strand, London WC2R 0RL, England • Penguin Ireland, 25 St. Stephen's Green, Dublin 2, Ireland (a division of Penguin Books Ltd.) • Penguin Group (Australia), 250 Camberwell Road, Camberwell, Victoria 3124, Australia (a division of Pearson Australia Group Pty. Ltd.) • Penguin Books India Pvt. Ltd., 11 Community Centre, Panchsheel Park, New Delhi – 110 017, India • Penguin Group (NZ), 67 Apollo Drive, Rosedale, North Shore 0632, New Zealand (a division of Pearson New Zealand Ltd.) • Penguin Books (South Africa) (Pty.) Ltd., 24 Sturdee Avenue, Rosebank, Johannesburg 2196, South Africa

Penguin Books Ltd., Registered Offices: 80 Strand, London WC2R 0RL, England

First published by Plume, a member of Penguin Group (USA) Inc.

First Printing, October 2008
10 9 8 7 6 5 4 3 2 1

Ⓟ REGISTERED TRADEMARK — MARCA REGISTRADA

LIBRARY OF CONGRESS CATALOGING-IN-PUBLICATION DATA

O'Donohue, Clare.
   The lover's knot : a Someday Quilts mystery / Clare O'Donohue.
      p. cm.
   ISBN 978-0-452-28979-6
   1. Quilting—Fiction. 2. Quiltmakers—Fiction. 3. Quilts—Fiction. 4. Murder—Fiction. 5. New York (State)—Fiction. I. Title.
   PS3615.D665L68 2008
   813'.6—dc22   2008016909

Printed in the United States of America
Set in Granjon
Designed by Eve L. Kirch

PUBLISHER'S NOTE
This is a work of fiction. Names, characters, places, and incidents are either the product of the author's imagination or are used fictitiously, and any resemblance to actual persons, living or dead, business establishments, events, or locales is entirely coincidental.

BOOKS ARE AVAILABLE AT QUANTITY DISCOUNTS WHEN USED TO PROMOTE PRODUCTS OR SERVICES. FOR INFORMATION PLEASE WRITE TO PREMIUM MARKETING DIVISION, PENGUIN GROUP (USA) INC., 375 HUDSON STREET, NEW YORK, NEW YORK 10014.

To my mom, for teaching me
to love words and live life

$\mathcal{A}$CKNOWLEDGMENTS

Writing may be a solitary process, but this book would not have been written without the aid of quite a few people—a few are listed here. First of all, I'd like to thank Allison Dickens and Branda Maholtz, my wonderful editors, Nadia Kashper, and the team at Plume. My agent, Sharon Bowers, and everyone at the Miller Agency. My sister Mary for serving as head cheerleader, first editor, and unofficial publicity director. My friend and fellow writer Kara Thomas, who nudged and nagged me to sit down and write. Alex Anderson for her friendship, advice, and quilting knowledge. Laura Chambers and the producers and guests of *Simply Quilts*. Cindy O'Donohue, Allison Stedman, Kelly Haran, Alessandra Ascoli, Joi De Leon, Amanda Young, Aimee Avallone, Bryna Levin, Kevin Dorff, and V for friendship, support, and for not letting me slack off. Margaret Smith, for serving as official photographer. Peggy McIntyre, for a lifetime of friendship. And my family, Dennis, Petra, Mikie, Jim, Connor, Grace, Jack, and Steven.

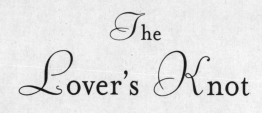

CHAPTER 1

"I'm fine," I said between sobs.

"I know you are, dear." My mother's worried voice on the other end of the phone made it clear she knew just the opposite. "Call Grandma. You can go up and stay with her for a few days."

"I will."

"And try to get a good night's sleep."

That was out of the question. I'd scheduled crying for the next few hours, followed by fits of anger, loneliness, despair and denial. An intense desire to call Ryan would likely keep me occupied from midnight to three. Then, if all went according to plan, I'd fall into an unsatisfying sleep and wake up with a splitting headache and a bed full of tissues.

I pushed the wedding invitations off the bed and watched them fan out over the floor. The envelopes bent and the response cards landed in dust. What did it matter? They were headed to the garbage anyway.

How had this happened? This morning I was happy. I had everything—almost everything. And the one thing that was missing had arrived in the afternoon.

✄

Six months ago when I announced my engagement, my grandmother Eleanor Cassidy, the formidable matriarch on my mother's side of the family, called me with a question.

"What colors do you want?"

I immediately knew she was speaking of my wedding quilt. My grandmother owns a small quilt shop in upstate New York. She has made me a quilt for all special occasions, from my first day at school to my college graduation to my first apartment. Some are large enough for a bed, but most are wall hangings—intricate, modern, and usually in her preferred bold, bright colors.

So when she asked me to choose the colors, I knew exactly how she'd react.

"Neutrals," I replied. I had already decorated the bedroom in my mind and decided it would be a soothing, restful place full of neutral colors.

"Neutrals?" I could hear the annoyance in her voice.

I laughed. "Yeah, you know tans, beiges, whites, creams. Can you do it? If not . . ."

"I can do anything." And with that she hung up. My grandmother is not a woman to waste time.

✂

When she called me and told me she was sending the quilt, I was so excited that I took a vacation day just to stay home and wait for it. Not an easy conversation to have with the boss, but I didn't care. The quilt was not only going to be beautiful, I was sure, but it was tangible proof that the wedding was approaching.

At about one o'clock, my doorbell rang.

"Good afternoon, Nell Fitzgerald. That's a huge box you're getting," the deliveryman said.

"It's from my grandmother," I told him as if he had been dying to know. "It's my wedding quilt."

Before the deliveryman had even left, I ripped open the box. At first all I saw was one large piece of fabric with an embroidered label: "Machine sewn with love by Grandma. Hand quilted by the Friday Night Quilt Club."

I pulled it out and flipped it over to the front. It was the most beautiful quilt I had ever seen: a lover's knot pattern, little strips of fabric sewn together to form interlocking diamonds. The background strips were in fabrics of soft whites and ivory, the others in subtle shades of tan and beige. It was as if the quilt were already a hundred years old—its quiet, seemingly faded colors whispering a tale of a long and happy love.

I cleared my fading comforter off the bed and spread the quilt over it. I carefully straightened and smoothed it, running my fingers over the patches and the tiny handmade stitches. My grandmother often would say that when several people work on a quilt, you could see the differences in their stitches. If you looked hard enough, she told me, you could count how many people contributed to a quilt. But as I stared, I could only see perfect stitches, one just like the next. It seemed impossible to me that five different women, the members of my grandmother's Friday Night Quilt Club, each could have worked on it.

My bed, a futon really, was only a double, so the quilt draped onto the floor, but it was beautiful enough to make even my crappy furniture look dressed up. I lay on it and closed my eyes, feeling the soft fabric with my fingers. I knew that the only thing that would make this more perfect would be the moment when my fiancé, Ryan, and I made love under this quilt for the first time.

But that was eight hours ago. Before Ryan stopped by, before he looked guilty and scared and unsure. Before he told me what he had been waiting to say for, apparently, weeks. Before the life I'd planned turned to dust.

CHAPTER 2

The train left at 12:05 p.m. Even though I had gone to Grand Central, bought a ticket and boarded the train, I still had no idea what I was doing running away to Archers Rest, and to my grandmother. What was it going to solve?

I could have stayed home, pulled the covers over my head and pretended it was a nightmare. My face was red, with the remnants of yesterday's makeup still visible. My eyes were so puffy they could barely open. My long hair, which yesterday had been neatly pulled back, was now ratty. I hadn't showered, washed my face or brushed my teeth. I looked like the sort of woman that any man with the slightest amount of common sense would leave. And yet, even looking the way I did, I knew I had to get on the train and go to the prickly comfort of my straight-talking grandmother.

As the train moved north, I tried to hide by slouching down in my seat and staring out the window, but it didn't matter. I didn't see the streets of Harlem passing by outside my window. Instead there was a horrible movie playing in my head, over and over, and I couldn't make it stop.

✄

Ryan and I met two years ago, on my first day at Garvey Publishing. We waited for the elevator together in the lobby of the building. I noticed him immediately. He was tall with neatly cut brown hair and deep brown eyes. He seemed sure of himself, without being cocky. When the elevator arrived, he waved me on first and we smiled politely to each other. He had a lovely smile, wide and sincere and welcoming. I was attracted to him the minute I saw him, but I played it cool. I stared at the elevator buttons and tried to think of something to say. But he talked first.

"Where are you going?" he asked.

"Thirty-fifth floor . . . doing layouts."

"Do you work with Amanda?"

"Yes. I guess. I don't know anyone up there. It's my first day."

At that moment the door opened to his floor, but instead of getting out, Ryan smiled and waited for the doors to close. "She's great. I'll introduce you."

We went up the additional five floors and into the layout department, where I met Amanda, a beautiful twentysomething woman who smiled quickly when she saw Ryan. I was about to be jealous until I saw a framed photo of Amanda and a *GQ*-looking man displayed on her desk. Ryan left me in her care with a wink and a softly spoken good-bye.

"I'll see you around."

When? I wanted to ask, but instead I muttered, "Sure."

From that day on he pursued me relentlessly. He called me his girlfriend on our third date, said "I love you" by the fifth, brought up the subject of marriage long before I'd even thought of him as marriage material, and proposed six months ago without so much as a hint from me.

All along I felt slightly undeserving, as if I'd won a twenty-million-dollar lottery on the only ticket I'd ever bought. But Ryan had always seemed so sure. Of me. Of us. Of everything.

But last night when he came over, he didn't seem sure of anything. He didn't really kiss me when he walked in the door, just grazed my lips absentmindedly. He walked around the place as if he had been invited for the first time, unsure of where to go.

"You're almost completely packed," he kept saying.

"We're moving into the new place soon," I reminded him.

He nodded, lightly touched a few of the boxes, and did everything to avoid my eyes. It was clear there was more than the new apartment on his mind. Not that he was talking.

So I talked. "I picked up the invitations," I said. "And I was thinking that we could spend Saturday addressing envelopes and have Sunday to do something non-wedding-related."

He nodded again. Lately he seemed to zone out every time I mentioned the wedding. "Typical cold feet" was what everyone told me. And I guessed that was true, except . . . it kept nagging at me. Something was different, more polite, more formal. But I couldn't bring myself to ask him, and he didn't seem willing to tell me. So I ignored it the best I could and kept talking.

"I was thinking that if we did invite Carla and James from work, we really don't have to invite Diane. I know they work in the same department but . . ." I knew I was rambling, but a part of me was afraid to stop talking.

He was staring at the quilt. Sitting on my bed, he had looked down and noticed that the still-draped quilt was covering the bed and half the floor.

"Isn't it great? My grandmother's wedding gift. My grandmother made the top. I told her I wanted neutrals, you know, beiges and tans and stuff, and she told me it would take months and months to get the right ones. I guess it's really hard to get neutral fabrics, even if you do own a quilt shop."

I was talking really fast, the way people do when they're nervous. First date nervous—with a man you like who may, or may not, like you. I had forgotten that feeling, and let me tell you, it did not feel good.

Ryan seemed equally ill at ease, which was actually starting to frighten me. He just kept staring at the bed. I couldn't tell if he was hearing me. He looked like he was on the verge of tears. I was hoping, just for a second, that he was overcome with love and excitement, but that seemed unlikely. He was almost panicky. I could have asked him what was wrong, pointed out the obvious, but why do that? That might lead to an open, frank discussion about our future, and who wants that with a man you're about to marry?

So I just kept talking. "It's all hand quilted by these women who come to her shop on Friday nights. They just sit around and have coffee and talk and sew. And they pitched in with the quilting so it would be done in time for the wedding. It's hand quilted. Did I tell you that?"

Now he was staring at me. And there were definitely tears in his eyes. My heart was pounding. I felt like saying "I don't want to know." But I couldn't say anything.

So he spoke first. "I'm not ready."

"Not ready for what?"

"This," he said, pointing to the quilt.

I chose deliberate stupidity, the only defense I could muster.

"It's just something to sleep under."

He made a face. I was making this hard for him. Good, I thought. I'll keep making it hard.

"What it means."

"What does it mean?" I knew he meant marriage. He knew I knew, but I couldn't let him off the hook without saying it.

"I'm not ready for marriage."

And now he had said it. I had made him say it, and now I wished more than anything I hadn't.

We both stared in silence. To an outside observer it might look as if our eyes were locked. But we were looking just past each other. I guess I was supposed to talk next, so I asked the question. The question that if you have to ask means things are not going your way.

"Is there someone else?"

"No. God no," he said quickly. "I want to be with you."

Confusing but hopeful answer. "As what?"

"I just want to wait. Get married later, when I'm ready."

He looked up at me. If he was looking for agreement, he wasn't going to find it.

"What are you asking me to do?" I asked. "Date you?"

"For a little while longer," he said, a small amount of relief in his voice.

"I feel like you're asking me to interview for a job I've already been offered."

He shook his head. But he didn't look at me, didn't say he loved me, didn't offer any further explanation. He just sat in silence. And I stood watching his silence. There was a soap opera scene in there somewhere, but I was damned if I was going to play it out.

"I think you should go," I said quietly.

He looked at me for all of a second, and then, without protest, he got up and left. And that, more than anything, broke my heart.

✂

Sitting on the train on my way to my grandmother's the next day, I knew if I kept replaying that scene I would cry again. So I took a deep breath, listened to the rhythm of the train, and concentrated on the view outside my window instead of the pictures in my head. Just as I did, the clutter of city buildings gave way to the Hudson River, wide and blue and peaceful.

The trees near the river were just beginning to turn from green to deep shades of orange, red, and purple. The whole scene was postcard lovely, and it made me feel alone.

Archers Rest was a long way from my tiny home, and there would be nothing to do except wander through my grandmother's quilt shop. I wasn't sure it would have anything to distract me or entertain me, but that didn't matter. The town had one thing that all of New York City didn't. It was Ryan-free, and that was what I needed most right then. When I left my apartment I'd grabbed my purse, a few clothes, and some makeup—but no cell phone. If Ryan called, I wouldn't be able to pick up the phone. And if he didn't, I wouldn't be there to hear the silence.

"Next stop, Archers Rest," a computerized voice came over the speaker.

I got out of my seat and waited for the train to stop, the doors to open, and my weekend of tough love to begin.

"Nell. Over here." My grandmother was waving at me as if we were still in crowded Grand Central and she had to struggle to be seen. I was the only one getting off at this stop. She was the only one waiting on the platform. I could have seen her if she stood behind a tree.

"Hi, Grandma," I said tiredly.

"You look like hell."

"Don't sugarcoat it."

She dismissed me with a wave. It was always a source of amusement to me that I had been named after her. Eleanor. It's a strong, grown-up name, and it suited my grandmother perfectly. It was how I thought of her—not cuddly, kind Grandma, but unbreakable force Eleanor. Despite sharing the name, I was not an unbreakable force. Someone must have realized that early on, since I was nicknamed Nell almost from the time I was born.

"You're supposed to say something comforting, like 'You look gorgeous,' " I teased her.

"You don't need any more lies, do you?" Eleanor smiled as we walked to her car.

"I need sleep."

"Sleep you can have. And lunch. What are you in the mood for?"

"Anything fattening."

I really wish I were one of those people who couldn't eat in a crisis. My coworker and now friend Amanda went on the "heartbreak diet" every time she ended a promising romance (which was usually every four months). When we met she was madly in love with a blond Adonis, until four months later when his picture was in the trash. It was all she could do to eat an apple. Amanda dropped ten pounds in the month it took her to meet a handsome banker. When his picture ended up in the trash six months after that, she was off food for three weeks until the next one came along. Last week she'd been eating Hostess Cupcakes at her desk so I knew she was in love again, but I hadn't yet met the latest.

I wished I could follow her system, but I was beginning to see I had one all my own. Break my heart and I'll eat everything in sight.

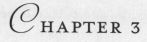

CHAPTER 3

As we turned into my grandmother's driveway I felt, temporarily, better. She lived in a huge, white Victorian, where she'd raised my mother and uncle. It had four large bedrooms, three fireplaces, a library, butler's pantry, two secret passages, and one dog, Barney, the latest in a long line of golden retrievers.

Normally the house was picture-book ready, with flowers crowding the beds in front and immaculately trimmed bushes lining the drive. But this time the view was marred by a scratched and dented red pickup truck and piles of roofing debris on the lawn.

"What . . ." I started to ask.

"Marc Reed," she said, as if I had any clue who he was. I made a face at her to express my confusion.

She beeped her horn and pointed up. So I looked. On her roof stood a brown-haired, shirtless man in his thirties—a man who looked as though he'd earned every muscle from hard work. He waved.

"Marc Reed," she said again. "Fixes roofs, builds furniture, does odd jobs. Very handy." She pulled up in front of the house and stopped the car. "Not hard on the eyes either."

"Grandma!"

She shrugged. "I'm not recommending him, mind you. Not unless you want more trouble than you already have." I said nothing, but I did look. "I need to see how he's getting on with that patch," she continued. "You go inside."

She walked off to talk with Marc, who climbed down the ladder, smiling at me as he descended. Up close he looked just as fit and tanned as he had on the roof. His hair was cut short, and seemed dark red in the sun and light brown as he moved into the shadows. He had small lines outlining his deep blue eyes and long eyelashes that curled slightly as he blinked. He was the picture of laid-back good looks, but there was something in his eyes that made me uncomfortable.

Embarrassed at being so easily rattled by the slightest bit of male attention, I mumbled something about being hungry and headed into the house.

✂

"I have some cake left over from Nancy's birthday," my grandmother told me as she walked inside, finding me still in the hallway. "You remember Nancy? She's the woman who helps out at the shop."

"I've met her dozens of times." I smiled. "Are you starting to forget things?"

"One of the pleasures of old age," she answered with a wink. "Do you want coffee or tea?"

"Tea, I guess. Where's Barney? Why didn't he come to the door?"

"Vet says he's going deaf. Getting old like me," she said. "Try the living room. And tell him to come into the kitchen for lunch."

I turned left into the enormous living room. Eleanor kept the furnishings sparse. There was only a couch, two chairs, and one table to fill the room. As a child it was a perfect place to play tag, and my sister and I often ran circles around the couch, trying frantically to get to the "safe" spot—the marble fireplace with an ornately carved mantle. It was also the place where Eleanor kept some of her more precious quilts. Two made by Grace Roemer, the woman who had taught my grandmother to quilt, and three she made herself. I'd always loved her quilts, but before today I hadn't realized just how much comfort I took in looking at them.

I ran my fingers along a quilt with brightly colored stars against a black background. (Amish style, Eleanor had once explained to me.) The pieces that made the stars were small, no more than two inches each, and the quilting was an elaborate echo of the pieced pattern, making it seem as if stars were bursting all over the quilt. But because the quilted stars were stitched only in black thread, they stood silent against the background. All that work for something that you couldn't even see unless you were two inches from the quilt. I wondered why anyone would bother, and yet I wanted desperately to have created something that held such quiet surprises.

"Nell," I heard my grandmother call, in that insistent "stop wasting my time" voice. "The food is ready. And bring Barney."

I was so caught up in the quilt that I hadn't noticed who lay by the windows at the far end of the room. The afternoon sun was bringing a glow to the entire room, and basking in it was my grandmother's companion, Barney.

I walked over and knelt beside him, and he turned his head back to see who it was. He was, at first, startled, then embarrassed at being caught unawares, then within seconds unreservedly joyous at seeing me. Nearly twelve years old, gray around the snout, and happily plump, he still had the joy of a pup. Old or not, that dog could wag. We kissed and hugged and played until I heard my grandmother's voice again.

"Nell," she called.

I got up and started toward the kitchen. Barney bounded after me. When we reached the kitchen, his excitement began again at the sight of Eleanor. She reached down and patted his head.

"What's all the fuss, old man?" she asked him. "Did you think I'd left town or something?"

Barney wagged his tail even harder in response. When he was sufficiently petted, he settled into a large bed stuffed with toys. My grandmother's uncluttered decorating style clearly had not rubbed off on the dog.

✂

There was more than cake on the table. There was a spread of ham and turkey, bread still warm from my grandmother's oven, a green salad and a homemade potato salad, as well as the cake, two éclairs, and piping hot tea.

Without a word, I piled my plate with a bit of everything and devoured as much as I could. Suddenly I was starving.

"It's a good sign that you're hungry." Eleanor winked at me.

"It's good food," I said between bites.

She watched me eat for a few minutes. "I'm going to head to the shop. I can't expect Nancy to hold down the fort for too long. Poor girl. She's very sweet, but no head for business."

"I'm going to take a nap, then," I said.

"It will do you a world of good." She nodded. "And if you want, when you get up you can walk over to the shop."

"I won't be up for several hours."

"Doesn't matter. It's Friday night. Sometimes we're there until midnight."

She got up and Barney got up with her. "I'll leave him with you for company." She motioned for him to stay. "But bring him with you if you come."

"Is he one of the regulars?" I smiled.

She rolled her eyes. "Those girls have made more quilts for Barney than they've made for their own grandchildren." She pointed to Barney's bed. Now that the dog was up again I was able to see at least five small quilts lining the bed, each with dog fabrics or appliquéd bones. Above the bed was a quilt with a likeness of Barney sleeping on the bed, with a dream bubble of a Russell terrier with a pink bow.

"Who's she?" I asked.

"Nancy's dog, and his girlfriend." She rolled her eyes. "Get your sleep and I'll see you later."

CHAPTER 4

After Eleanor left, I helped myself to a second slice of cake and two more cups of tea until even I couldn't eat anymore. I spent twenty minutes debating with Barney whether I should call my cell phone to check for messages. I could tell by the way he rested his head on my lap that he was against it. So I got up and headed upstairs.

The house had once belonged to a pretty wealthy New York family who used it on weekends. I'm sure most people thought it was too large for a single elderly woman, but somehow Eleanor filled the space. Her bedroom was a sparsely furnished one at the top of the stairs, with photos of my grandfather Joe and their children and grandchildren on the walls, and a large blue and white check quilt on the bed.

With Barney by my side, I walked to the other end of the hall, to the massive sewing room that had once been a master bedroom. It was the only place in the house that could be called cluttered. There were at least a half dozen unfinished quilt tops, three sewing machines, including a black Singer Featherweight, and probably more fabric than Eleanor had at the shop. It looked a bit chaotic, but I knew it all made sense to my grandmother.

On either side of the hallway next to the sewing room were two small rooms. One had been my uncle's, and was now an office with a desk and sleeper sofa. The other had once been my mother's and still held some of her dolls and other toys. But more important, it had a comfy queen-size bed in the middle of it and two quilts piled on top. It was the perfect guest room, and I looked forward to it every time I came to visit.

Suddenly my body felt heavy and tired, so I pulled the thick velvet drapes closed, shutting out the light and the world at the same time. I climbed into bed, got under the covers, and closed my eyes.

The last sound I heard as I fell into a deep, hard sleep was Barney circling and collapsing on the floor.

✂

Four hours later when I finally returned to consciousness, the room was completely dark. Aside from the sound of Barney's breathing, everything was quiet. For someone used to city noise, with honking cars and people talking and laughing in the street below, the house had become almost spooky. And very, very dark.

I felt around for a light and turned on a small Tiffany-style lamp on the nightstand. That much was easy, but getting out of the warm bed was proving to be more difficult. According to my watch it was almost nine o'clock. I knew there wasn't much to do in this house, or in the town for that matter. By nine o'clock every business would be shut down for the night. Except Someday Quilts. And that I couldn't face. Inside the shop were my grandmother's friends. Women who didn't even know me but had labored over a wedding quilt for me. And now I would never use it.

Rather than lay there and feel sorry for myself, I got out of bed and headed down the hallway. In my apartment I kept the television on for company almost constantly. But the only television in Eleanor's house was in the kitchen, so my grandmother could watch the news in the morning while she made breakfast. Other than that, she didn't see the point in, as she saw it, wasting valuable time. The kitchen was as good a place as any for me, though. I could have another snack.

I hadn't even found the remote for the television before Barney woke and came after me, nudging me and whimpering. I've never owned a dog, but even I understood the meaning. Barney wanted out.

"Give me a second," I told him. I was about to grab his leash when I thought about what my grandmother had said about my looking like hell. "I'll wash my face and we'll go for a walk."

Barney whimpered in response. He looked at me, his happy face showing stress and anxiety. Either he really had to go or there was something in the darkness outside that demanded his attention.

✂

Barney was already at the front door by the time I'd found my shoes. It had been warm in New York in the morning, and among the many things I'd neglected to bring was a jacket. I reached inside the coat closet in the entryway and found one of my grandmother's wool cardigans, gray and intricately knitted. There were patches on the elbows, to cover spots worn from years of use. It smelled of my grandmother and it comforted me. At that moment if I could have borrowed her unwavering ability to face life, good and bad, I would have, but I settled for the sweater.

Barney did his business quickly but made it clear he was not going back to the house. Instead he trotted ahead of me, sniffing happily and turning occasionally to make sure I could keep up. I'd forgotten to take his leash, so I had no choice but to follow him and hope he knew where he was going. But as we got farther and farther from the house I realized he knew exactly where he was going, and I didn't like it one bit.

"Come back, Barney," I called out. "We have to go home now."

Instead, he kept walking. I wasn't sure if this time he ignored me because of his hearing problem or because he had his own plans. I walked a little faster, but I couldn't quite keep up. Barney seemed to be making a game of it, staying just a little out of my reach, going up the road leading into town.

When we arrived on Main Street, Barney took one last look at me and slowed his pace a little. He looked as if he might stop at the diner next to my grandmother's shop. If I could catch him while he was in front of the diner, then I might be able to drag him away before anyone saw us. In all the times I had visited my grandmother I'd managed to avoid her Friday Night Quilt Club. It wasn't that I had any objection to the club or to the women who made up the group; I just didn't want to sit around being polite to a bunch of my grandmother's friends. I tried to explain this to Barney. He must have understood because he teased me by sitting right outside the diner, directly in front of a huge FOR LEASE sign in the window. Three more steps and the light from the quilt shop would ruin my plan. I moved slowly. Barney watched me, the corners of his mouth turned up into a slight grin. I inched toward him. And just when I was about to grab his collar, he barked, jumped up, and bounded for the door of Someday Quilts. I didn't move. I clung to the hope that I might be able to escape.

"Are you okay, miss?"

I looked up to see a man walking toward me. As he passed the shop, he stopped for a moment to pet Barney, who wagged delightedly and jumped all over him. They were clearly old friends. The man's suit looked as though it had just come from the cleaners, but he didn't seem to mind getting it messed up. He looked about thirty, with dark hair and small, intellectual-looking glasses. I would have guessed history teacher or accountant, but when he leaned over I saw a metal object underneath his jacket. As I looked at it, I realized it was a gun.

"Yes, I'm fine," I said. I didn't know whether to be scared. Barney clearly wasn't. But then I was becoming alarmed about something else. His presence was attracting attention from inside the quilt shop. The man waved at someone in the shop, then looked back at me.

"I'm Jesse Dewalt," he said to me as he stretched out his hand. "You're Eleanor's granddaughter, I guess."

"How did you know that?" I asked as I shook his hand.

"It's a small place."

"And who might you be?" My eyes were on the gun peeking out from under his suit coat. He adjusted his coat to hide the gun.

"Sorry, I should have introduced myself," he answered in a quiet, serious tone. "Chief of Police here in town. I'm out making my nightly rounds."

"You don't look like a cop," I said stupidly. "I mean, you're not in uniform or anything."

"No, not tonight." He didn't crack a smile.

I smiled, if for no other reason than to show him how it was done. But he didn't return the gesture, just waved at Barney, nodded toward me, and kept walking. He hadn't exactly been friendly, but Barney liked him and that was as good a reference as a person can get. I found myself watching Officer Jesse walk off into the darkness.

And that was a mistake. It was just the opening Barney was looking for. He scratched at the entrance to the shop and barked a friendly hello. There was really no way to leave Barney there and sneak home. My grandmother would be upset if she thought I'd let the dog go off on his own. And it was clear now, thanks to my momentary interest in Officer Jesse, that Barney was outside. I was left with no choice. So I made the best of it. I opened the door.

Inside the shop my grandmother was laughing with the women sitting in a circle around her. For a half second I wondered if they were laughing at my broken engagement, but I knew that was only my bruised ego talking.

"Look who's here," my grandmother said as she waved me to come in. "How was your nap? It was a long one."

"Just what I needed."

I moved in a little but still stayed close to the door. Barney, on the other hand, bounded into the middle of the circle to greet each of his ladies in turn. I don't think any of them noticed me until they were done greeting him. When they did they each smiled enthusiastically.

"The granddaughter," the oldest one said. I remembered her from my childhood visits. Maggie Sweeney, one of Eleanor's dearest friends and a stern presence to a ten-year-old, and to me now. She looked the way old women used to look before they were running corporations and skydiving at eighty years old. She had gray hair pulled back in a bun and wore one of those Laura Ashley–style dresses, with a black floral print and a white lace collar. She had a warm face, though, and the greenest eyes I'd ever seen.

"She is," my grandmother said, and looked around the room with a warning. "And nobody give her a hard time."

The women nodded and smiled at me again.

"Sit down," said another, and someone took some fabric off a chair in the corner and moved the chair to the circle. The whole group inched closer to leave enough space for me to join them.

I sat and tried to meet their smiles with my own. It was all very uncomfortable.

"These are the girls," Eleanor said with a sweep of her hand. "Except Nancy. She couldn't come tonight."

"She's missed a lot of meetings lately," said one woman.

"Well, I suppose she spends enough time at the shop as it is."

"Enough about who isn't here. Let's talk about who is," Maggie said.

"Hi, Mrs. Sweeney," I said, "it's nice to see you again." Then I turned to the others. "I'm Nell."

"Everyone knows that, dear," said a blonde with deep blue eyes and heavy makeup, who looked to be in her fifties. "Eleanor filled us in on all the details."

I shot an angry look toward my grandmother, who smiled at me innocently. The rest of the women seemed to be studying me, waiting for me to launch into a story or burst into tears or otherwise entertain them. Instead I sat with an idiotic smile on my face and an embarrassed look in my eyes, trying to feel less strange in a room full of strangers.

"Leave her alone, Mom," came a voice from the back. Finally, someone on my side. I turned to see a woman about my age coming up from the basement. "I'm Natalie. Don't worry. They're just excited to have a new recruit," Natalie assured me. She was the picture of her mother, blond and blue-eyed, but Natalie wore no makeup at all, and she didn't need to. "They won't rest until every man, woman, and child knows how to quilt."

"Are you interested in quilting?" Maggie turned to me, suddenly excited.

"She's got talent but no discipline," my grandmother offered. "I've tried to teach her."

"I was twelve," I said in my own defense, then regretted it because I knew what was coming.

"Well, if she has talent, then there's hope," said another woman who had been quiet up until then.

"I don't have a lot of time," I said. A weak excuse, but something.

The heavily made-up blonde answered with a dismissive wave. "You're in," she laughed. "And once you're in, there's no getting out. Unless you die."

They all laughed. I laughed a little too, but it was a nervous laugh.

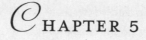

CHAPTER 5

For the next dizzying hour I was introduced and reintroduced and then quizzed by each member of the club. It didn't surprise me that Maggie was the leader, even with Eleanor in the room. A former librarian, she had raised eleven children and now had twenty-five grandchildren. Every one of them had at least one quilt, hand sewn by Maggie, who didn't believe any machine, even a sewing machine, could do as good a job as a person.

Natalie was twenty-eight, only one year older than me, and the mother of a ten-month-old. She had a husband everyone in the group described as "tall, dark, and handsome," which made Natalie roll her eyes. Her mother, Susanne, was the one with the makeup counter on her face. She turned out to be the artist of the group. Her quilts had won ribbons at national shows, and one had even been featured in a magazine.

"I got married very young," she said to me. "Too young, I think. Didn't have a chance to figure out who I was, as they say."

"Have you figured it out yet?" came a voice from the other side of the group. Bernadette, known in the group as Bernie, was a hangover from of the sixties, now in her sixties. She was another familiar face among the crowd. I knew I had been introduced and reintroduced to her over the years, but the only thing I'd ever learned about her was that she owned the pharmacy in town and she had a warm, friendly face.

Susanne smiled toward Bernie. "Have I figured myself out yet?" she laughed. "I don't think I want to know anymore. I certainly don't want to know who my husband is."

The others laughed with her. "I was nineteen," said Maggie. "I found out pretty quickly it isn't always roses and I love yous."

"You got roses?" shouted Bernie. "I don't think any of my husbands got me roses."

"Why would you marry men who were so unromantic?" Natalie asked.

"The sex was good," Bernie retorted. All the woman roared with laughter.

"Bernie, we have a newcomer in the room," my grandmother admonished.

Bernie looked at me. "She won't be a newcomer for long." Bernie leaned in. "I have stories that could make even a girl living in New York blush." Then she looked toward Eleanor. "But I won't." She turned to the fifth member of the group. "Carrie here, she has a romantic story to tell, if that's what you're looking for."

Carrie was, it looked to me, in her late forties. She began to tell me about herself but was interrupted by Bernie and Natalie, who felt they could tell Carrie's life story much better. Apparently she had married right out of college, divorced three years later, and spent the next fifteen looking for Mr. Right, while amassing a small fortune as a New York stockbroker. When he didn't appear, she decided to have a child. She quit her job, moved to Archers Rest, and scaled her lifestyle back so she could work as a consultant and stay home with her baby. It was a good plan, but she soon found a better one. Months after she gave birth to her son, she married his pediatrician. Now they also had a daughter.

"It wasn't quite what I expected," she said to me. "But it worked out." All the women voiced their agreements. It was a not very subtle nod to my uncertain future, but it was much appreciated.

>%

Every Friday, these woman cleared out a small amount of floor space amid an overflowing stock of fabric, patterns, rulers, and quilt-related books. Then they sat in a circle to gossip, eat sugar-laden treats and drink (only caffeinated) coffee. They passed around their latest quilting projects and complained about what they called UFOs, or "unfinished objects," as Maggie explained.

"It happens when you start something with a great deal of excitement and then run out of interest about halfway through," Maggie told me.

"Are we talking about marriage again?" Susanne laughed.

"Stop putting marriage down," her daughter Natalie protested. "Some of us are happily married."

Maggie let out an exaggerated sigh and continued. "The trick is not to get stubborn about it. If the project doesn't work, then you have to let it go."

"That must be frustrating," I said.

Bernie's eyes lit up and she leaned toward me. "It's freeing," she said, exaggerating the length of the words to, I'm guessing, make their importance clear. And they must have been important words, because the others all nodded in agreement. "With every quilt you make you have a picture in your mind of what it *should* be," Bernie continued. "Then you start. You pick fabrics, you cut the fabrics, you sew the pieces together. All along there are compromises, mistakes, inspirations. When it works, then you are truly holding your dreams in your hands. When it doesn't . . ." She shrugged.

"You just throw it out?" I asked, looking to my grandmother

for confirmation. Eleanor saved bags of two-inch pieces of fabric, "just in case." She kept a plastic bag with fabric and a needle to sew whenever she had time to kill. I couldn't believe my grandmother would endorse wasting hours of work for artistic reasons. But she was nodding along with the rest of them.

"We trade sometimes," Carrie admitted. "Or sew them into charity blankets."

"I have a lot, so I usually give mine to Nancy," Natalie admitted. "She finishes them off and sends them to her son's college friends, who I guess don't really care what the quilts look like as long as they're warm."

Maggie patted Natalie's hand, as if to comfort her for having so many UFOs. It was an odd pair. Watching seventy-five-year-old Maggie laughing easily with Natalie, nearly fifty years her junior, made me a little envious. Aside from quilting, the two seemed to have little in common, but quilting was enough to bind them together. I wondered if my friendships were as tight.

But envy was one thing; joining the group was an entirely different matter. Suddenly, all I wanted was to head back to the house and sleep. I yawned.

"Oh, she's tired," Carrie pointed out.

"You should get her home, Eleanor," suggested Bernie.

"The poor thing, she needs her rest," agreed Susanne.

"I am sleepy," I volunteered, and yawned again.

My grandmother nodded and patted Barney's head. "Barney, take her home."

Barney got up, went one more time around the circle to say his good-byes, and led me to the door.

"We'll see you next Friday," the group said in unison.

"Oh," I stammered, "I don't think so. I'm only here for the weekend."

I opened the door and was almost free when I realized that

all night I'd forgotten something. I turned back. "Thank you all for the quilt you made me. It's more beautiful than I could have imagined."

They each looked at me as if they were about to cry. As I left the shop, I knew the subject of my breakup had started up again.

CHAPTER 6

Morning came too soon. I could hear my grandmother down-stairs and I knew it was only a matter of time before she came up looking for me.

Instead she sent her assistant. My door started to open slowly, and a blond furry snout sniffed in the opening. There was a grunt, more pushing, and then Barney was in the room, wagging his tail and sniffing at the bed for signs of life.

There was no point in staying in bed with this hairy alarm clock drooling and whimpering. I got up and made my way toward the kitchen to find myself some coffee.

"Are you up?" My grandmother stood at the door to the kitchen.

"Nope." I smiled. "Still in bed."

"Then you should get dressed."

"I was going to eat first."

"No food," she said, and she walked past me to the front of the house.

No food? There was always food at her house. And not just food. Hot out of the oven blueberry crumble, melt in your mouth pot roast, garlic mashed potatoes. How could there not be food?

I love my grandmother, but one of the reasons I came to visit was the food. In New York, I'd gotten used to grabbing a muffin for breakfast, a salad for lunch, a slice of pizza for dinner. I had a kitchen the size of most people's linen closets, so aside from making coffee, my cooking skills—such as they were—went unused. My grandmother, on the other hand, was a maestro in the kitchen. And though she also lived alone, she cooked every day. She cooked for herself, of course, but also for several senior citizens who, as she put it, "needed a little help to get going every day." She cooked for school bake sales, town picnics, and for the charity drives of all three churches in town. If someone needed help, my grandmother was there with a pie.

Except, apparently, today.

✂

I went after her to at least get her to make me some scrambled eggs. I found my grandmother by the front door talking quietly with Nancy.

"Well hello." Nancy smiled as I walked toward her. "I wondered whether our paths would cross this weekend."

"Hi, Nancy." I hugged her lightly. "It's been a while."

"Well, a city girl can't be expected to find many reasons to come up here," she said.

"Thanks," my grandmother responded sarcastically.

"Don't take offense, Eleanor. It's good she has her own life." She looked me up and down. "Are you staying for a while this time?"

"No. I'm leaving tomorrow."

"See, what did I tell you. A life of her own." Nancy picked up a bundle of small quilts, each about two feet square. The top one was an appliquéd autumn tree with leaves in at least a dozen shades. The piece was simple but it had such depth.

Nancy's work was a combination of sewing, threadwork, and beading. She made landscapes, scenes of people at play, animals, and abstracts. I'd seen Nancy's beautiful handiwork before, and it always amazed me. Before she could stop me, I grabbed the bundle and began looking at the others.

"This is a work of art," I told her.

"Nonsense," she said, taking the quilts back from me. "It's just something I do as an outlet."

"You could sell those," I said.

"I've been saying that for years," my grandmother agreed.

Nancy just blushed. "I make them for my children," she answered, patting the quilts smooth.

My grandmother changed the subject. "Nancy volunteered to open up the shop today, so we can spend some time together." Then she nodded toward me. I understood the gesture immediately. My mother used to do the same head nod when my uncle gave me a piece of candy.

"Thanks, Nancy," I said obediently and looked toward Eleanor, who smiled.

"No worries at all. Happy to do it. I'd do anything for your granny, you know. Just like most people in town."

Nancy headed for the door, and so did we.

"Did you take the deposit to the bank last night?" my grandmother asked as Nancy was leaving. "You know I hate leaving money in the shop overnight. Makes a great target for thieves."

"Honestly, Eleanor," said Nancy with a laugh. "I'm the one who makes the deposits. And I did it last night like I do every night." She left quickly, not waiting for Eleanor's usual sharp reply.

My grandmother just muttered to herself and handed me something. "It's chilly. Take this."

It was a worn-out leather men's jacket, the sort of jacket that would sell in Manhattan for hundreds of dollars, and in Archers Rest would be donated to charity.

"Where are we going?"

"I thought you were hungry" was all she would say.

It was a beautiful fall day. As we walked, I found that I was enjoying the sunshine, the falling leaves, and the quiet of small-town life. And then I thought, how romantic it was, and I was depressed again.

Heartbreak requires concentration. If you forget for a moment that you've been dumped, you might enjoy a bit of sunshine and then, *wham,* you remember. Then you feel bad about being dumped all over again. I needed to stay depressed, but I couldn't think of anything in Archers Rest that was bad enough to keep me that way.

CHAPTER 7

Archers Rest, like a lot of towns on New York's Hudson River, was first established in the 1600s by Dutch settlers. The head of the group was man named James Archer, who died the first winter. He was buried in a small field on the edge of a town that in the nearly four hundred years since grew into a large cemetery, with almost seven thousand graves. Since Archers Rest had only five thousand living residents, there were more dead than alive in the little town.

I thought it was a delightfully morbid fact about the town, but my grandmother dismissed me. "It's big enough that you don't know everyone but small enough that even strangers have friends in common," she had told me once. And everyone had friends in the cemetery.

Archers Rest runs along the river, so we followed the river's edge from my grandmother's house to Main Street. We turned down the street past the hardware store, a pharmacy, and the post office.

As we got to the end of the street I saw Someday Quilts just ahead. Inside lights were on and Nancy was in the doorway changing the sign from CLOSED to OPEN.

"Why doesn't Nancy come to your quilt club?" I asked.

"She does when she can," Eleanor said tiredly, as though this were old territory for her. "Her husband isn't well and it's difficult for her." She seemed to be choosing her words carefully. "Sometimes she likes to leave a little early on Friday. She closed the shop an hour early yesterday."

"She just wanted to get home?" I asked.

"Perhaps." Eleanor looked at me. "I believe you said you were hungry. So I expect you to eat plenty."

My stomach was making quiet rumbling sounds that were about to get a whole lot louder. But in a typical bit of grandmother irony, we arrived at the one restaurant in town that made me nearly lose my appetite—the diner next to her shop.

✄

The place seemed old and tired. At the front were four small Formica tables with two chairs each, and every one was taken. Past them were booths on either side. The seats were reddish-brown leatherette, but small rips at the seams revealed hints of the bright red they must have been thirty years before. There was a sign on the wall that announced the special of the day, meatloaf. It looked as if that had been the special since the diner's opening. There was no decoration anywhere, unless you counted what was obviously a thin layer of dust covering everything. I didn't care, though. I just wanted food.

"I can't believe this place still exists," I said. "Has the food improved?"

"It's not about the food. It's about the people," my grandmother said as we walked in. "The owner was good to me when I opened the shop, and I like to support her."

Natalie and Susanne were at a table near the back, with Natalie's ten-month-old son, Jeremy, in a high chair. They waved us over and handed us menus, which I immediately began studying.

"It's a shame this place is closing," my grandmother said.

"Carrie was talking about opening up a coffee shop. This would be a good space," Natalie offered.

"Oh, she's just talking," Susanne disagreed, and then as if explaining to me, she continued. "Carrie sometimes misses being a high-powered businesswoman."

"Who wouldn't?" interrupted Natalie. "It must be so exciting to live in New York City and have a cool job and go out to fancy restaurants all the time."

"Yeah, it must be," I laughed. "Most of the time I eat a salad in my cubicle."

"What are you talking about? Eleanor said you work at a news magazine. I don't read it, but it sounds glamorous. My husband and I are pretty simple high school graduates." She laughed. "A hairdresser and a mechanic. Nothing glamorous, like your life."

"That's nonsense. There's nothing simple about either of you," her mother interrupted. "Anyway, where does glamour get you? Carrie gets ideas in her head all the time about opening a business. Last year it was an antique shop, this year it's a coffee shop."

"Last year it was a child care business. The antique shop was the year before," Natalie corrected her.

"Regardless," said Susanne, "she never follows through."

It was like being at a tennis match, going back and forth between mother and daughter while my grandmother silently drank her coffee.

"She doesn't go through with it," Susanne continued, looking just at me, "because as your own grandmother can tell you, owning your own business is a twenty-four-seven job."

Then they switched topics, talking about a favorite quilt show they all watched. My food had arrived, so I kept busy wolfing down pancakes and bacon. Only baby Jeremy had less concern for etiquette.

"How do you stay so thin?" marveled Natalie, watching me.

"Depression eating." I laughed, but I put down my fork.

"You're allowed," Susanne reassured me.

Both Susanne and Natalie gave me that "poor thing" look that I had seen last night at the shop.

"Yes. This weekend." My grandmother suddenly sounded stern. "After this weekend you have to get on with your life. He made a big mistake, and gaining twenty pounds won't change that."

She was right, of course, but rather than admit it, I changed the subject. "What will happen to this place if Carrie doesn't buy it?"

"She won't," said Susanne, a little too sure. "Probably someone from New York will take it. Someone coming up in search of a nice quiet life."

"Turn it into a hip little restaurant like they must have in your neighborhood," said a suddenly excited Natalie. "Put in WiFi and serve chai tea."

"Are you speaking English?" Susanne looked at her completely perplexed.

Natalie just rolled her eyes. "They'll make it like a city place, is what I'm saying."

I looked around. It wasn't impressive. Even though it was a diner, it would still have to be stripped to the joists to turn it into the kind of trendy place the women thought it would become. I had a better idea.

"Why don't you take it?" I asked my grandmother.

"Me? What do I need with a diner?"

"Expand the shop." I looked around again. Since it needed a major remodeling, it could be anything. "You could knock down the wall between your place and this and double your selling space."

"Someday is packed to the rafters, El," agreed Susanne. "You could put in a classroom. You've always wanted a classroom."

Eleanor looked around the diner. "Needs work," she said.

We all nodded. It was impossible to ignore that it was a big job. "Well, maybe it is too much for you," I started to agree.

She looked at me. Even Natalie and Susanne recognized that I had challenged my grandmother, and she would find it irresistible.

"Could be done," Eleanor finally admitted. "Where's the bill? I need to go to work."

✄

Susanne, Natalie, and Jeremy had already said good-bye and left, and I walked to the door, but my grandmother hesitated. I could see that she was quietly examining the diner. I knew what I saw— torn leatherette booths and soda machines—but I could tell by the look in her eyes that in her mind the place was already filled floor to ceiling with fabric.

CHAPTER 8

We walked next door to the shop my grandmother had owned for more than thirty years. And looking at it, it might seem as if she hadn't gotten rid of anything the entire time.

The quilt shop had a treasure hunt quality to it. While there were organized shelves with bolts of fabric lined up by color, there were just as many bolts leaning up against the wall. Fabrics of colorful flowers, cute baby animals, and Christmas prints were piled on top of one another near the cash register at the front.

To get to the rest of the shop, you had to make a semicircle around a dangerously overloaded rack of books and down an aisle that was one person deep.

If you did, you would be rewarded with a dazzling display of quilts. Eleanor had made the large, wildly colorful ones with abstract patterns that appeared to follow no rules. Nancy, on the other hand, was clearly the creator of the small, carefully constructed and elaborately quilted pieces. In the center was one of Eleanor's favorites—a small, bright log cabin quilt that Grace, the woman who taught her to quilt, had made. Each was enough to inspire even me to take up quilting.

Nancy caught me staring at the quilts. "Are you ready to make one of your own?"

"At some point," I admitted.

"Well, I'd be happy to help you learn, if you like." She reached her hand out and touched one of her wall hangings. "Making a quilt can be the answer to so many problems."

Then she sighed, grabbed a ruler from a nearby basket, and headed back to the front of the shop. I'd liked Nancy from the moment she came to work at my grandmother's shop more than ten years ago. She seemed rooted to Archers Rest. I don't think she'd been more than fifty miles from it for years, but she'd made sure her sons had the chance to go off to bigger things if they wanted. One was in medical school and the other, Nancy proudly told me, was planning to spend his junior year of college in Italy.

"What are you doing?" My grandmother's voice snapped me to attention. "Are you caught in a trance over there?"

I turned quickly, knocking over a display of scissors and rotary cutters.

"You could definitely use more space," I said to justify my clumsiness. "If you knocked a wall down you could put up more shelves and get some of this stuff off the floor."

"Knock a wall down?" Nancy asked as she moved back in our direction.

"I was telling my grandmother that she should lease the diner space and expand the shop."

"What a nice idea. Eleanor, do you think you will?"

"For heaven's sake, Nancy, I have enough on my hands with this space, let alone taking on more expense and trouble." My grandmother walked away from us to help a woman pulling bolt after bolt of fabric off a shelf.

"I think she's worried that she's getting too old for so much work," Nancy said in a low whisper.

"Really?" was all I could say. To me, my grandmother had always been old and always ageless. When I was born she was almost fifty, and now she was in her midseventies. Even now she seemed to have more energy than I did. Or maybe it was just that she used her energy in more focused ways.

"I think it would be exciting to expand the shop." Nancy looked around. "Give it a little face-lift."

"If you want a face-lift . . . ," Eleanor started as she finished up with her customer.

"Too late to do me any good," Nancy laughed. "I just think it would be fun."

It would be, I thought. I considered writing down some ideas, making myself useful.

"I know we have more six-inch rulers." My grandmother was done dreaming and had returned to the business at hand. "But I can't find any."

"Downstairs," said Nancy. "I'll get them."

As she said that, two more women came into the shop. And behind them Carrie entered with two small kids in tow.

"I'll get it," I volunteered. "You guys are getting busy."

"Will you know what they are?" my grandmother asked, concerned.

"Six-inch rulers are rulers that measure six inches, right? Or is that some clever quilting code to fool nonbelievers?"

My grandmother was not a fan of sarcasm. Well, that's not true. She wasn't a fan of my sarcasm. She was perfectly fond of her own.

"They're in a box by the back corner," said Nancy. "I think they're under a pile of other boxes. Just bring up three or four. We haven't room for more."

"Just be careful," Eleanor said.

"What's the worst that could happen? I'm in a quilt shop," I threw back at her as I headed toward the stairs.

At the very back of the shop stood a long, narrow staircase that led down to a small storage room and office. With space at a premium, even the stairs were piled with boxes. A small chain with an EMPLOYEES ONLY sign was supposed to keep out the customers, but the regulars always ignored it, as there was a bathroom downstairs.

The stairs were not only narrow but also steep. I slowly went down, with one hand on the wall for safety. This was not something I wanted my grandmother to see—my being careful—but these were not stairs for the faint of heart.

At the bottom, I stood amazed at the sea of boxes. Both Nancy and Eleanor were fans of keeping the latest new tools and fabric in stock, but with the shop already crowded, it meant that only one or two of each design made it upstairs and the rest waited in the basement. As something like six-inch rulers sold out, they had to make a trip downstairs for more. With the shop as busy as it was, that could mean as many as a dozen trips a day.

It took me several minutes to find the box of rulers in the back corner and several more to find the six-inch ones. I had the brief idea of bringing up a twelve-inch ruler as a joke, but decided it would amuse only me. Instead I grabbed what I had been sent for and started back upstairs. But before I'd reached the third step, I'd almost tripped over a bolt of fabric. I put the rulers down and cleared the steps, moving everything to the corner of the basement.

"Nell," I heard my grandmother call.

"Coming."

With that task done, I perched on a chair behind the register for the next hour and watched Eleanor wait on person after person. Everyone that came in gravitated toward her, and she seemed to have exactly what each person wanted. I liked my job most days, but I didn't excel at it like this. I didn't love it. One more way my life wasn't working. Could I be any more self-pitying? My namesake would have been proud.

When I saw her stop to talk with Carrie, I made my way over. Carrie's children were having quite a time tossing books from the low shelves of the book rack, but neither of the women seemed to notice.

"It was something my granddaughter thought up," Eleanor was saying. "It seems like a lot of trouble."

"What's that?" I interrupted. If the word on the street was that I thought up something that was a lot of trouble, it was enough of an invitation to join the conversation.

"The diner," said Carrie. "Susanne mentioned to me that Eleanor might take it over."

"Just talk," Eleanor said. I got the feeling she was reassuring the woman. "It's just that we are getting crowded in here."

"Well, you could use the space," admitted Carrie. "But, of course, we could also use a good coffee shop in town." She turned to me. "The only place to get espresso in Archers Rest is at the pizza parlor. And it's instant."

"I think a coffee shop is a great idea, too," I responded, trying to be nice. No sense in stepping on anyone's dream.

"Well, it's a lot of work," Carrie said, seeming to back off the idea. Carrie's daughter was tugging at her leg, and Carrie was ignoring her. "My husband thinks it would be a waste of money since I don't really have the time."

"Nor do I," agreed Eleanor. And then my grandmother reached down without looking and caught a bolt of fabric that Carrie's son was about to pull down on his head.

Since I was doing little but stir up small-town controversy, I slowly headed toward the door. The shop was getting busy. People were coming in alone and in groups. Mostly women but some men. Some of them had fabric swatches or books to reference. Some seemed focused, heading right toward a section or a color. Others wandered around, pulling fabrics here and there, waiting to fall in love with something. Everyone seemed filled with anticipation and creativity, and rather than sit on the sidelines, I decided to leave.

"I'm heading to the house," I called back to my grandmother.

"Barney will want a walk," she called back.

Carrie's little boy beat me to the front door, with a frustrated Carrie, her daughter in her arms, following closely behind. I grabbed the little boy before he could make it into the street.

"I used to be a vice president." Carrie shook her head. "On Wall Street. I thought I could handle anything." She nodded toward her children, running in circles around her.

"They're lively. Kids are supposed to be lively," I said as her son jumped up into the backseat of Carrie's car, stepping over her daughter to do it.

"I guess," she sighed. I turned to leave. "It's a good idea, your idea to expand the shop," Carrie said almost shyly.

"She could use the space." I hesitated. "But I feel bad if you had plans for the diner yourself."

"No, not plans. I just was talking about it with someone . . . Marc . . . you know Marc."

"Yes. He's helping my grandmother."

"He's great, isn't he? Just so many ideas," she practically gushed. "He's really very talented . . . in so many areas."

"Like your kids." I pointed to the two children climbing over the backseat into the driver's seat.

"Oh, God," she said as she reached into the back of her car, doing her best to restore order.

✄

I crossed the street and found myself in front of the town bakery. A familiar-looking man with glasses and a serious expression was holding the hand of a small girl. The child, maybe five years old, was happily struggling to fit a giant chocolate chip cookie into her small mouth. Several times he leaned down and patiently wiped the chocolate chip stains from her face.

I was almost on top of them before I recognized him.

"Officer . . . ," I started.

"Jesse . . . Dewalt." He stood up and smiled a little, but just a little. "This is my daughter, Allison."

For just a second it seemed strange that he was a father. But I reminded myself that I didn't know anything about this man, except that Barney liked him. The fact that he was quiet and sullen didn't mean some woman couldn't have fallen head over heels for him.

I waved to Allison. "It's a good day for a cookie," I said to her. And since her mouth was full, she just nodded.

"She thinks every day is a good day, but we try to save it for a Saturday afternoon treat, right kid?" Allison looked up and laughed at her father, and he laughed back. The delight he took in her lit up his face, and I suddenly was struck by how handsome he was.

"Well," I said, feeling a little awkward, "I should be heading back to my grandmother's."

I started to turn before Jesse spoke. "How long are you staying?"

"Until tomorrow."

Allison tugged at his hand, but he kept his eyes on me. "You should come up more often," he said. "I know Eleanor would love it."

"Maybe I should," I said. And for the first time when I smiled at him, he smiled back. "I'll let you guys get back to your Saturday." I looked down at Allison, whose face was now covered with chocolate. "But I'd clean her up before you head back to your wife."

When I looked back at Jesse, his smile had faded. I nodded good-bye and turned toward my grandmother's, leaving the serious man to the not-so-serious task of keeping a little girl from dropping her cookie.

It seemed like just the sort of crime prevention a cop in Archers Rest would be qualified for.

CHAPTER 9

When I got to the house, Marc's truck was out front and he was putting up the ladder. He was wearing a flannel shirt, and I was, as embarrassing as this is to admit, a little disappointed not to find him bare-chested again.

"Hey there, granddaughter," he waved.

"Nell," I said.

"Marc." He smiled a dangerously cute smile. "Eleanor at the shop?"

"Yes. I can call over there if you want."

"No." He picked up a heavy load of roofing tiles. "It's just she usually makes me something to eat when I'm working for her. And she's a good cook."

"Sorry. I'd offer, but you don't want my cooking."

He smiled and looked at me. Not stared, exactly, but looked long enough to be studying me. It was a look of confidence, bordering on arrogance. But there was also something sad that betrayed the cool guy persona he was trying so hard to achieve. A bad boy with a touch of wounded puppy.

Suddenly I was self-conscious. "I should get inside," I said.

The spell was broken. He looked away. It seemed like he blushed, but maybe he was just sweaty from the work he'd been doing. In any case, he nodded and turned away.

Barney greeted me with the usual excitement, for which he got two of his favorite doggy cookies. I let him out in the yard and he wandered out of sight, likely down to the river. I sat waiting for him to return, but ten minutes went by and then twenty. No Barney.

A cloud moved over the sun and suddenly it turned the afternoon chilly and gray. I walked in the direction Barney had gone but there was no sight of him, just a few squirrels who scrambled up trees as I came close.

"Barney," I called out. Nothing. "Barney," I said a little more insistently this time. Still nothing.

I veered off the path I usually took to the edge of my grandmother's property and started toward the thicket of trees that we romantically called the "black forest." Although there were only a few dozen trees, they were old and even as they dropped their leaves, they still blocked out most of the darkening sky.

"Barney," I practically screamed.

There were more than five acres of property, but Barney was lazy. He wouldn't have wandered around. He would have done his business and come back to the house, knowing dinner was waiting for him.

"Barney," I finally screamed.

I heard rustling behind me and spun around. I saw nothing.

A storm was now brewing in an ever-darkening sky, and I hadn't brought a flashlight with me. With the tall trees and the encroaching evening, I felt blackness descend around me.

"Barney," I called toward the rustling. I could hear a slight panic in my voice. Even though I knew it had to be the squirrels, a small voice inside me said it didn't sound like squirrels. I was momentarily frozen, staring at the spot where I heard the sound. I wasn't sure whether I was scared that something had happened to the dog or was about to happen to me.

"Nothing happens in this town," I told myself. "Good or bad."

With common sense taking the lead, I turned back toward the house. I would give Barney an hour to get hungry and come home, and if he hadn't, I'd come back out with a flashlight.

I took a dozen steps and heard a sound behind me. It was more than just rustling leaves. It was footsteps. I clenched my fist into a pathetic attempt at a weapon and turned.

"Who is that?"

Nothing.

"Who is that?"

"Hey," a male voice came from the other direction.

"Marc?"

"Yeah, you okay?"

I was, I guess. "I thought someone was behind me."

Marc came toward me. "I saw. You were about to do battle with a vicious squirrel. Or maybe a bunny." I turned and saw a squirrel rustling in the leaves before it scampered up a tree. Marc started laughing and I turned every shade of red from light pink to brick.

He smiled. "I heard you calling for Barney." He stepped toward me. "I came to tell you he's in paw-to-paw combat with another squirrel out front. Takes after you, I guess."

He took another step, and I instinctively stepped back, more out of extreme embarrassment than anything.

"Did it scare you that bad?" he asked.

"No." I hated being the silly girl. Maybe it was stupid to punish Marc for my self-consciousness, but I couldn't help myself. We walked for a minute in uncomfortable silence.

"It's an amazing old place, isn't it?" Marc stopped and looked at the house just up ahead.

"Sometimes I love it almost as much as my grandmother does."

"I bet she'd leave it to you, if you asked her," he said as he turned to me, his eyes sparkling.

"Eleanor will be in this house for years," I said, a little offended. "Years and years."

"I suppose. I've always wanted to go through the place, though. You know, see what's hidden in the attic."

"I don't think anything's hidden up there. And you know my grandmother. She wouldn't want someone poking around her house even if the crown jewels were in it."

He smiled and nodded. "I suppose. I guess I just like going where I don't belong." He winked at me, as if I knew what he meant.

I moved ahead and Marc followed. By the time we reached the back door, we were side by side. His arm casually brushed against mine, and something about it made me jump a bit. Barney, looking a little worried, caught sight of us and ran to my side.

"Why didn't you come when I called?" I asked him as he jumped at me so excitedly that I nearly fell over.

"Didn't Eleanor tell you he's losing his hearing?"

"I guess I forgot."

Barney jumped up on me once again. Before I could crouch down to let the dog have his way, Marc pulled him off me roughly. Barney winced at the move.

"Don't do that. You'll hurt him," I yelled.

"Dogs shouldn't jump on people," he said flatly, and released Barney.

"I have to feed him," I said. Leaving Marc at the back door, Barney and I went inside.

✄

Barney had barely begun his meal when the doorbell rang. I opened the front door to no one, but on the porch were a half dozen of my grandmother's flowers banded together with twine. Resting on the twine was a note: "Sorry I scared you. Mr. Squirrel."

In the driveway, Marc had turned on the headlights of his truck. He waved at me. I waved back. "I'm going to clean up here before I leave," he called, gesturing toward the pile of old roof tiles that littered the front lawn.

"Thanks," I said, and held up the flowers. He smiled and I smiled back, then closed the door. I don't know why I'd reacted so strongly to Marc. He hadn't really done anything but remind me that I was easily spooked, and even more easily embarrassed.

I grabbed the flowers and brought them inside. I couldn't put them in a vase. If my grandmother saw that someone was picking through her flowers, she wouldn't be happy about it. But I didn't want to throw them out either. I took them into my bedroom and put them on the nightstand. I lay on the bed and stared at them for a while, then I turned my attention to the ceiling.

Tomorrow was Sunday, and that meant going home. If I took the 4:40 train back tomorrow afternoon, I'd be in Manhattan around 6:30 p.m. and at my apartment no later than seven. I would have survived a whole weekend without talking to Ryan.

But going back meant going to work and either seeing him, or spending the day only a few floors away and not seeing him. Neither option exactly thrilled me.

I had to come up with some kind of game plan for what I would say if I saw him. I had to figure out my response to any messages he might have left on my voice mail. *If* he left messages on my voice mail.

And it also meant finding a place to live. I couldn't afford the place Ryan and I had planned to move into together, and my apartment had already been re-rented.

It was too much to think about, so I did the only thing I could think of—I went to sleep.

CHAPTER 10

I was standing in my wedding dress, looking down the aisle at the church. It seemed like the aisle went on for miles. I looked around, but none of my bridesmaids were with me, and that was a bit annoying. Why couldn't they be on time for my wedding? I didn't know whether I should just go ahead and walk down the aisle by myself or wait for everyone else.

I took a few steps and stopped. I couldn't make out who was at the end of the aisle. Was it Ryan? It looked like Ryan, but not completely. The man at the end of the aisle had lighter hair. Maybe. It was hard to tell. Should I walk down the aisle or not? I walked back to my starting point. I didn't know what to do. Hopefully someone would get here soon and tell me.

I heard a phone ring. My parents, maybe, or my maid of honor. I looked around, but I couldn't find a phone, and when I looked up the aisle to the altar, there was no one there. If I could find the phone maybe someone could explain to me why no one was taking my wedding day seriously.

The phone stopped. I was alone in the church in my wedding dress, and now my flowers were a mess. The beautifully arranged bouquet had become a freshly picked group of flowers tied together with twine. The phone started ringing again. Off in the distance Barney barked. His barking got closer and closer.

I opened my eyes slowly. It was dark outside, I was on the bed and my grandmother's phone was ringing incessantly. I got up, feeling heavy and groggy. There was a phone in the kitchen, so I headed in that direction.

"Hello," I mumbled.

"Nell, dear, it's Nancy. There's been an accident."

I wasn't sure I was awake yet.

"Nell," Nancy said again. The fear in her voice snapped me out of my fog.

"An accident. What happened? Is it my grandmother?"

"She was going downstairs to get needles and she slipped on some fabric on the third stair from the bottom. I called the paramedics."

"I'll be there in a second." I hung up the phone and searched the kitchen for my grandmother's car keys. They weren't here. They had to be here. She hadn't driven to the shop. Okay, I needed to get hold of myself. I could walk to the shop by the time I found the stupid keys.

"Grandma's hurt." I tapped Barney on the head and he jumped up. We both ran out the front door into a rainy night, and into Marc, who was still cleaning up.

"Hey there," he said casually.

"My grandmother fell, at the shop. And I can't find the stupid car keys."

"Hop in." He jumped into the driver's seat of his truck as Barney and I climbed in, sharing the passenger side. "What happened?"

"She slipped on the stairs."

"Those are dangerous stairs."

"I know," I said, more worried than ever.

"How is she?"

"I don't know," I said. In my rush, I hadn't even asked. I took a deep breath and told myself she was fine. She had to be fine.

We were at the shop in less than five minutes. An ambulance, its lights blinking, was parked out front. I jumped out and ran, but

Barney passed me by and headed straight into the shop, leaving Marc behind to park.

When I got into the shop, I saw Nancy talking to Maggie, but I couldn't see my grandmother.

"Where is she?" I was frantic.

"She's downstairs," said Maggie calmly. "She's okay. She may have broken her hip, but they aren't sure."

I nodded and took my first deep breath since I'd gotten the call. She's okay. I rushed to the stairs.

✄

At the bottom, my grandmother was being lifted onto a stretcher. Barney was hovering around her. He was getting in the way, but I knew he wasn't going anywhere.

"This is ridiculous," Eleanor told the paramedics as they strapped her onto the stretcher. "You'll never get me up the stairs this way. You'll kill us all."

"Ma'am, we're very experienced."

"You're twenty-three years old, George. When you were five you ran away from home to this store."

"Mrs. Cassidy, I really do know what I'm doing," the paramedic said confidently. "You've broken your leg. We don't know about your hip."

"I can walk."

"Well, you're not going to," he said, rather strongly.

Once I got a good look at him, I had to admit he did look young. And neither he nor the guy with him looked particularly strong. My grandmother might have a better chance walking. But I took their side anyway.

"Let them do what they need to do," I called down.

"Nell," she called, craning her neck to see me. "I'm fine, dear. Tell Nancy to close up the store without me."

"I think she has that covered," I said. I wanted to add, you insane woman. Screw the store. You could be dead at the bottom of these stairs.

The paramedics slowly moved up the steps, one at a time. Each step they pulled her up and the stretcher seemed to sway slightly. Don't drop her, I nearly said out loud, but I didn't.

"Need help, guys?" Marc was suddenly behind me.

"Yeah," said George, straining.

My grandmother wasn't a big woman, but the stairs were steep and Barney was nipping at everyone's heels. Marc walked down and grabbed part of the stretcher.

"Bad day, Eleanor?" he asked with a smile.

"I've had worse."

"That's the spirit, Mrs. Cassidy," George said, smiling.

"Concentrate on getting me up these stairs," she scolded.

In a few minutes they were upstairs and headed out of the shop. Nancy, Maggie and I followed as they put her in the ambulance, while she complained about the fuss. Barney tried to climb in after her, but Marc stopped him.

"Barney, come here," I called out. He couldn't hear me, but when the ambulance pulled away, he came walking over anyway, distraught and confused. I leaned down and wrapped my arms around him.

"She'll be okay," I whispered in his deaf ear.

CHAPTER 11

Marc drove me to the hospital. Nancy and Maggie brought Barney home and then came to join us. Within twenty minutes the other members of the Friday Night Quilt Club had assembled. Susanne and Natalie brought Bernie. Carrie arrived alone but with a thermos of coffee.

"Better than hospital stuff," she said.

Bernie brought cookies, and Susanne had egg salad sandwiches. It was exactly what my grandmother would have done in their shoes—circle the wagons around whoever was in need, and provide whatever comfort could be provided. I wanted to cry at the kindness of it, but instead I ate a sandwich and three cookies.

For the next hour we all waited, with most of the quilt club talking about how annoyed Eleanor must be and how she would be furious to know that there were so many people waiting in the lobby. Marc, though, was silent. He couldn't have been that upset about Grandma. He was only her handyman. I thought about telling him he didn't have to wait, but when I looked toward him, I realized he wasn't waiting for news. He was slouched in his chair staring angrily at Natalie, Maggie, and Susanne, who sat across from him.

A nurse, who had ignored every question I'd asked when we first arrived, finally came over to me. "Your grandmother would like to see you."

"Don't tell her we're here," advised Bernie. "She'll have a fit."

✂

My grandmother was in a nice private room, but she wasn't enjoying it. "Tell him I can go home," she ordered me.

A tall, thin doctor looked toward me with an exasperated smile. "I'd love nothing more, Mrs. Cassidy. But I'm keeping you here for a couple of days."

She had broken her leg near her ankle and done some damage to her kneecap, but her hip was merely bruised, and after six to eight weeks of recuperation she would be just fine. I was relieved. She was furious.

"I can't sit around doing nothing for six weeks. I have a business to run. Doesn't he understand that?"

"Grandma, the doctor didn't push you down the stairs, so stop being mad at him."

"Thank you." The doctor smiled, then caught an angry look from my grandmother and fled the room.

"I can't believe I was so stupid." She was straining to get comfortable, and frustrated by the large cast that made that impossible.

"How did it happen? I cleared the stairs."

"You did? I don't know. I think I may have missed a step." She was shaking her head in disbelief, as if she were discovering for the first time that she wasn't infallible.

"I'll call Mom and Uncle Henry and let them know . . ."

"Don't you dare. I'm fine."

"I'll let them know you're fine."

"Nell. I know you're trying to do the right thing, but I don't want everyone getting on a plane to see me hop around in a cast." Her voice was losing energy and she suddenly looked as if she needed me.

I had to smile. "Okay. I'm going to let you rest."

She touched my hand lightly and seemed unwilling to let it go.

"I'm sorry, Nell. You didn't need this. And on top of it, you've been waiting out there alone all night."

"I haven't been alone." It was out before I remembered Bernie's advice and did my best to cover. "The nurses, the doctors, patients all over the place. It's more crowded than Manhattan."

She smiled weakly and let go of my hand. I hesitated, but it was time to go. She did need her rest.

In the hallway outside her room, everyone was waiting.

"She's fine. She's tired," I told them.

"Of course she's tired," said Maggie. "We all need some rest."

Maggie wrapped her arms around me and I found myself hugging her tightly. Then each woman hugged me, and hugged each other, until we made a sloppy, relieved mess of tangled huggers. Twenty-four hours ago these women were strangers to me, and now we were reassuring one another like old friends. We walked out together into the parking lot and stayed talking for another twenty minutes. Nancy would open the shop tomorrow. I'd spend the morning at the hospital and call Natalie to let her know how Eleanor was doing and when she'd be released. Natalie would initiate the phone chain they had in place for quilting emergencies. I didn't ask for the definition of a quilting emergency.

All I could think about was spending the night in that big house without my grandmother.

CHAPTER 12

The ride back home with Marc was silent, and that was fine with me. When we got to the house I started to hop out with barely a good-bye, but Marc grabbed my hand.

"Are you going to be okay in there alone?" The friendly smile was back.

"I have Barney."

He laughed. "Yeah, great watchdog." He reached into the glove compartment and pulled out a business card. "Take my number and call me if you need anything."

I nodded and watched him drive away before I went inside.

✄

Barney was waiting by the door, sitting at attention. When he saw me he wagged his tail, but his heart wasn't in it. He kept looking past me to the front door.

I went into the kitchen and put on the kettle. After a few minutes Barney came in, looked around, and walked over to me. His head was up, but his tail was hanging low between his legs.

"I know, love." I patted his head. "Believe me, she wants to come home just as much as you want her here."

I made some tea, cut myself a piece of cake, and sat at the table, then realized I was too tired to eat. I offered Barney a dog biscuit, but he just sniffed at it and lay at my feet.

My eyes were starting to close, and the effort to open them again seemed pointless. I left the tea half-finished, the cake untouched, and headed up to bed. The stairs creaked as I walked up, and the entire second floor was dark. There were no streetlights by my grandmother's house, so without a full moon, there was no light outside. And it was quiet. Not even crickets were doing whatever crickets do to make that noise.

Barney settled on the floor and I crawled in underneath the pin-wheel quilt that covered the bed. I reached my hand out, turned off the light on the bedside table, and lay back. I stared off into space for a while, waiting to go to sleep. Then . . . something. It sounded like someone at the front door. The sleepiness of just a minute before was gone. I sat up and listened. Quiet. I looked over at a sleeping Barney and was comforted for a moment that he hadn't been alarmed, until I remembered he couldn't have heard anything. I lay down again, but I made sure to face the bedroom door. Just in case. Minutes passed. I started to close my eyes when there was a definite noise, like a door flying open, but it seemed to be coming from the kitchen this time. I had locked the doors, hadn't I? I couldn't remember if I had locked up. Every muscle tensed and I froze.

I turned on the bedroom light. If someone was in the house, he'd know that he'd been heard. I threw a pillow at Barney, who raised a sleepy head in my direction.

"Get up," I whispered. "Go downstairs."

Barney got up and started wagging his tail. He lay his head on the bed next to me because he clearly believed that I had woken him up to pet him. You had to admire his optimism.

I got up slowly, shaking with each step, and walked to the door of the bedroom. I couldn't hear anything but wind and rain.

Now I really missed my cell phone. I could walk to my grand-mother's bedroom, where I thought she had a phone, but if I called the police and it was nothing, then everyone in town would be telling the hilarious story tomorrow.

But I couldn't just stand there shaking all night. My grandmother wouldn't. I grabbed Barney's collar and we headed to the top of the stairs. If someone was going to kill me, he was going to kill me standing up. I wasn't going to be found cowering by my bed so everyone could say "poor thing, first she gets dumped and then she dies alone and scared." No, they were going to say "poor thing, first she gets dumped and then she dies stupidly fighting off an intruder."

Barney walked beside me as we slowly descended the stairs. He couldn't hear what I was listening for, but he knew I was scared, and that was enough for him to stick close. Together we made it into the downstairs hall, turning on every light I could find. My grandmother didn't have much in the way of weapons, so I grabbed an umbrella out of the stand and walked into the kitchen.

I turned on the light. The back door was open.

✂

The room was empty. Barney walked lazily over to his bowl and started picking at the last of his dinner. Even a deaf dog would sense danger, right?

I grabbed a knife from the counter to replace my pathetic umbrella weapon and slammed the kitchen door shut, locking it tight.

Walking back out into the hallway and toward the living room, I saw no one. I opened all the closets, checked all the doors and windows, turned on all the lights.

Had it just been the wind?

✂

Barney found me standing by the front door and looked at me with sleepy eyes. I knew what he was thinking, and he was right, probably. I had forgotten to lock the kitchen door and a strong wind blew it open. Still, I left the lights on downstairs while Barney and I headed back up.

CHAPTER 13

The next morning, a loud car horn woke me before the alarm or Mother Nature had a chance to. I walked over to the window ready to scream at whoever was making that racket. A red-haired woman in jeans and a bright blue sweater stood in the driveway next to a truck with a medicine bottle logo on the side.

"Bernie?" I yelled. "What are you doing?"

"Hey there, sweetie," she yelled back. "I brought you breakfast."

As annoyed as I was by the early morning intrusion, she had brought food, so I lumbered downstairs, followed by an equally sleepy Barney, and let her in.

"You didn't have to do that," I said as I took the plate of Danishes off her hands.

"Oh, I just did it as an excuse to check on you, dear," she said, smiling. "Did you sleep okay or did this spooky old house get to you?"

As we sat in the kitchen with Danishes and coffee, I told her about the creepy noises and the total darkness that kept me from getting a good night's sleep. I did not mention that I had hoped to sleep in a little—a plan she had spoiled.

"I think Eleanor's crazy to keep this place all by herself, but crazy in a good way, you know?" Bernie laughed heartily. "After my first husband died, I moved into a small apartment with the kids. And after my divorce, I moved in with a friend. Couldn't live alone in a place like this."

"How many husbands have you had?" I asked, probably impolitely.

"Three, so far," she laughed again. "Three husbands, two fiancés that didn't make the cut, and more lovers than I can remember. Which is a shame, since they would be very good memories."

"I guess I have some catching up to do."

"Best way over a broken heart is a romance," she said as she leaned back in her chair. "But guessing by the interest you've generated, you may already have figured that out for yourself."

Interest? I blushed, then realized what she must have meant. "No. Marc just drove me to the hospital."

She waved me off. "Marc is a lovely distraction. But he's not a romance. There's a darkness around that boy."

"I sensed that he wasn't well liked by some of the women in the club."

She smiled. "He's not well liked by some, too well liked by others, but everyone can choose their own friends." She poured herself the last of the coffee. "Make a fresh pot dear," she ordered, which I did without argument.

She watched me, smiling. "The girls laugh at me, but I'm a bit of a psychic," she said. "I sense things."

"Like what?"

"I don't think you've seen the last of your wayward fiancé."

"No, I haven't. He'll be at work tomorrow."

"That's not what I meant."

I laughed. "Bernie, I hope you're right. I think."

She finished her coffee and got up. "Just be careful, Nell. Make sure you keep your eyes open." She smiled at me, then turned away. "Tell Eleanor I'll be by later."

Though the game plan was that I would spend the morning at the hospital, I knew I had to make one stop first. The car keys that were so elusive the night before were now hanging on a hook by the back door. Didn't I look there yesterday? I tried to remember, but it was all a frightening blur. It didn't matter now. I grabbed them and headed to Main Street.

The shop wasn't open when I arrived, so I let myself in. Normally my grandmother and Nancy would have cleaned the place in the evening, putting fabrics and notions back where they belonged, so the next day would start fresh. But in the excitement of last night, all of that was left undone. Bolts of fabric lay on the cutting table and magazines were spread out on the counter. Even the cash had been left in the register.

I walked to the back of the shop and stared down the stairs. They were empty, just as I had left them. Carefully I walked down one step, then another. I wasn't looking for anything in particular, but it just didn't feel right. To everyone else it was a case of an elderly woman who slipped on steep, narrow steps. Something that happened all the time. But I had cleared the stairs because I had been afraid of something like that happening. And something about it just didn't make sense.

I slowly walked step after step, looking for a loose board or a nail that might be sticking up, something Eleanor had tripped on. Something I could fix. But I couldn't find anything. Then, with only four steps to go, my foot came out from under me and I went, butt-first, down into the basement.

✄

With nothing but my tailbone and my dignity injured, I got up and walked back up to the fourth step. I pulled at it, but it wasn't loose. There were no nails sticking up. I ran my hand gently over the wood. The step felt sticky, almost greasy, but not quite. I rubbed my fingers on the spot and sniffed. No smell. It felt a little like wax, but it didn't have the thickness of wax. What was this stuff?

I heard the door open upstairs. Footsteps came toward me.

"Who's there?" a voice called down.

"Nancy?" I shouted back. She appeared at the stop of the stairs.

"Oh, it's you, Nell. Are you all right? What are you doing?"

"There's something on the step. Something slippery." I held up my hand, as if that were proof.

She came down the stairs quickly and stopped just above me and, reaching down, she ran her fingers over the wood.

"Someone must have spilled something. Do you think that's what Eleanor slipped on?" she asked.

"Probably. What could it be?"

Nancy looked around at the empty stairs and shrugged. "I don't know. Come upstairs, carefully now. I'll get something to clean it up."

She started back up the stairs and I followed her, skipping the fourth stair. While I waited for Nancy to finish cleaning the step, I looked around at the messy shop. The place looked as if a pack of three-year-olds had gone through it.

"How do grown women do this to a business?" I swept my arms dramatically at all the bolts that were piled on top of each other.

"Quilters have to touch the fabric. They have to take it out, look at it, feel it." She laughed. "They just don't always feel the need to put it back."

"Can I help?" I didn't really know how to help, but I thought I should ask.

"No thanks. Eleanor will be anxious to see you." She glanced at the clock and stepped up her efforts.

"I feel bad about leaving you so close to opening time, but it's not like you're going to get a rush." I smiled, but Nancy just raised an eyebrow.

"You'd be surprised," she said with a smile.

I walked toward the door, still thinking about the stairs. "Who could have spilled something?" I asked.

"Me, I guess. Your grandmother." She paused. "One of Carrie's kids."

"What would one of her kids be doing on the stairs?"

She raised her eyebrows. "They're not always supervised in here. Yesterday I saw the little boy head for the stairs and Carrie go after him in a mad dash. It was five minutes before she could get the boy back upstairs again. And the whole time I had to keep her daughter from pulling every fabric off the shelf."

Just then, with minutes until ten, a woman knocked on the door. Nancy waved at her and pointed to the clock. The woman nodded but didn't budge.

Maybe they did get a rush.

CHAPTER 14

"How does anyone stay home during the day and watch television?" My grandmother greeted me with annoyance and flipped off the TV.

"You're obviously feeling better." I dropped her favorite cardigan on the hospital bed. "In case you're cold."

She quickly scooped it up. "It's freezing in here. And," she took a deep breath, "I'm sure Nancy is frantic at the shop."

"Grandma, Nancy has worked at the store for years."

"With me beside her every step of the way."

"She's very smart," I said, not really knowing whether she was or not.

"I know that," Eleanor huffed. She made an actual noise that sounded like "huff." "I'm just worried how we're going to manage. Nancy's never run a store."

"I'll stay," I volunteered before I realized what I was offering. I really wanted to get back to New York, to see if Ryan and I could somehow figure our way through this, but now the words were out. And if I were needed here . . .

My grandmother looked into my eyes, with sweetness usually saved for animals and children. "Oh, dear," she said as she took my hand. "You've never run a store either."

As soon as I was out of the hospital I reached into my pocket and pulled out a business card. I dialed the number on it without even thinking whether I should.

"I have a favor to ask you," I said right away.

"Name it."

"Meet me at my grandmother's house in twenty minutes."

He agreed and hung up without asking a question.

✂

Twenty minutes later I pulled into the driveway. Marc was already at the house, leaning against his car reading a piece of pink paper.

"I brought lunch," I said as I got out of the car, holding up a pizza box.

"You learn how to make that from your grandmother?" He folded up the paper and put it in his back pocket. Then he came toward me with a smile. He did have a nice smile. Different from Ryan's, but equally as charming.

Once in the house, after pizza and ten minutes of play with a still-worried Barney, we set to work. We took my grandmother's bed, piece by piece, into the living room, pushing back the furnishings to make room. Marc extended the cable wire so we could bring the TV from the kitchen into the living room, and we took the rugs, and anything else she could slip on, out of the downstairs bathroom and kitchen.

When we were done the place looked comfortable if slightly chaotic. But even with the bed in the living room, it wouldn't be enough. There was one more thing left to do.

"You ready?" Marc leaned against the fireplace and lowered his eyes so they met mine.

I shrugged. "Not really, but I don't have any other ideas, do you?"

"I like your plan, but we should go now if we're going to do this in one day."

✄

Once Marc and I were in his car driving south toward New York, I started to worry. It had seemed like a good idea to pack up my apartment and move in with my grandmother for a few weeks. I needed a place to live, and time to think, and she needed help—whether she would admit it or not. But what if I was using her problems as an excuse to run from my own?

"You've gotten quiet." Marc turned down the radio. I realized I had just been staring out the window, so I turned to him, trying to think of something to say.

"I was just thinking how nice it was of you to spend your whole Sunday helping me."

He smiled and seemed pleased by the compliment. "I'm a handyman. I fix things."

"Oh, how are you at relationships?" The words popped out of my mouth and I suddenly felt self-conscious, but Marc didn't seem to notice.

"Yeah, I heard you got dumped."

"I wouldn't call it dumped," I protested, but only for a moment. "Yeah, okay, I guess I got dumped."

"Been there. It's the worst. You feel as if you got kicked in the stomach, and by the one person you trusted completely." He stared straight ahead and spoke quietly, almost to himself. "You just have to get past it."

"How?"

Marc rested his hand on my leg for just a second, but it felt good. "You're doing it, Nell. You're not sitting around waiting for him to decide if he wants you. You're making decisions. You're making plans for your future." He shifted a little in his seat. "It's none of my business, but the guy is an idiot."

I touched his leg just where he had touched mine, and left it there for more than just a second before I turned back to the window.

✄

When Marc and I got to my apartment in New York, I immediately went for my cell. Three messages—one from Amanda and two from Ryan, one Friday and one today. I held my breath as I listened to his voice.

"Nell, it's me. I don't know if you want to talk to me or not, but I'd like to talk to you. I just want to know if you're okay with everything. If you're okay, period. Give me a call." Beep.

"Nell. It's Ryan. I know you're hurt and you're probably angry at me." *Probably angry?* "But I think it's unfair not to call me back and just let me worry about you. Please just call me, or I'll keep calling you." Beep.

"Everything okay?" Marc still stood in the doorway, watching me.

"Fine." I attempted a smile, and threw the phone in my purse. "Come inside. I'm pretty much packed up, so it shouldn't take long." I grabbed a box and handed it to him.

The only furniture I really had was my futon and TV; everything else was disposable or easy to pull apart. He had the truck packed and ready to go in less than two hours.

"I'm getting coffee for the road," he said. "Want anything?"

"Coffee sounds good."

"Take these," he said, and threw me a small set of keys—just two, a car key and what looked like a house key—on a worn leather key chain. "I'll be right back."

I went upstairs to see the place one more time and check that everything was in the truck. In the corner I had left one box. I wanted to carry it down myself, sort of a symbolic good-bye. In it was the lover's knot quilt I'd received just a few days earlier. Strange to think how much had changed in so little time.

I thought I would burst into tears. I'd planned it. But I felt nothing; I just was anxious to get on the road and breathe in some clean, crisp air.

When I walked out onto the street I could see that Marc was talking with someone. I took three steps and realized who it was—Ryan.

"What are you doing here?" I asked, genuinely confused.

"What are you doing?"

"She's moving, pal." Marc stood between Ryan and me.

"She's my fiancée, *pal*." Ryan moved around him.

"Not anymore." Marc moved toward me.

"All right, guys. That's enough." I pulled Ryan a few steps from Marc. "I was about to leave you a message," I told him.

Ryan moved close to me, very close. More for Marc's benefit, I knew, than either his or mine. "Who is that asshole?"

"My grandmother's handyman." Ryan looked Marc over. Marc stared back. I loved Marc for acting all knight-in-shining-armor over a woman he hardly knew. "And my friend."

"You're making new friends already?" If he had meant to sound tough, he'd failed. I could see his eyes getting watery. Ryan gently touched my hair.

"Have you changed your mind?" I knew better than to ask the question, but I wanted to give him every chance.

He just stood there looking embarrassed, then he reached for my hand. I pulled it away.

"You didn't call me back," he said.

"I forgot my phone," I answered.

"How did we get here?" He stared at me.

"You," I said quietly. "You got us here."

He nodded. "So you have to move? Because I need more time, you have to pack up and leave?"

"My apartment was rented, remember?" He suddenly remembered. "What am I supposed to do, crash on Amanda's couch until you're ready to get married?"

"No," he said sharply. "I just don't think we're going to solve anything with you all the way up there." I could feel Ryan's breath on me and I started to feel confused. I moved a few steps away from him.

"I don't have anything to solve," I said. "You do. And maybe what you need is time alone to figure out what you want." I didn't know whether to be mad or hurt or disappointed. But I knew I had to leave. Marc was right. I couldn't sit around and wait for Ryan. I had to make my own plans. And I had to make them now, before I changed my mind.

"My grandmother needs help," I said. I stepped away from him and climbed into the passenger seat of Marc's truck. Marc immediately jumped in the driver's side.

"You have your cell phone with you this time?" Ryan called after me.

I nodded.

"Then I'll call you," he shouted.

"Don't make any more promises until you know you can keep them," I said, but I wasn't sure Ryan heard me. As Marc drove away, I watched Ryan standing on the street looking as hurt and confused as I felt.

CHAPTER 15

We were halfway to Archers Rest before either of us spoke.
"I'm sorry to have dragged you all the way into the city,"
I said by way of apologizing for Ryan.

"I love New York. I don't go there too much now, but I used to
live there. I went to Columbia for a couple of years."

"Really? What did you study?"

Marc made a face. "Biology, if you can believe it. My father's a
doctor in town and he really wanted me to follow in his footsteps. I
liked science, so I gave it a try, but medicine was not for me. I'm not
cut out for postponing gratification." He winked at me. "Nearly
killed my old man when he saw my grades. He gave me this lecture
about how he wasn't spending hard-earned money so I could go
drinking." He laughed. "Sure was fun, though."

"How did you end up . . . I mean . . ."

"As the town handyman?" He looked over at me. "It's cool. I
don't know. I like working with my hands. I'd love to build a house
someday, maybe a smaller version of your grandma's, right on the
Hudson, and build furniture."

"Have you built anything I could see?"

He got shy for a moment, then admitted, "Yeah, I guess, if you
want to. I've got some tables and chairs and stuff. I like to build
old style. I use a lot of hand tools and I make some reproductions.
That's my real love. I'd like to build something someday that my

son, my children, and grandchildren could use and know that I made it."

I looked over at him and noticed for the first time that his smile was slightly crooked and that he had a dimple on his right cheek. When he saw me watching him, I could see he was blushing a little, but he said nothing and neither did I. He was sweet and full of his own dreams. I liked him. And as simple an emotion as it was, that seemed very complicated to me.

We chatted about his future furniture-building business the rest of the way home, and then spent twenty minutes moving my stuff into the guest room at my grandmother's house. It was hard to believe that what had taken up an entire New York apartment hardly made a dent in the floor space of one room in this house.

✄

The next day, when Eleanor was released from the hospital, she didn't criticize either the new arrangement or the fact that I'd taken a leave of absence to help her out. I took this as approval.

"A lot of work for one person," she said as I helped her into bed.

"Marc helped me."

"He has a good heart, when he wants to use it."

"That's a little unkind."

She waved me off. "How are you getting off work?"

"Sick grandmother. Desperate for my help."

"Now who's being unkind?"

"What was I supposed to tell my boss?" I protested. "That I'm running away from a broken heart? One of us had to be needy and pathetic for me to get time off, and it wasn't going to be me."

She took my hand. "It isn't you. You're helping me, and I'm glad you're here. What about some dinner? If I know my friends, there are five casseroles and ten pies in that kitchen."

"At least."

"First thing you do is tell people to stop bringing food."

I wasn't about to tell people that, especially since it wasn't likely my grandmother would be cooking anytime soon, and she wouldn't want to eat what I could whip up. I heated two plates of a noodle dish that Susanne had dropped off and arranged them on a tray with glasses of water and dinner rolls.

From his position next to my grandmother, Barney wagged and wagged as I carried the tray into the living room, but he wasn't about to leave her side.

"I didn't think he was allowed on the bed." Barney had his head on a pillow, stomach up for easy petting.

"You tell him," she said as she gave his tummy a pat. They were a good couple, Barney and my grandmother. She pretended to be annoyed by his dependence, and he pretended to dislike her rules. All the while they clearly adored each other. If he had been a person, it would have been an enviable match. Truth was, I envied them anyway, despite the difference in their species.

✂

We watched the news while we ate, then *Andy Griffith* on Nick at Nite. I settled into the bed and felt the tension in my body release as I watched Andy outsmart a big city crook two episodes in a row.

"This is a bit less exciting than you're used to," Eleanor said.

"That's a good thing. I've had enough excitement." I told her about the scene between Marc and Ryan.

"Good enough for him," she said. "Did he think you would wait forever?"

"It's been less than a week."

"Long enough." I had to agree with that idea. "Ryan didn't think he was making a decision," she continued. "He thought he was delaying one. He didn't think about how it might change everything."

"Because he's selfish," I suggested.

"I don't think that's it. Scared, maybe. People make most of their worst decisions because they're afraid."

I sat up. "I don't know whether I'm supposed to hate him or feel sorry for him."

She smiled. "I felt the same way about your grandfather after he died. One too many beers and he wrapped his car around that tree, changing my life, your mother's, even yours, in a way. Of course, your grandfather couldn't have imagined that his decision would have that kind of effect. Just like now, Ryan didn't think that postponing the engagement would send you off with another man."

I blushed and stammered for a minute until I could figure out what to say. "Marc's not another man, he's a friend."

She sighed. "I don't mean to interfere."

"You're not. Well, you are." I smiled. "But I could use a little wise interference. It could be your way of paying me back for all the help I'm going to give you around the house."

"And at the shop, if you can. I took a lease on the diner to expand the shop."

I practically jumped. "You did what? When?"

"Why are you so surprised? It was your idea."

"You've been in the hospital."

"I had access to a phone." She rolled her eyes, but I could see she enjoyed being one step ahead of me. "I thought about what you said, and it made sense, so I made a few calls. I had nothing else to do, just sitting there like some sick person."

I settled back down next to Barney. "Wow" was all I could get out.

She patted my hand. "And it worked out perfectly, with you here to help. That will keep you busy."

I stretched myself out on the bed, wrapping my arm around a sleeping Barney. "Not too busy. I have a limited amount of energy." I closed my eyes and was asleep to the sounds of Opie and Aunt Bee talking about their day.

CHAPTER 16

My grandmother's alarm went off at six-thirty in the morning, but I was awake for several minutes before. Barney had woken up and jumped off the bed, stepping over me in the process. My grandmother reached for her crutches and dropped them, saying in a loud whisper, "Damn," a word she'd never used before, at least not in my presence.

"Let me help." I got up and the day began.

I scrambled eggs according to my grandmother's strict instructions, and they weren't just edible—as they were when I made them in New York—they were quite good. I walked Barney, did the dishes, and brought down unfinished quilting projects so my grandmother could do some hand sewing. I made a list of all the needed groceries and errands she wanted me to run. When I got back, she told me, I would need to pack some of her old clothes into boxes for a charity drive.

"One more thing," she said as I was walking out the door with half a dozen lists. "Stop at the shop. See if Nancy needs any help." I was exhausted, and it wasn't even ten o'clock.

✂

When I walked outside I half-expected to see Marc's truck and his ladder to the roof. I found myself a little disappointed when they weren't there. I wondered if he was finished with the roof, which would be a good thing, I told myself, since it looked like rain.

I did most of the errands and managed to grab a cup of coffee at the diner before I walked to Someday Quilts. From the outside it looked quiet, but when I opened the door, I walked straight into a very frazzled Nancy.

"We have to shut down the store," she said instead of hello.

"What? Why?"

"Ask him." She pointed to Marc, who was coming up the stairs with a toolbox and a measuring tape. I smiled, a little too happily, I knew, but I was glad to run into him.

"Nancy," he chided, "Eleanor wants this wall knocked down as soon as the diner closes tonight. I can't do that with people walking around. There will be dust everywhere, power tools. If you don't care about the customers, think about the fabric." He was having fun with her, I could see, but Nancy wasn't interested.

"Did she hire you?" I turned to Marc. "She didn't say anything to me."

"She called me this morning. She said to get started right away. I think you were out running errands." Marc shifted a little but stood his ground.

Nancy looked at me. "I'm sorry," I said. "She just told me last night that she leased the shop. And you know my grandmother. Once she makes up her mind, she doesn't like to wait."

"Look, I'm all for this renovation," Nancy sighed. "But this one shows up without any warning when I'm trying to run a store." Nancy tilted her head toward Marc but looked at me. "I admire enthusiasm, but you don't want someone going off half-cocked."

"Hey, I'm here." Marc leaned toward Nancy. "I could be at the track with your husband."

Nancy rolled her eyes. "You could hardly do more harm there

than you're doing here." She smiled at Marc as though he were a slightly mischievous puppy. "And before you get smart with me again, young man, remember I've known you since you were a small child. There's no fooling me with that charm of yours."

"Yes, ma'am." Marc pretended to look contrite, and then smiled. Then he turned to me and shrugged. "What now, granddaughter?"

I blushed, and I knew he could see it, so I looked around the shop trying to think of something to say. "The diner's closing tonight?"

"After the lunch crowd. The owners told Eleanor she could have it all. Not that she wants a bunch of old kitchen equipment." He smiled. "Didn't Eleanor tell you all this already?"

"No," I said. "Why don't you start work on the diner, then, pulling out the old stuff and getting it cleaned up. How long will that take?"

"A few days."

"Fine," I continued. "We'll close Wednesday, do inventory, and bring everything over to my grandmother's. Everyone in town knows where she lives. We can run the shop out of there for a few weeks. And Marc can wait until, say, Saturday to knock down this wall. In the meantime, we'll pack up whatever we can."

"Fine with me," Marc said. "I have a doctor's appointment Thursday anyway."

Nancy turned to me. "I'll call our regulars," she said, "and let them know we're moving to Eleanor's for a while."

"You do that," I said. "And don't worry about Marc. I'll make sure he doesn't do anything without my supervision. Okay?"

She laughed. "Good luck with that, dear." She drifted to the stairs and disappeared to the office below.

"Good thinking." Marc threw an arm around me. He leaned his head in and rested it on mine. "I like the idea of you supervising me."

I let out a nervous laugh. "Work fast," I said, then pulled away. "And don't cause any trouble."

"Man, you are just like your grandmother."

✄

Less than twenty minutes after I arrived, Carrie was in the shop to confirm what Nancy had, apparently, told her on the phone. Several minutes later, Maggie arrived. Then Bernie. Then Susanne. Only Natalie was missing.

Carrie said twice to me and once to Susanne, "Well, the shop needs to be bigger. I agree with that. But it's a shame to lose a place to get some coffee."

"What about setting up some tables and making a little coffee shop in the store?" I suggested by way of compromise, and was verbally beaten in response.

"We'll have coffee all over the fabric," said Nancy and Susanne.

"You can't run two businesses and do them both well," declared Bernie.

"Have you ever had Eleanor's coffee?" whimpered Carrie. I had actually had my grandmother's coffee. And while it wasn't a half-decaf soy latte, it was quite good.

I could see that no one was interested in a coffee and quilt shop. "Just throwing out ideas," I said in my defense. "I'm sure my grandmother knows exactly what she wants in the space."

"She certainly does," Marc finally spoke.

"Thank you, Marc, but we'll talk with Eleanor about her plans." Maggie gave him an icy stare I hadn't thought she was capable of. Only Carrie smiled at Marc and said she'd be interested in hearing what he had in mind.

"Can I start doing anything now, boss?" Marc asked, smiling broadly.

I looked around at the shop. "We can move stuff away from the wall you're going to open up." I looked toward Nancy. "But only while I'm here helping." She nodded her approval.

"Why don't you bundle up some of the out-of-season fabric?" Maggie suggested.

Nancy leaned against the checkout counter. "I want to go through that for inventory first. Maybe pack up here, behind the register."

Marc moved toward the register, but I stopped him. "You grab a box and Nancy and I will take the stuff out of here."

"I'll help," Carrie volunteered, and stepped next to me.

I reached my arm into the deep shelf underneath the register, while Carrie hovered nearby.

"Be careful," Maggie said. And no sooner had the words come out of her mouth than something bit my hand. I pulled it out immediately. Blood was running from my fingers.

"Oh, dear," Carrie gasped, and grabbed antiseptic and a bandage from her tote bag. "One good thing about having small children is you're prepared for anything."

I went downstairs to the bathroom and tried to wash the blood away, but it kept coming. Just the tips of two fingers had cuts in them, but they were deep. I finally gave up trying and put the antiseptic and bandage on it, then went back upstairs.

Nancy was holding a flashlight and scanning the dark shelf. "Found it," she said. Carefully she held up a rotary cutter—a tool that looks like a pizza cutter but is designed for quick cutting of fabric. "It was open." She turned to me, a concerned look across her face. She put a cover over the sharp blade. "These are really dangerous. You're so lucky it wasn't worse."

I nodded. "Maybe that's enough for today," I suggested. "Marc, just clean up and we'll worry about all this stuff after Wednesday. I'm going home."

"I want to drop in on my son Brian," Maggie announced as

she picked up her purse. "Nell, can you give me a lift? It's on your way."

While Nancy and the others stood watching Marc, he just smiled at me and went back to measuring. I grabbed my keys and headed for the door, wondering just what I had gotten myself into by volunteering to stay in Archers Rest to help my grandmother.

CHAPTER 17

Maggie gave me the directions to her son's house as soon as we got in the car, and then we drifted into an uncomfortable silence. She fidgeted with her purse and looked out the window. I stared straight ahead at the road. Alone with her for the first time, I felt a little like a school child, afraid to talk in case she "sssh'd" me. With the members of the quilt club she seemed like a different person, relaxed, younger. But with me, she was every bit the stern librarian she'd once been.

"Is this the son who's a state representative?" I finally asked.

"It is, but that's just a stopping point. He'll be governor one day," she said proudly.

"My grandmother told me you have quite accomplished kids. Your son, plus a doctor, two lawyers, and an artist."

"Sheila isn't a artist. She owns a kind of art gallery. She doesn't actually make the art herself." There was a vague disapproval in her voice, but it quickly softened. "She does have a good eye, though. She always finds something."

"I wanted to be an artist when I was a kid. I used to love to paint. In fact, when I moved to New York I wanted to work in an art gallery," I confessed. "Hanging out with artists all day seemed really fun. But I couldn't find a job, and I guess I sort of took a different road."

"You have time to choose whatever road you like." She took a deep breath and changed the subject. "I wonder if Eleanor knows what she's doing. She takes people at their word, an admirable quality if she isn't being lied to."

"What do you mean?"

"That's it on the left," directed Maggie, and I pulled over to a pretty brick house with a well-tended garden.

"Maggie, can you please tell me what you meant?" I asked again.

"I didn't mean anything, except I think that Eleanor needs to be careful, and if she won't be careful, then you need to be careful for her."

"Well, that certainly clears things up for me," I said as Maggie got out of the car.

"You have her sarcasm," Maggie said. "Never cared for that in Eleanor." She started to frown, but instead she shook her head and smiled. "You really are like her."

I laughed. "Is that a compliment?"

Maggie laughed back. "Sometimes," she said, and headed toward her son's house.

✄

"I hear that you've been getting me out of trouble," my grandmother shouted to me as I walked in the house. "And getting yourself into it."

I peered into the living room, but she wasn't there. I walked back to the kitchen. She was hobbling around on her crutches, making sandwiches.

"What trouble am I in?" She pointed to my bandaged hand as she took a slice of bread from the loaf.

"I can do that. You shouldn't even be out of bed." I took the bread out of her hand. "What trouble did I get you out of?"

"At the shop. I guess Marc was a little enthusiastic. I hear you smoothed things over with the girls."

"I did good?" I was not about to let a possible compliment go unnoticed.

"No, you were just happy to see Marc, but you got me out of trouble anyway by putting off the renovation until Saturday. It gives everyone a chance to get used to it."

For just an instant I felt the need to deny my interest in Marc, then I decided it was better to let the comment pass. My grandmother was right, and she knew it. There wasn't any point in trying to explain something I didn't even understand myself. "You kind of surprised me too, hiring Marc," I said as I cut a pat of butter.

"You're doing it wrong." Eleanor had moved on to my sandwich-making skills.

"How could I be doing it wrong?" I was spreading butter on bread, not exactly a skill requiring an advanced degree.

"Less butter, and do both sides—it keeps the sandwich moister that way."

"Have you ever stopped to consider that we simply have different, yet equal, sandwich-making techniques?"

"Not really, no."

I buttered both sides her way, put the turkey and tomato slices on the sandwich, and cut it on the diagonal, as instructed. Eleanor sniffed at it a bit, refused to say anything nice about it, but finished it in seconds.

"I'm dying to hear what you and Marc have planned for the shop," I finally admitted.

A glint came into her eye. "We'll cut a hole in the wall, make a doorway to the other side, and add shelves for more fabric." She started sketching on a napkin. "And here in the back we'll build an office where the kitchen was, and next to it there will be a small classroom."

"Is Marc doing all this?"

She made a face at me. "Don't get too attached."

"I'm not attached. I just wonder if he's up to the task."

"Well, when he called me he was so enthusiastic. He really wants the chance to prove his worth, and I like that. No one thought I could run a quilt shop, a widow with two small children and no experience running a business. But I did okay. Sometimes you have to give people a chance."

"I don't think Maggie likes him. Or Natalie."

"Well, they have their opinions." She turned back to the napkin and a subject she clearly preferred. "I want to put up a whole wall of quilting tools, but I can't decide where."

"I have some ideas," I said. Eleanor smiled and handed me the pen, and together we arranged and rearranged the shop until every detail was worked out.

"This is a great plan, but it's a little ambitious, especially for the crew you've got. Marc isn't a real contractor, Nancy's never run a business before and, let's face it, I don't know anything about any of it."

"I'm not worried about any of you," she said, and then smiled. "Well, I'm not worried about Marc or Nancy. Your sandwich-making abilities are a little sad."

CHAPTER 18

Over the next several days I split my time between doing my grandmother's errands and being her spy at the shop. Nancy complained hourly about the noise Marc was making next door as he pulled old booths and kitchen equipment from the diner. For each regular who came by to express her excitement about the shop expansion, another would predict dire consequences—it was too much work for Eleanor, it would be difficult to make enough money to pay for expansion, it would ruin the coziness of the place.

✂

We closed the shop on Wednesday and I drove Eleanor over to sit in a corner and bark orders while Nancy and I did the inventory. Nancy spread boxes on the floor and began sorting the fabrics into categories from Christmas to children to plaids. When I incorrectly identified a fabric with ducks on it as children's, rather than Easter, I was taken off fabric duty. Instead Eleanor had me sort through the quilting tools. It was amazing to me that despite the seeming chaos, everything was catalogued and accounted for. When the inventory was done, there wasn't one missing pack of needles or thread color anywhere.

"I'll make one more check downstairs," I said.

"Be careful, Nell," Eleanor shouted after me. "I mean it."

She didn't have to warn me. Not since I'd fallen down the stairs myself, not that Eleanor knew that. Nancy had done an amazing job of bringing all the boxes upstairs and the place was clean and empty. But when I peeked into the little office on the side, I found another story. Boxes were half-packed with old files and binders, and a large box in the corner was filled with cut-up pieces of fabrics and threads. It seemed like a job for Nancy, who would have a better idea which, if any, of this stuff was worth keeping.

✄

"We should start taking stuff to the car," I said as I came back upstairs.

"Remember to put supplies for the quilt club in a separate box," Eleanor directed.

"Like what kind of supplies?"

Nancy handed me an empty box, then began pointing out a variety of rulers, rubber mats, and rotary cutters. "You'll also need a good pair of these," she said, and handed me heavy metal scissors.

"Thanks," I said. "I can use these to cut some poster board and make a CLOSED FOR REMODELING sign."

"No, you cannot," Eleanor snapped. "Cutting paper will dull those scissors, and fabric scissors need to be very, very sharp."

"Sorry," I said, and placed the scissors at the top of the box. "I'll get the hang of all the quilting rules one of these days."

Nancy and I took as many boxes out to Eleanor's car as could fit, and then filled up the back of her car. But the shop still had a dozen or more boxes left to go, as well as the quilts that hung on the back wall and the junk in the office.

"I'll take a trip over to your place, Eleanor," Nancy said. "Then if you two set up the shop there, I'll come back for a second load."

✄

On the drive to her house, Eleanor hummed to herself cheerily.

"What's up with you?" I finally asked.

"I'm just amazed at how easy this has been so far," she said.

"Of course it's easy," I said. "You'll be happy to be back running the shop, even if it is in your dining room. And Nancy will be happy to be working with you. And I can have some peace and quiet overseeing things at the shop."

"You enjoy being right," she said dryly.

"Wait—I'm right about something?" I laughed. "This has to be a first."

"I'm just saying that it was a good idea to expand the shop, that's all. And I'm glad you'll be there to make sure it all turns out right." Her smile made me suspicious, but it left me no room to keep arguing. She was like that, innocence and manipulation with a smile, and I admired the hell out of it.

At the request of all of the members of the Friday Night Quilt Club, my grandmother agreed to open the shop for one last meeting in the old space. We had done a pretty good job of pulling the place apart the last few days, and no one had bothered to sweep up. On Friday morning I walked over to make sure that the place would be clean and safe. One broken leg was all I could handle.

As I got to the door I passed a flustered Carrie on her way out.

She looked embarrassed to see me. "Forgot the shop was closed?" I asked her.

"No, no, of course not. I just wanted to talk with Marc. See what kind of work he was doing."

"Why?"

"I wanted to see, that's all," she said defensively. "I was passing and I thought I'd stop in. I might open my own place one of these days. I miss being in business, you know."

I nodded, but I didn't know. I'd never thought about owning my own business, or even running anyone else's. These last few days did have a certain element of fun to them, I had to admit, but I was riding this bike with my grandmother grasping the seat firmly. I had no interest in seeing if I could pedal all on my own.

I wanted to ask her why, if she wanted her own business so much, she didn't just open one. But I realized I probably knew the answer. I'd been saying I wanted to be an artist since I was a kid, and so far I had nothing to show for it. So instead I said good-bye and watched Carrie walk down the street. She walked quickly, looking around to see who else she might run into, but when she disappeared around the corner, I opened the door to the shop.

Inside the place was almost empty, aside from a few boxes Nancy hadn't been able to fit in her car. Marc was alone drawing an arch on the wall that divided the shop and diner.

"Is that the opening? It seems small," I said.

"In order to maintain the structural integrity of the place, I have to keep the arch pretty small, but it's big enough for two people to walk through." He grabbed me and we leaned up against the wall, both fitting into the space outlined for the arch. "See?" he said. I saw. "Maybe it's too much room. Maybe I should make it smaller." He pulled me closer. I couldn't tell if he was flirting with me because he liked me or making fun of me because maybe I liked him, so I just moved away to another section of the wall.

"If you're not tearing the whole wall down, you'll need to take care of that." I pointed to a hole in the wall near the corner.

"That mouse hole?"

"If that's a mouse hole, then he has a glandular problem. I could put my fist in it."

"I never saw it before." Marc leaned down to examine it.

"It had shelves in front of it, and piles of fabric."

"I'll fix it, boss," he said, smiling. He was excited to be there, I could tell. And maybe even excited to see me every day. Or maybe that was just my wishful thinking.

"Why don't I get some coffee?" I suggested.

"I could use the caffeine," he nodded.

"Late night?" I wasn't sure I wanted to know.

He blushed slightly. "I was up late, going over the plans for this place."

"Oh, please. I've heard about your reputation."

"I've heard it too. I wish I got laid as often as people say, but I actually I spent my night alone." He smiled briefly, then looked down. "I better get back to work."

"I better get that coffee." I had to get out of there because I knew I was smiling and I couldn't stop. I was almost out the door when I heard a banging.

"We're closed," I called back. There was a sign on the door that said CLOSED in big black letters, but some people must need more than that to take a hint. The banging started again.

Prepared to be polite and firm to whatever fanatical quilter I would find on the other side of the door, I pulled it open. Ryan was standing there.

"Hi," he said as he stood just outside the door. "Your grandmother said you were here." He looked toward Marc but didn't acknowledge him. Marc even waved hello but got no response. Ryan started to take a step inside with the same angry expression he'd had on the sidewalk in New York, but I put my hand on his stomach to stop him.

"What do you want?"

"I came to see you. I thought we could talk."

I looked back at Marc, who was watching the scene with a big grin on his face. I wanted to stay and figure out what was so funny to him, but I knew it was better to get Ryan out of there. "Let's go for a walk," I said.

"I'll start knocking down the wall," Marc called after me.

"Tomorrow," I shouted back. "Tonight is the club and I don't want any plaster or nails falling on anyone's head. And don't get any dust on that pile of quilts by the cash register. Nancy will kill me if the quilts get dirty."

"Whatever you want," Marc said. The grin even wider. Ryan moved toward him, but I pushed him out the door.

"What are you doing?" I demanded.

"What am I doing? What is it with you and that guy?"

"That guy? The guy who is renovating my grandmother's shop?" Ryan wasn't even the jealous type, or hadn't been until he dumped me and Marc came along. Of course, until he broke off the engagement I had been one of those in-love saps who didn't notice any other men on the planet. But if I was noticing one now, it wasn't really any of Ryan's business. "I don't want to have this conversation standing on the street," I said.

"So let's walk," he said as he took my hand. Since I had no choice, I followed as he led me down the street. We turned toward the river, walking two blocks to the edge of town. The river was looking gray and still, reflecting an unusually dark midmorning sky. It was about to storm. "How long have you known that guy?"

"Oh my God, Ryan. I met him the day after you broke up with me. I told you already. He's my grandmother's handyman."

"I don't like him. I don't think you should."

I thought for a second, but only for a second. "Well, I do like him. He's nice. He's funny. He's really into old buildings and making furniture." Ryan rolled his eyes. "Okay, then. He hasn't hurt me, and I like that in a man."

"Sleep with him, then," Ryan spat.

"Maybe I will," I shouted. At that moment I would have slept with Marc just for the revenge.

Ryan walked away from me, back in the direction we came

from. The sky opened up and rain started falling on my head, but I couldn't move. What was I doing? I loved Ryan. I wanted to marry him, didn't I? Maybe he'd had a change of heart and I didn't give him the chance to tell me. Marc was a nice distraction, but was a flirtation with him really worth putting a future with Ryan in jeopardy?

I headed up the street toward him. I would catch up and we would talk. I would listen, without being angry or hurt or defensive, and whatever he told me I could deal with. I hoped.

CHAPTER 19

I hurried back toward Ryan, but I couldn't find him. Hoping he was looking for me, with the same need to clear the air, I went back toward the shop. And I was right. When I turned the corner I saw Ryan outside the shop. But I had gotten his intention all wrong. He was standing over Marc, who was flat on his back on the sidewalk.

"Stay away from her," Ryan shouted and stormed off.

I ran over to Marc.

"Are you okay?" I helped him to his feet.

"Fine. Nice guy, your fiancé."

"Ex-fiancé," I said as I watched Ryan get in his car a few blocks down and drive away. "I'm so sorry. I don't know what to say."

"Don't apologize, for starters," Marc said as he gingerly touched his jaw and winced.

"Why would he hit you? Did he say?"

"No. But he didn't have to," he laughed. "He sure takes it badly when somebody gets in his way."

I was as much embarrassed by Ryan's behavior as I was touched by Marc's reaction. A few seconds ago I was running after Ryan, and now I was watching him walk away while I stood by Marc. The whole situation seemed to be getting out of hand.

✂

Marc didn't seem to need bandages, and I wanted to do something for him, so I headed to the local grocery and grabbed a six-pack of imported beer. Maybe it wouldn't make up for Ryan's behavior, but it was something. And I'd have something fattening to calm my nerves.

When I got back Marc was sitting on the floor, leaning against the checkout counter. There was the box of quilting tools left in the shop for tonight's meeting on the counter, next to a pile of neatly folded quilts that had been hanging on the back wall. I took the box of tools and set it on the floor between us, hoping that the rotary cutters and scissors would ensure my chasteness.

It worked, at least for a few minutes. We both quietly drank a beer and I wondered if he noticed how awkward I felt.

"He's never been like that before." I finally brought up the elephant in the room.

"Don't worry about it. I tend to bring out the best in people." As he smiled, he winced.

"I don't know. You've made me feel pretty good." The words popped out of my mouth before I'd decided if it was really the right thing to say.

Marc took my hand and held it in his. "Thanks. I don't know what it is about you, Nell. You make me want to be the guy you think I am."

I watched how his fingers stroked mine. It felt dangerous and sexy, and I leaned in closer. He looked up at me. He looked as if he might kiss me, but he was taking his time about it. So I leaned in farther. I pressed my lips against his lightly, waiting for permission. Just when I was sure none was coming, he suddenly put his hand behind my head and pulled me in closer.

The rain was pouring down when I left Marc at the shop. We had sat like two teenagers and made out on the floor of the quilt shop. While the storm had kept most of the foot traffic off the street, it was still daytime and we were sitting in full view of a picture window and hadn't noticed or cared. It wasn't until Marc waved to me through the shop window that I realized that our private moment was actually open to anyone walking past.

I was a block from the shop when I saw Ryan's car parked at the curb. Clearly our conversation wasn't over, and I figured now was as good a time as any to continue it, but he wasn't in the car. I realized I was relieved. Being with Marc had put me in a good mood, and I had a feeling a conversation with Ryan would bring it to an end. Still, I walked the rest of the way home knowing I had to deal with my feelings for both men, and the sooner the better.

When I got to the house my grandmother and Nancy were helping Natalie pick out some flannel fabrics for a quilt she was making for her son. Barney was too engrossed in the fabric selections to do anything but lift his head toward me and wag a little.

"Marc at the shop?" Eleanor asked.

I held my breath, wondering if somehow word had reached her about my afternoon. Then, as innocently as possible, I answered. "Yeah, he's dying to knock down the wall between the stores. I told him to wait until tomorrow, but who knows if he'll listen."

"We don't want debris all over the place tonight for the club meeting."

"That's what I told him."

"Hopefully he'll listen." She picked up a bolt of blue cowboy fabric and showed it to Natalie. "Ryan was here."

"At the house?"

"Yes. He seemed upset."

"I saw him, at the shop," I said. "He must have come here afterward."

"Did you talk?"

"Shouted, actually."

"Well, at least you're communicating." Her voice was so monotone I couldn't tell if she was being sarcastic, but I let the comment pass.

"Everything's ready for tonight," I said as I left the dining room. "I'm just going to lay down for a bit, and we'll head back at six-thirty."

The three women smiled, then turned back to the fabric Natalie held in her hands. I took it as my cue to head upstairs and try, at least for a little while, to pretend I wasn't making a mess of my life.

CHAPTER 20

At precisely six-thirty I started the car and pulled it as close to the front door as possible. It was still raining and I had nightmares of my grandmother sliding on the pavement, but she managed to get to the car with me on one side and Barney on the other.

"Be careful," she said at least six times in the six minutes it took to drive to the shop.

"You want to drive, Bigfoot?"

"Didn't your mother teach you to be nice to your elders?"

"I don't believe she mentioned it," I smirked. "Maybe she wasn't raised right."

"Don't have too much fun or I'll tell the girls you want to make a quilt."

We pulled up in front of the store before I could come up with a ripping response. Outside the shop Bernie, Maggie, Susanne, Natalie and Carrie were all huddled under umbrellas.

"Get inside," Eleanor shouted.

"I have the key," I reminded her.

"Then hurry and open the door."

I left Natalie and Carrie to help Eleanor out of the car and ran to the front door of the shop. I tried the key. Strangely, the door wasn't locked, just difficult to open. Marc must have forgotten to lock it and now something was jammed up against the other side.

"Help me push," I said to Bernie, and we shoved ourselves against the door.

I stepped inside and reached for the light, nearly tripping on whatever had blocked the door. Eleanor was now standing just outside and getting wet. I turned on the switch and looked around to help her inside.

"Oh my God," I heard her say.

I looked down. There was a man lying at my feet. It was another second before I realized it was Marc.

"Call 911."

"See if he's breathing."

"There's blood everywhere."

One after another the women of the quilt club took action, checking Marc's pulse, calling for an ambulance, helping my grandmother to a seat. Bernie, a fan of crime shows, advised everyone not to touch anything. I stood there staring at Marc's body. He was on his stomach, with a pool of blood coagulating around him.

Sirens were wailing in the distance, then drew closer and stopped in front of the shop. Paramedics jumped out of the ambulance and raced in. They were frantic for only seconds before deciding there was nothing for them to do. A police car pulled up, and Barney's friend, Officer Jesse Dewalt, got out. Dressed in jeans and a dark sweater, and looking even less like a cop than the night we met, he stood talking with a officer who had also just arrived. He wasn't wearing a jacket, a foolhardy move on a rainy September evening, but he didn't seem cold. Or in much of a hurry. He talked with the paramedics. He made a phone call. Finally, he hung up and walked through the door into the shop.

He glanced down at the body.

"His name is Marc . . . ," I started to say.

"We went to high school together," he interrupted without looking up at me. "You okay, ladies?"

"Jesse, dear, what happened?" asked Maggie.

Jesse put on latex gloves and moved closer, being careful not to step in the blood. He leaned over Marc. He seemed to be studying his face and hands. I could see there was a dark bruise on the side of Marc's jaw from where Ryan had hit him. But there was also a fresh cut on his cheek and scratches on his hands. The scratches had drawn blood, but they hardly seemed enough to cause death or create the pool beneath the body. Jesse grabbed Marc's shoulder and pulled it toward him. The source of the blood was immediately clear. A large pair of scissors lay under Marc's body and there was a dark wet hole in his chest. Near his body was Eleanor's favorite quilt, stained with blood.

"I think I'm going to throw up," I heard myself say. I ran down the stairs to the bathroom.

✂

I leaned my head over the sink and waited. I waited to faint, to throw up, to burst into tears, but nothing happened. I just stood there.

Marc was dead. Not two feet from where we had been kissing, he was lying in a pool of blood.

Upstairs I heard footsteps. I heard my grandmother talking. She sounded strong and in charge. I heard her say my name. She wasn't calling to me, though. She was talking about me. But I couldn't quite hear what she was saying. As much as I didn't want to go back upstairs, I didn't want to be fragile and fall apart while my grandmother was upstairs handling things like a grown-up. I took one last deep breath and headed for the stairs.

CHAPTER 21

When I walked upstairs, Marc's body was still there, only now it was being photographed. Half a dozen uniformed people were milling about, looking busy and official. In the corner, all the women of the Friday Night Quilt Club were huddled around talking with Officer Jesse. My grandmother had her hand on Natalie's arm, but Natalie didn't seem to notice. She stared straight forward as if no one else was there. Maggie and Bernie sat on either side of Susanne. Only Carrie was standing, and she couldn't seem to take her eyes off Marc. I walked over to the women, nearly tripping on a hammer that lay in the middle of the floor, several feet from Marc's toolbox.

"He wasn't a very nice person," Susanne was saying.

"Don't speak ill of the dead." Bernie leaned into her.

"Why not?" said Susanne, pointing to Jesse. "You know what he was like."

Jesse nodded.

"Are you talking about Marc?" I walked closer to them, and all heads turned me. "He was a very nice person."

"We're aware you thought so," Susanne commented dryly.

I knew my face had turned a bright red, but I tried to ignore it. I leaned toward Susanne as if I had some menacing comeback, but the truth was I didn't know what to say. I looked at my grandmother, who reached out and touched my arm. I stepped back from the group and stood there watching them gathered in their tight circle, just as they had been a week ago when we met. They were open and welcoming then, but I didn't feel any of that tonight. No one moved over to let me find a place in the circle. I felt as if I had walked up to the most popular girls in school and they were making it very clear I didn't belong. Despite my best efforts, tears started rolling down my cheeks.

Jesse turned his body fully toward me, standing directly between me and the rest of the group. For a moment he studied me, then said, "You're right, you know. Marc had his good points."

"Well, someone didn't think so, or he wouldn't be in that position, would he?" Susanne said sharply.

"I think it had to be the husband of one of his girlfriends," said Bernie. "There was that woman over in Peekskill. What was her name?"

"I don't think you need to go as far as Peekskill to come up with a suspect," Maggie said. "Besides, he just started this job. You would have to be from town to know he was going to be here tonight."

"And if you intended to kill him," Eleanor jumped in, "you would have brought your own murder weapon with you. That's a pair of my good scissors."

"But you cleared everything out of the shop. Why would your scissors be here?" Maggie asked.

"We left a box of supplies," I interjected. "In case anyone needed something at tonight's club meeting."

"That was so thoughtful of you dear," said Bernie. "You really have a knack for thinking of others. Just the way you've come up here to take care of your grandmother . . ."

Carrie burst into tears. "Oh my God," she muttered, never looking away from Marc's body.

Jesse cleared his throat. "Why don't you ladies go home and I'll take your statements tomorrow. We have a lot of work to do here and I need to call Marc's father and brother."

Susanne and Bernie jumped up to help Eleanor to her feet. Maggie touched Carrie lightly, and for the first time since I had come upstairs, Carrie's eyes moved away from Marc. Instead she looked toward me. But there was no kindness there, no sadness. Just a hard stare that made me feel guilty and embarrassed, without knowing why.

"I made lemon squares," Bernie said to Jesse. "I don't think we'll be eating them, so tell the other officers." She offered the wrapped plate to Jesse, who quickly unwrapped it and took a large bite out of one.

"Mrs. Avallone made lemon squares," Jesse announced, and several other officers and paramedics walked over.

"We didn't have time to make coffee," Bernie apologized to the group.

"We'll get some later." Jesse smiled at her. "It's going to be a long night. Sugar and caffeine are exactly what we need." Then he leaned over and kissed Bernie on the cheek, leaving a little imprint of powdered sugar behind.

Bernie blushed. "I'll stop in at your mother's and tell her you'll be here, working late into the night."

"Thanks. She wasn't expecting to keep Allison overnight, but she'll have to now."

"Poor little thing, she'll miss you."

"Are you kidding? They play dress-up, eat cookies, and watch movies all night. Allie much prefers the company of her grandma to her boring old dad." His smile was broad now. The dead body behind him seemed to be forgotten amid playful conversation and lemon squares.

Bernie just waved him off. "I've never seen a father and daughter closer. Lizzy would be proud."

"Excuse me," I said a little more meekly than I intended. "What about Marc?"

Jesse nodded. He finished the lemon square in two quick bites. "You're absolutely right."

"He was working on the shop," I said. "He was here in the afternoon, but when I left he said he was going to head home for a few minutes. I don't know where he lives . . ."

"A block from here," Jesse said. "He said he was coming back?"

"Yeah. I asked him to clean the place up before everyone came tonight." My face turned white. I'd asked him to come back and clean up. If I hadn't . . .

"It's not your fault, you know," Jesse said in a quiet and kind tone that finally made me see him as a police officer. He might not be the guns blazing kind you see in the movies, but anyone in trouble would be calmed by his reassuring certainty, just like I was now. "You should get out of here, take your grandmother home."

Jesse gave me a soft smile, but as I smiled back, his faded and he leaned over Marc once more.

✂

By the time Susanne and I had gotten Eleanor out the door, Maggie and Bernie were standing down the street exchanging theories about who had a reason to hurt Marc. "Enough of a reason" was how Maggie put it. Carrie was on her cell phone filling someone in on the news. Natalie was gone. None of the other ladies had seen her leave or knew which way she went. Even her mother seemed surprised.

"Let's go home," Eleanor said wearily.

I nodded. "Just what I was thinking."

✂

Eleanor stared out the passenger window most of the ride home, making it clear she didn't feel like chatting. Neither did I exactly, but I did want to know what it was about Marc that made his death seem so inevitable, even to nice women like Bernie. But my curiosity was fighting it out with something else. Maybe it was better not to know, I thought. Marc had been there for me, made me feel less thrown away, less expendable. This afternoon he had even made me feel desirable. Whatever everyone else thought about him, he had been nice to me. Maybe that was all I really wanted to know.

✄

My grandmother's house was dark in the distance as we pulled into the driveway. I would have left on a porch light or something, but Eleanor saw such indulgences as a waste of electricity.

"Nothing in the dark that isn't there in the light," she would tell me when I would leave lamps on. She said it with absolute certainty, but I never quite believed her. The dark, at least to me, was filled with things that dissipate at the flick of a switch.

If a porch light had been on, I would have seen the car parked near the house, but until my headlights hit it, I saw nothing. I parked behind the car and left my grandmother sitting in the passenger seat while I got out to investigate.

"Let me see who it is," I said, but I knew. I knew by the make of the car, by the dark silver paint color, by the scratch near the license plate. That car, or rather its owner, was the last thing either my grandmother or I needed to deal with after the evening we'd had. I looked around, but no one was there.

Eleanor rolled her window down. "What are you doing? Help me out," she demanded.

I walked over to the passenger side, got her crutches out of the backseat and leaned over so she could support herself on me as she got out of the car.

"We really should leave a porch light on," I said more to myself than to Eleanor.

"It's probably a neighbor." She nodded toward the car, but she didn't sound sure and I knew she was wrong.

We walked up the steps to the front door and I struggled with the lock. I wanted to get inside, but for some reason the key wasn't cooperating. I looked down and saw that my hand was shaking. Eleanor saw too. She took the key. In seconds the door was open and she hobbled inside. I was almost in myself when I heard steps behind me.

"Nell," said a soft but familiar voice.

I turned around. Ryan was standing inches away. Suddenly the porch light went on. In the light, I saw the blood on his hands.

CHAPTER 22

"What are you doing here?" I said loudly, surprised by how frightened I felt.

Ryan's voice was shaking. "Is he dead?" he asked.

I almost couldn't answer. "Yes." I finally got the words out. "Yes, he's dead." I stood frozen, not wanting to ask how Ryan knew Marc was dead.

"God," he said. "Oh my God."

Lights were going on all over the downstairs area of the house, flooding the porch. The front door creaked open. Barney came out fast, barking and growling at Ryan. Eleanor stood at the doorway.

"You should come inside. Both of you," she said.

So we did.

Eleanor and I sat at the kitchen table, silent and waiting until Ryan came down from the upstairs bathroom. He had washed the blood off and looked relieved that it was gone. He sat on one side of the table and my grandmother and I sat on the other. Barney stood guard between us. I felt like we were Ryan's jury, waiting for the evidence to convict or exonerate. But in this case, beyond a reasonable doubt wouldn't be enough. I wanted to know beyond all doubt that Ryan had nothing to do with the scene at Someday Quilts.

"I saw you," he said to me. He glanced over at my grandmother as if he were embarrassed to have her in the room. But I wanted her there, and it was clear she wasn't going anywhere no matter what. "I was walking back toward the shop to talk to you, and I saw you and that guy kissing."

Eleanor turned toward me, but since I couldn't bring myself to look her way I had no idea what kind of a look she was giving me.

"I know it's stupid of me to be so jealous," he said.

"You've never been before," I said.

He shrugged. "You've never given me a reason." He sounded tired—more than tired. "I don't know. Lots of things have been going on lately. I came up here to tell you. Then I guess I saw that guy—and you—and I felt like the biggest fool on the planet."

"I didn't even know him two weeks ago," I muttered, finding it hard to believe that so much had happened in such a short span of time.

"That's true," Eleanor broke in. "She met him after you called off the engagement."

"Postponed," Ryan corrected her, then shook his head. "Whatever, it doesn't matter."

"What did you do?" I finally asked the question that had been hanging in the air since his arrival.

"Nothing. I swear I didn't think I hit him that hard."

"You hit him," Eleanor said as if she were a detective trying to take his statement.

Ryan got up and walked over to the sink.

"Would you like some tea?" Eleanor asked.

"No, he wouldn't," I said. I didn't want to waste any time with hospitality. I wanted to know what had happened.

"Yeah," Ryan said at the same time, and filled the kettle with water.

✂

We all stopped talking, waiting for the kettle to whistle. When it did, Eleanor, Barney and I watched Ryan put three tea bags into a teapot and fill it with hot water. He opened the refrigerator as if he had lived there all his life and poured milk into a jug. He brought the milk, tea and three mugs over to the table.

"Do you take sugar?" he said to my grandmother, who shook her head.

It was all very surreally civilized. When Ryan sat down again and tea was poured, the break was over. My grandmother said again, "You hit him."

"Yeah. I walked back to the shop to find Nell." He looked down. "I saw the two of you." I felt guilty for a moment, then stupid, then just scared. Could Ryan really have killed Marc because of a few kisses?

"What did you do?" I asked again, with an impatience in my voice that surprised even me.

"I walked around. I went to some Irish bar on the next block and had a beer."

"Moran's," my grandmother clarified.

"I guess. I decided that I had to talk to you, Nell, to find out what was going on. So I walked back over to the shop. He was by himself."

"Marc," I interrupted. "His name was Marc."

"Okay. Marc was outside." I could hear anger rising in his voice, but just as quickly it was gone, replaced by tiredness and fear. "We started talking. He said something. I pushed him. I hit him. He hit back. I guess he fell against the building. He got a cut on his cheek. It looked bad. I just left him there." Tears welled up in his eyes. "I walked around for a while, trying to think. Then I decided I needed to know, so I went back to the shop to ask him." He paused and looked at me. "To ask him about his intentions with you."

I saw Ryan was waiting for a reaction, and I thought about commenting, but I decided it would only delay his story. "Then what happened?" was all I could get out.

"Well," he continued, "when I got back to the shop I saw an ambulance and police. I asked one of the cops what had happened, and he told me there was a guy inside who was hurt. He wouldn't tell me any more." Ryan sat back. "He was woozy. I should have called someone, but it didn't look bad enough to kill him."

"It didn't," said Eleanor. "He was stabbed."

Confusion, and then what looked like relief, moved across Ryan's face.

"Are you sure?" he asked her.

"Very," she said. "He must have gotten up and gone into the shop and someone came in and stabbed him."

"Come on," I said. "I get that Marc wasn't the town favorite, but are you honestly telling me that on the very day that a jealous boyfriend knocks him around someone else stabs him?"

Both Eleanor and Ryan looked at me like I was a stranger.

"Do you want me to have killed that guy?" Ryan asked.

"No," I said, and backed down. But I didn't exactly believe his story either.

CHAPTER 23

My grandmother excused herself ten minutes later, saying something about her tired leg. Ryan and I stayed in the kitchen and cleared up. We didn't say anything, so the only sounds were running water and the clanking of dishes. Barney, who had stayed close to Eleanor since her return from the hospital, was now glued to my side. I didn't know what to feel standing next to Ryan—safe, scared, angry or just numb.

So while Ryan washed the mugs, I took Barney out into the night for short walk. We walked down to the river and stared out at the blackness. The rain had stopped but the weather hadn't improved. I could feel a frost around me, but despite the cold and the darkness, I didn't want to go back inside. Instead, I took Barney along the edge of the river.

✂

A thousand years ago I was a bride-to-be. I had a man I loved who would always love me. I had a new apartment to decorate and turn into a home. I had a lover's knot quilt I would pass on to my children. Now what did I have? I looked out at the river, listened to the quiet and waited for an answer. None came. Resigned and feeling the cold, I turned back to the house.

✂

Ryan and I went upstairs, with Barney following close behind. I walked past the open door to my room toward the office at the end of the hall.

"I don't know how comfortable it is, but there's a pullout bed in that couch," I said to Ryan.

"I'm sure it's fine." I could hear the exhaustion in his voice, and wondered if I sounded just as empty and tired.

"I'll get you some sheets and a quilt," I said.

Ryan grabbed my hand as I was about to walk out of the room. For a second we stood, holding hands, then I pulled away.

✂

Once Ryan was settled for the night, I closed the door to my room and sat on my bed. I couldn't take it all in. What I knew was bad enough—I didn't even want to consider all that I didn't know. One minute I would reassure myself by saying that I knew Ryan, I knew he wasn't capable of murder. Then the next I would be reminded of the scene at my apartment just a couple of weeks ago when he blindsided me by postponing the wedding. Did I know him? My mind kept playing the question over and over. And then a more terrifying question crept in. Is there a murderer in the house?

✂

Nothing would be solved, I knew, by my sitting on the bed, so I got into my pajamas, switched off the light and lay under the covers. I don't know how long I lay there staring at the ceiling, the image of Marc's lifeless body in my mind, but eventually I must have drifted off. At some point in the night I felt as if I had entered a nightmare. My room looked like my room, but a shadowy figure was moving toward the bed. I jumped up.

"I'm sorry." I heard Ryan's voice in the darkness.

I switched on the light. "What are you doing?" I snapped.

Ryan stopped where he was standing, a few inches from the foot of my bed. "I couldn't sleep."

"Ryan, it's just not a good idea . . ."

"Why not? All I want to do is sleep next to you." He seemed hesitant, nervous. "Is that okay?"

I took a deep breath and nodded. Just a few hours before I'd been wondering if Ryan was a murderer, but now I was relieved he was in the room. It didn't make sense, but nothing was making sense. One minute I wanted nothing more than to be Ryan's wife, the next I was imagining a life without him. A life that included kissing other men. In that second I realized that maybe it was unfair to be so angry at Ryan for being confused, when I was so confused myself.

I pulled back the sheets and made room for Ryan in the bed. He climbed in and lay down with an audible sigh. "Good night," I said as I turned my back to him.

But he was having none of it. "I have to touch you," he said. He moved his body close to mine, putting one arm under my head and the other over my waist, spooning me. I could feel his chest against my back, his legs against mine. I wanted so much to relax into his arms, but I also needed to guard myself. I stared straight ahead and tried to find no comfort from the way his fingers moved down my arm.

He moved his head so that his breath was just above my ear. "I love you, Nell," he told me, just as he had so many times before.

I couldn't bring myself to say anything. For a few minutes I just lay there staring at the hand that reached out from under my head, feeling his breath on my neck.

"Did you do it?" I said almost to myself.

"No."

He kissed my ear. This was what I had wanted to happen from the moment he had called off the wedding. I turned around and let my lips meet his. My kisses with Marc had been schoolgirl, uncertain and strange. But Ryan's mouth, his hands, the feel of his skin, were all familiar to me. He moved on top of me without saying another word.

For much of the night, with a nearly deaf dog snoring on the floor beside us, we made love underneath our wedding quilt. Just as I had dreamed we would.

CHAPTER 24

I woke up to the front doorbell ringing. Ryan was asleep, still half on top of me. The bell rang again. I knew it would be a struggle for my grandmother to answer it, so I jumped up, put on my clothes from the night before and ran down the stairs.

Jesse was standing on the other side of the door.

"You have a visitor." He pointed to Ryan's car.

"My fiancé," I said, accidentally leaving out the ex. "He came up last night." Jesse raised an eyebrow but said nothing. "Do you want to come in?" I asked as if nothing strange had happened last night.

He walked through the door and looked around. "Is your grandmother up?"

"I don't know. I just got up. Let me check."

"Oh, you were in bed," he said, surprised. "You're wearing what you wore last night."

"It was the closest thing to me." I was suddenly embarrassed by his attention to detail. "Go into the kitchen. I'll get my grandmother."

✂

In the living room, Eleanor was not only awake but dressed and on the phone. When she saw me, she wrapped up her call.

"Who was at the door?"

"Jesse."

A worried look crept across my grandmother's face. "Nothing else has happened, has it?"

"I don't think so," I said, suddenly anxious at the thought. "How much more could happen?"

She grabbed her crutches. "I'm beginning to wonder that myself."

Barney, looking sleepy and confused, came walking down the stairs and joined us. He sniffed at my grandmother and walked behind her as she hobbled to the kitchen on her crutches. Then he turned his attention to Jesse, who got down on his knees and roughhoused with the old dog. Barney made it very clear he loved every second of it.

I stayed out of the way, making coffee and looking for something I could serve. We had already eaten most of the pies, cakes, casseroles and pasta dishes that friends had brought by, but there were some brownies. Hardly breakfast food, but I put them on the table.

"We're going to have to keep the shop closed for a few days, Mrs. Cassidy," Jesse said as he got up off the floor.

"It was closed anyway," she answered.

"He was remodeling the place?" Jesse asked.

"Expanding," I broke in. "My grandmother is taking over the diner next door."

Jesse looked at me. "I heard that. A big job for Marc." He turned back to my grandmother.

"I don't know," she said. "He did good work around here. Repaired the floor in the dining room last year and that looks nice."

"He loved the old houses," Jesse agreed. "And I know he loved that building your shop is in."

"He was excited about the remodel," I said, and a wave of sadness fell over me.

Jesse nodded and reached his hand out toward mine, but then

seemed to think better of it. Instead he took out a small tape recorder and placed it on the table. "I've got very bad handwriting," he said almost apologetically, pointing to the recorder. He turned it on and looked at my grandmother.

"Do you mind if we go over some details from last night?" he asked her.

"No, I'd like to," she said. "I'd like to be able to make sense of it for myself."

He nodded and turned to me. "It would be better if you weren't here."

"I'll be in my room," I said, and got up from the table.

Jesse nodded, turned to my grandmother and asked plainly, "Can you tell me what you saw last night, when you got to the store?"

As she started to talk I stepped back into the hallway. I wanted to check on Ryan. There was no hiding that he was here—that had already been established. But it would be better if Jesse didn't see the cuts on his hand, didn't know about the fights.

I went upstairs and into the bedroom as quietly as I could. Ryan was still asleep, draped across the bed as if he were passed out.

I wasn't sure why I wanted to protect him. Maybe I didn't need to. If Ryan was telling the truth, then he didn't need my protection. The smart thing would have been to wake him up and send him downstairs to tell his story. But what if he wasn't telling the truth?

✂

"Hey." Ryan opened his eyes, a smile creeping across his face.

"The police chief is here to take statements," I said.

"I should get dressed." He jumped up and put his pants on just as there was a knock on the door.

Jesse was standing in the hallway. "Is this your room, Nell?"

he said through the open door. I nodded. He walked in, looking around, first at the unmade bed and then at Ryan as he finished dressing. "The fiancé?"

"Yeah," said Ryan, and automatically extended his hand. They shook, but Jesse didn't let go. He turned Ryan's hand over and looked down at the bruised knuckles.

"Got into a fight?"

"Yes." Ryan pulled his hand back. "Two, actually. Both with that guy."

"The murder victim?" Jesse asked.

"He was after Nell."

Jesse nodded. "That was his style," he said. "Go after the vulnerable."

"Excuse me?" I interrupted. "The vulnerable?"

"The way I heard it," Jesse continued, "it was over between the two of you." He gestured at Ryan and me. "You came up here to nurse a broken heart, and Marc was helping you with that."

"The way you heard it," I repeated his words, feeling oddly uncomfortable that Jesse was aware of my friendship with Marc.

"It's a small-town, Nell," Jesse said quietly. "That's how I knew about the fight between your . . . fiancé here and Marc."

"Who told you?" I demanded.

Jesse smiled. "That quilt shop is in the center of town. And it has a picture window. Normally there are quilts hanging all over it, blocking the interior. But with those gone, anyone walking down the street can get a clear view of people fighting . . . or kissing . . . or anything."

Got it. Jesse, Ryan and everyone in town knew what I'd been up to yesterday afternoon. Suddenly I felt like the biggest fool all over again. I took a deep breath. "Then someone must have seen Marc's killer," I said.

"Afraid not. It probably happened after dark, and downtown

is pretty quiet in the evenings," he said. He turned back to Ryan. "Ryan, is it?" Ryan nodded. "First I need to get your fingerprints, then your statement if that's okay?"

Ryan sat on the bed, and Jesse took out what looked like a blank index card and a small inkpad and put it on the dresser. "I'll need to get your prints, to compare against several we found in the shop," he said to Ryan.

Then he put his tape recorder next to them. "And I'll need your statement. Is it okay if we do it here? I assume you wouldn't want to come to the station when it would be quicker, and quieter, here." Jesse looked up at me with a flash of sympathy in his face that made me feel he was trying to save me from being even more of a subject of local gossip. Then his expression changed to an unemotional stare. "You should see if your grandmother is okay."

I was sure that Ryan would tell the same story to Jesse he'd told me last night, but I wanted to hear it again. It was clear, though, that Jesse wasn't going to start asking questions while I was in the room.

✂

I walked out into the hallway. Jesse closed the door behind me. As much as I wanted to lean against the wall and listen in, I knew it wasn't right. Besides, in old houses like this one, the walls are thick. When I tried, all I could hear were indecipherable mutters.

I went to the kitchen to consult with Eleanor.

CHAPTER 25

"You won't believe what he's doing upstairs," I said to my grandmother as I walked into the kitchen. She was at the sink, balancing on one crutch and washing ink off her hands. "You too?"

"Me too, what?"

"He took your fingerprints. You don't think that's a little ridiculous?"

"He's conducting an investigation. He's trying to see whose fingerprints were on the scissors."

"Everyone's fingerprints were on the scissors," I spat out, but I knew that wasn't true. Mine were, as were my grandmother's, Nancy's and probably the entire quilt club. But Ryan's fingerprints shouldn't be there. As far as I knew he had never even been inside the shop. "What do you know about that cop, Jesse?"

"A little. He's a local boy. Went to New York and became a cop, got married and had little Allison. Then his wife got sick and they came back to town. She died about two years ago."

"That's not a little. You know his life story."

She shrugged. "Why are you interested?"

"He's questioning Ryan." I plopped down at the kitchen table.

She nodded. "Ryan didn't do anything wrong, so there's no reason to worry." She said it with certainty and a touch of reproach.

I paused and then asked the question I'd wanted to ask her since last night. "How do you know?"

Eleanor considered it for a moment, then said firmly, "It was in his eyes. And his voice. Everything. I'm not an expert on people, but I've lived awhile, and Ryan was genuinely surprised when I said Marc had been stabbed." She hobbled back to the kitchen table and with some difficulty sat down and rested her injured leg on a chair. "Didn't you think he was surprised?"

I sat back. "I guess I was too freaked out to pay close attention," I admitted.

"Well, you have so many emotions mixed up with Ryan and Marc that it would be hard to see it objectively."

I nodded. She was right, I decided. I would feel better when Ryan went back to New York and I could sort out my feelings—and mourn Marc—without him.

✂

Eleanor grabbed a pile of red fabrics that lay on the table in front of her. Slowly and with annoying patience, she began neatly folding them into triangles. With nothing else to do, I grabbed a piece of red fabric and copied her. We sat in silence, waiting for movement from upstairs. At least I was waiting. My grandmother seemed content to fold.

"What are we doing?" I asked, suddenly impatient with the silence.

"Folding fat quarters." Without waiting for me to ask the next, obvious question, she continued. "Fabric comes forty-four inches wide, standard. If you get a yard, you get a piece that's forty-four inches wide and thirty-six inches long. If you get a quarter yard, then you get a piece that's forty-four inches wide and nine inches long."

"These aren't forty-four inches wide."

"No, they're not," she said slowly as if I were a not-too-bright child. "A quarter yard of fabric is useful, but it has its limitations. If you only need a little fabric, but you need something longer than nine inches, you get a fat quarter, which is twenty-two inches, half the length of a normal quarter, and eighteen inches, twice the length."

"Why not just buy a half yard?"

"Because you don't need a half yard."

"But the shop would sell more fabric that way."

Eleanor moved my pile of folded fabric and replaced it with un-folded rectangles. "When we reopen, let Nancy run things." She patted my hand and smiled.

Two sets of boots could be heard walking down the stairs, but only one person came into the kitchen.

"Can I talk to you now?" Jesse's tone was still flat but it was clear that he wasn't asking me a question.

"I guess," I said and left my pile of red fabrics. "What do you want to know?"

"How about a walk?" Jesse seemed determined to take each of us out of earshot of the other.

We walked outside without speaking, crunching the leaves underneath our feet. I had nothing to hide, but I was unnerved anyway.

"Ask me," I quietly demanded after a minute or so of silence had passed. I couldn't take his patience, his quiet demeanor anymore.

"Ask you what?"

"If I killed Marc."

"You didn't."

"I know I didn't," I said immediately, then stopped and turned to him, realizing what he'd said, but his caramel eyes betrayed nothing. "How do you know I didn't kill Marc?"

"The coroner puts his time of death at around six p.m. You were with your grandmother at that time," he said with a slight smile. "And Eleanor wouldn't lie about that, even for you." His eyes stared directly into mine. "Besides, you had no motive to kill him. You didn't know him well enough."

If he was being sarcastic, I couldn't tell. "All right, what is it that I'm missing about Marc? Everyone in town seems to know something about him that I don't."

Jesse was looking straight at me, his voice calm and even. But I was struggling to stay composed. "Did your fiancé ever explain why he punched Marc?" he asked.

"Over me," I said quickly, but I realized I'd never asked Ryan exactly why a normally nonviolent man had gotten into two fights in the same day. "No, he didn't tell me." I felt exhausted by my confusion. "Why did he?"

"Marc apparently made some comments about you."

"So what?"

Jesse hesitated, clearly unsure of how much he should tell me. "About how Ryan had gotten you primed for Marc to go in for the kill." Jesse hesitated again and looked back toward the house. He took a breath and finished his thought. "Marc liked women who were vulnerable."

"You keep using that word. What do you mean exactly?"

He nodded. "He helped himself to their affections . . . and to their bank accounts."

I stared at him in disbelief. "I have a hundred and forty eight dollars in my bank account," I stammered.

"You have access to the shop. And to the house. And what's in it."

I wanted to laugh. I wanted it to be a joke, but Jesse didn't seem like a guy who would joke about such things. All I could do was stand there.

"I'm not saying he was only interested in getting his hands on Eleanor's stuff," he said quickly, "although I'm sure it crossed his mind. But Marc liked to play all angles. Maybe he thought he could get some money out of your grandmother if he left you alone. Or maybe he thought there was something valuable in the shop he could take if he had access to the place without your grandmother being here."

"And I'm that much of a sucker? Some guy smiles at me and I give him the keys to the place?" I said the words as sarcastically as I could, but as I was asking Jesse, I was also asking myself.

"Marc didn't go after just anyone." Jesse moved closer, a look of concern on his face.

"Just the really stupid ones."

"No. Smart, actually. He liked his women smart. He was a bit of a con artist, but he had good taste."

I knew he was trying to give me a silver lining for my cloud, but it seemed like insult upon insult. A smart woman would have seen through the flattery and puppy dog eyes.

"Maybe," I said, "one of the other . . . women found him at the shop."

"Maybe." He locked his eyes on mine, but they revealed nothing. "It's too early to tell."

"Officer Dewalt, you don't think Ryan killed Marc, do you?"

"It's Jesse."

"Okay, Jesse, do you think Ryan killed Marc?"

Jesse looked down at the ground, moving his boot in a circle in the dirt. It took only seconds for him to look up again, but it felt like hours.

"I think," he said slowly, "he had motive and opportunity. But I don't know yet what that really means." His eyes met mine but offered nothing but a slight amount of sympathy. "Do you think Ryan killed Marc?" he asked flatly.

I knew if I opened my mouth the words "I don't know" would have come out, so I slowly moved my head from left to right and back again. If I could get Jesse to believe Ryan wasn't hiding anything, maybe I could believe it myself.

CHAPTER 26

Ryan and Eleanor were huddled together at the kitchen table, deep in discussion, when Jesse and I came back inside. Eleanor had her broken leg up on one of the chairs and Ryan was adjusting a red and white quilt over her. The pattern looked exactly like its name, a bowtie.

"Everything okay?" I asked.

Eleanor looked up as if she had been caught doing something wrong. "Fine," she said stiffly. "Just waiting for you."

I looked at Jesse to see if he noticed the chill in the air, but he was looking through his wallet. He took out a piece of paper and put it on the table in front of Eleanor.

"That's a guy over in Nyack who does great remodeling work. He can probably start for you as soon as we're finished at the shop."

Eleanor studied the name on the paper. "Doesn't your brother-in-law do remodeling work in Nyack?"

"Yes, that's my brother-in-law . . . my ex-brother-in-law, I guess. He's a good worker."

She nodded. "Thanks for this. I'll give him a call."

Jesse turned his attention to Ryan. "You'll be available if I have any questions?"

"I'll be here."

"Here?" I said.

"He's staying with us for a few days," Eleanor said.

"In the house?" I said, now very confused.

"Your grandmother suggested I stay while this gets straightened out."

"Why? Jesse can always call you in New York if he has questions." I looked to Jesse for confirmation.

"Absolutely," he jumped in. "As long as you're available at the number you gave me in New York, I can call with any questions. I'm sure you have to get back to work on Monday."

"It's fine," said Ryan, a little too insistently. "I can take a few days off to help around here and answer any questions you have."

"But . . . ," I started.

My grandmother shifted in her seat. We had been talking over her head and it was clear she was making her presence known. "It's settled. It's my house and I've invited Ryan to spend a few days, which he agreed to."

She had spoken with the finality of a mother to her wayward toddlers. All three of us stood silent—unable to compete with her authority. Both Jesse and Ryan were looking to the floor, and I clenched my jaw and literally pressed my lips together so I wouldn't say anything I would regret in front of Jesse.

Eleanor just straightened the quilt on her lap and waited for one of us to challenge her. Finally, Jesse spoke.

"I need your prints, Nell," he said quietly, with a hint of apology in his voice.

I rolled up my sleeves, pressed my fingers one by one into the black ink and with Jesse guiding my hand, rolled each finger onto a blank piece of paper.

"I guess that's it, then," Jesse said. "I appreciate your cooperation."

"There was a quilt next to Marc's body," Eleanor said. "When can I get it back?"

"I don't know," Jesse said. "It had some blood on it. We'll need to keep it as evidence. Is it valuable?"

Eleanor shrugged. I knew that she was speaking of Grace's quilt, and I knew to my grandmother it was priceless. "Bring it back when you can," she said.

Ryan shifted his feet and looked up.

"I'll walk you out," he said to Jesse.

Jesse took the cue, nodding good-bye and walking toward the front door with Ryan.

✄

Now that we were alone, I unclenched my jaw. As I opened my mouth to yell something clever about meddling grandmothers, Eleanor moved her broken leg and made an exaggerated groan.

"I didn't have a choice," she said as she adjusted in the chair and winced from pain. It was amazing how, now that I was angry, she was suddenly in more pain than she had been since the accident.

"You didn't have a choice," I repeated. "Do you think I believe that?"

"If you trust me, you do."

"If I trust you? To do what? Decide my life for me?" I was over-reacting, and I knew it. But I couldn't stop myself.

Ryan stood in the doorway. "Nell," he started.

"No," my voice cracked. "I don't want to be manipulated by either of you anymore." I pushed Ryan out of the way and ran upstairs.

I slammed the door to the bedroom not once, but twice. I wanted to make sure that my grandmother got the point. I was well aware I was acting like a child, but Eleanor had to be equally aware she was treating me as one. It wasn't just that Ryan's presence was confusing, it was that my grandmother had decided for me that he should stay. I wanted her advice, not her interference.

I flopped on the bed, wrapping my quilt tightly around me. Eleanor always behaved as if she knew what was best for me. I suddenly realized Ryan had done the same thing. He'd introduced me to restaurants and people and a life that would be better for me than the life I'd been creating. I went along with him. Wasn't it time *I* decided what was best for me? I was willing to admit, but only to myself, that slamming doors wasn't exactly the best way to announce I could handle things from now on. But after everything that had happened, I was in no mood for rational discourse.

I could hear noises from downstairs, but I didn't know what was going on, and I wasn't about to venture out of the room to find out. I just lay on the bed with my quilt watching the sun outside.

I wasn't going to stay in the house, I decided. I needed space, and if Eleanor didn't understand that, then she could have Ryan as a houseguest, but she would have to live without me. I grabbed my cell and dialed my last loyal friend.

"Hey there, stranger," Amanda answered in her usual bouncy way.

"Can I sleep on your couch?"

"Anytime," she said immediately. "I thought you were staying at your grandmother's."

"I was. But I can't anymore."

I launched into a long and overly dramatic retelling of the events of the last twenty-four hours. How I kissed Marc. How Ryan showed up, fists flying. How Marc was found dead and I wasn't sure if Ryan had something to do with it. How I needed time and space and support, and was getting none of it from my grandmother, who had become Ryan's ally in the fight to win me back. If that was what Ryan was trying to do. I didn't really know what Ryan was trying to do.

"Do you want to get back together with Ryan?" Amanda interrupted.

Good question. Until yesterday, I had assumed the answer was yes. But I had also assumed it wasn't an option. But now with Ryan here, I wasn't sure.

"Do you think I should take him back?"

Amanda was silent.

"Are you still there?" I asked.

"I'm thinking," she finally said.

"Should I play some *Jeopardy!* music while you come up with your answer?"

"I think that Ryan hasn't been fair to you, and you should think about what you really want. If what you want is Ryan, you know I'll be behind you one hundred percent."

There it was, the coded warning of girlfriends everywhere: "*If it's what you want* (translated: it's a huge mistake) *I'll be there for you* (translated: I'll still listen to you whine about his faults, even though—to be clear—you are making a huge mistake).

"I need time," I said.

"Then take it." Amanda breathed heavily on the other end of the phone. "I'm sorry."

"You're the one person who doesn't owe me an apology."

She didn't respond.

CHAPTER 27

From the hallway, I could see that Eleanor was alone in the living room, propped on her bed.

In the few hours I'd been upstairs, things in the house had gotten quiet. Ryan was nowhere to be found, so it seemed as good a time as any to have the talk. I stood just outside the door and watched Eleanor sew quietly while the news played in the background. She was working so intently she didn't seem to notice me standing ten feet away. Barney was lying at the foot of the bed and the rest was covered with squares of pastel fabrics as Eleanor appliquéd animals on each square.

After several minutes and without looking up, she barked, "Are you going to stand in the hall or are you coming in?"

I walked into the room. "I'm the one who's angry, not you, so lose the attitude," I said with as much strength in my voice as I could muster.

The slightest smile crept on my grandmother's face. "You used to look just like that when you were three and I wouldn't let you play outside by yourself."

"I'm mad at you," I said, losing steam.

"Why are you angry?" she asked innocently.

I almost laughed. "Are you pretending to be senile?"

Eleanor put down her sewing and gave me a long, hard stare. "I'm not sure I'm pretending." She winked. "Nell, I'm sorry. You're a grown woman and I obviously have no right to tell you or Ryan what to do. It's just when you've lived as long as I have . . ."

I plopped on the bed. "Not the 'I'm older so I know more' line."

She patted my hand. "No. It's the 'I'm older so I've made more mistakes' line."

"You haven't made any mistakes. You've survived. You've succeeded. You're an example to women everywhere."

"Are you making fun of me?"

"Only a little." I lay down and starting petting Barney's belly. "I don't have your strength."

"After your grandfather died, I moved in here to look after Grace. You know about that," she said.

"Sort of."

"Well, Grace was an old woman and she needed a companion. I think a widow with two small children was more than she bargained for, but she was a wonderful person and she made us feel welcome." My grandmother shifted slightly, and continued. "I know you think I was strong and just kept going after your grandfather died, but the truth is I was scared and lonely. Once a week I used to get on the train and go to another town—Cold Spring, Beacon, anywhere. Once I even went into New York City and I spent the whole day walking around dreaming about living there."

"Then you came back."

My grandmother looked at me, as I was slightly addled. "Obviously."

I put my head on her shoulder. "The moral of your story is that you think I'm running away from dealing with Ryan."

"I think you had your whole life planned out, just like I once did, and now you're faced with the idea that your life might be very different. If I'm pushing you, I'm sorry, but I think it's time you dealt with that. Running away is not the answer."

"No," I said quietly, then shifted the subject to one I had the strength to discuss. "But quilting is, I suppose."

She smiled. "It was for me," she said, and went back to her sewing. I just sat next to her on the bed and watched her sew a little yellow duck onto a pink fabric background.

"Who are you making that for?" I asked.

"No one in particular." She held the block out for inspection. "I like to keep a few quilts handy. The quilt club gives them to the premature babies at the hospital."

"It's nice . . . that you do that." I took the fabric from her hand and she handed me the needle and thread. "Show me how."

"You catch a little bit of the duck with your needle and a little bit of the background," she explained as I took a large stitch.

I kept going until I had finished sewing the duck onto the background fabric. It was obvious this quilt had two sewers— one an expert, and the other someone who could be confused with a high-functioning monkey. But I didn't care how bad my stitches looked. I was proud of my work. I showed it to my grandmother.

"Not bad," she said, lying.

"Let's do another one."

She chose a square for herself and handed me a pink square of fabric and a small blue teddy bear, and I set to work.

"You are now part of a long tradition," Eleanor said as we worked.

"Yes, I know. Quilting goes back to the beginning of this country, to Europe before that and possibly to ancient Egypt," I recited. I had heard this speech before.

"Well, yes," she said. "But I was thinking that you are joining the great quilting tradition of using fabric and thread to calm your nerves and get you through a difficult time."

I had to admit that touching the soft flannel fabric had the same effect as petting Barney. I found myself completely engrossed in each stitch, moving at a slow but steady pace around the pattern, almost as if I were meditating.

"My first quilt—" My grandmother leaned in. "God it was awful. It was the fifties, and quilting was a dying art. Everyone wanted modern, sleek stuff. We were all caught up in gadgets, cooking TV dinners," she laughed. "The idea of doing something as old-fashioned as cutting up a perfectly good piece of fabric just to sew it back together again seemed, well, crazy."

"So why did you do it?" I asked as I finished my second square and moved on to the third.

"At first I was being polite. Grace quilted, and she was so kind to me and your mom and Uncle Henry. When she asked me if I'd like to learn, I said yes. I thought I wouldn't like it." She patted the fabric in her hands, smoothing the square. "But I realized," she continued, "a quilt could be whatever I wanted. It could be straight and square. It could be colorful and wild. I was in complete control of the process." She looked toward me. "There are certainly rules. In everything there are always rules. But it was the first time I realized I could follow the rules or I could break them, and neither choice was wrong."

"Sounds pretty rebellious."

"Anything you do that is truly yours is rebellious." She watched my stitches for a moment. "Now we're starting our own tradition. I'm the elderly woman being taken care of . . ."

"And now you're teaching me," I said, and showed her my teddy bear block. "What do you think, in fifty years will I quilt as well as you?"

She fingered the uneven stitches that held the teddy bear to the pink fabric. "Maybe not in fifty years," she said, and smiled.

After an hour of sewing small animals onto blocks, my fingers were starting to hurt. I stretched and wondered about what was in the kitchen.

I was almost out of the bed when Eleanor looked up. "Whatever his reason for calling things off, it was because of him, not you. Once you know that, you won't need to look for reassurance in whatever man comes along."

"Is that what you think I was doing with Marc?"

"Yes."

"There was more to it than that," I said, a little defensive. "That's just what you saw."

She sighed.

"What does that sigh mean?" I was now turning red. My grandmother said nothing, but I knew. "Did all the woman in the quilt club sit around discussing my relationship with Marc?" She said nothing. "You must have all thought I was very stupid."

"Nancy's husband has a gambling problem that means she probably won't be able to afford to keep paying for her boys' education. Carrie's husband prefers to be at work than at home with her and the kids. One of Bernie's husbands had a heart attack and left her for the nurse." She took a breath. "And Natalie's husband wanted time off from the marriage, whatever that means, about a year and a half ago, and poor Natalie got herself involved in a rather painful affair."

"Well, you're certainly up on the local gossip."

"My point is, no one judges you or pities you or thinks you were foolish. We all have our problems, and we all love the men in our lives, even when they disappoint us."

"I'll talk to him," I said.

"Whatever you want." She smiled, and raised the volume on the television. "Let's see what nonsense the world has gotten itself into today."

I decided against a trip to the kitchen and settled back on the bed. Instead I listened to the newscaster tell a story about a rising terror alert in Washington, followed by a report on a killer tornado sweeping the Midwest.

I felt very safe in this bed, in this little town on the Hudson. I closed my eyes, finally feeling a little peace, until I realized I wasn't safe, not even here. The image of Marc's lifeless body filled my mind. Then I saw picture after picture of Ryan standing over Marc, angry and jealous, just hours before Marc was killed.

Even more disturbing was the realization that not only did I probably know the killer, my grandmother may have just invited him to stay.

CHAPTER 28

When night came, I stayed downstairs and shared the bed with my grandmother and Barney. It felt comfortable and warm there, and I didn't want to risk another midnight visit from Ryan, not while I was feeling so unsure about everything. I got up early and walked Barney for longer than he wanted to be walked, then came back to the house and looked for something to do.

I stared at the contents of the refrigerator for several minutes, as if ingredients were going to jump up and make themselves into something delicious. I saw some strawberries and box of blueberries and was ready to have a simple, healthy breakfast of fruit salad when I got a better idea. After searching through my grandmother's recipe cards, I found one for blueberry muffins.

Following it exactly, I mixed the dry ingredients in a bowl that was too small and mixed the milk and eggs in a very large bowl. Then, after carefully checking the recipe to make absolutely sure I was doing it right, I mixed the two together, folded in the fresh blueberries, and had a taste. To my relief, it tasted like muffin batter. I had forgotten to preheat the oven, but by the time I found the muffin tin and poured the batter into the cups, I figured the oven was hot enough. Fifteen minutes later—much to my surprise—I took perfectly baked, moist muffins from the oven and set them down on the table with a pot of coffee. I hesitated, then tore one in half. Steam rose from the middle. It was a creamy beige, with small dots of a purplish blue throughout—just how a blueberry muffin should look. I pinched off a bit and put it in my mouth. A light cake surrounded a pop of blueberry flavor.

"My compliments to the chef," I said out loud to myself.

Ryan staggered sleepily into the kitchen and watched the domestic scene with clear surprise.

"I didn't know you could bake," he said.

"Apparently I can." I smiled, still impressed by my accomplishment. "Have one."

He cautiously took a bite, then greedily ate it all. "These are really good," he praised me with his mouth full of muffin.

I nodded and made a tray of coffee and muffins to take to my grandmother.

✂

Eleanor was up and hobbling around when I walked into the living room.

"I brought you breakfast," I said, and put the tray down on the bed.

She eyed the tray, then picked up a muffin. "It's still warm."

"I followed your recipe."

She took a nibble. "I could not have done a better job myself," she said, paying me her highest compliment. After eating the rest of the muffin, she turned to business. "I've called Jesse's brother-in-law. He'll meet us at the shop at noon."

"Are the police letting us back in?"

"Briefly. But Jesse called me to say the place will be all ours tomorrow."

"So they've found as much as they will find?" I asked.

"I assume, dear. Put some milk in the coffee, will you?"

I did as she asked. "Did Jesse say if he found anything?"

"No." She stopped. "He asked me about a hole in the wall."

"Marc was knocking it down."

"Yes, but there was a deposit bag stuffed in the wall from my bank." She sipped her coffee. "It was empty, but he wanted to know if I knew anything about it."

"Do you?"

"When are you taking your detective's exam?" She peered at me. "No, I don't know anything about it. Most likely it dropped behind the shelves lining that wall."

"And got stuffed into the wall? That doesn't make sense."

"Maybe a very smart mouse wanted a comfortable bed," she said. "I can't see that it has anything to do with Marc, poor boy." She got up and steadied herself on a crutch. "It's after nine. At my speed, it will take the next three hours to get ready."

Her plan was to be bathed and dressed and ready to leave for the shop by eleven-thirty. She had declined any help, other than asking Ryan to put a kitchen chair in the downstairs shower. Whether it took her longer or not, my grandmother was determined not to be, in her words, "a fussy old woman about it."

"I may not be able to do a lot of things," she said, "but I can take care of myself."

"Then you've got me beat by a mile," I sighed.

"Not true. You can sew a nice quilt square and can follow a recipe that makes a darn fine muffin."

"And in 1952, that would be all I needed."

"Yes," she replied, her sarcasm at full volume. "No woman had problems in 1952."

"Take your shower," I said, another battle of wits lost.

She grunted. "Close the door behind you."

Ryan and I waited awkwardly in the kitchen, talking about the tornado in the Midwest, and how, thankfully, it had done little damage and cost no lives. How quickly a relationship goes from intimate chatter to banal chitchat.

✄

When Eleanor was ready, I packed up the car with her crutches and an oversized sewing bag, then settled Barney in the backseat while Ryan helped her to the car.

"I'm going to walk to the shop," Ryan said suddenly as he closed my grandmother's car door.

"You don't need to be there," I said.

"Why not?" interrupted Eleanor. "It will be quite the party. I talked to Nancy this morning and she and the quilt club are heading over for a peek." She was interfering again, but I knew there was no point in making an issue of it.

"I'll bet Jesse will be thrilled," I said as I pulled out of the driveway.

"I think we all need to understand what happened," she said quietly.

"It feels like they all need to gawk. No one is exactly grieving, if you haven't noticed."

She nodded. "I suppose we owe Marc that. I do, especially."

"Why you?"

"He was in my shop, working for me. If I hadn't hired him . . ."

"He would have been killed somewhere else."

Eleanor turned her head away from me and looked out the window. "Maybe."

$\mathcal{C}$HAPTER 29

As Eleanor predicted, the shop—or at least the street outside it—was getting to be quite a party when we arrived. Susanne and Natalie were looking in the window. Maggie, Bernie and Nancy were exchanging theories on the crime, and Carrie, an ever-present coffee in her hand, was watching Jesse talk to another man.

"Jesse says only the two of you and his brother-in-law are allowed in the shop," Nancy complained as we arrived. "I really think you should insist I be allowed in. I do work there. I am affected by the design."

"I agree," said my grandmother reassuringly, though I doubted she felt she needed Nancy's—or my—presence in the shop.

Jesse nodded at both of us, but, as always, turned his attentions first to Barney. By the time the two were done with their greeting, Ryan was walking to meet us.

"Came by to help?" Jesse asked him.

"Observe, really," Ryan started to say, then looked around to see that all eyes were on him.

"You are Nell's . . . friend," Maggie said crisply, pausing just enough between "Nell" and "friend" to make it clear to Ryan that everyone present was aware of the entire history of our relationship.

"I am," said Ryan gamely, holding out his hand. "Nice to meet you."

Ryan met her suspicious eyes, and I could see she was quickly charmed by him. Then each of the quilt club in turn shook his hand, exchanged pleasantries and was won over by his easy smile. It was a sad, sick commentary on my feelings that I was both annoyed by the women's reactions and proud that Ryan could easily captivate such a difficult audience.

I decided not to pay attention to Ryan's growing fan club, and instead pretended to listen to the discussion between my grandmother and Jesse's brother-in-law, Tom. Tom was a solid man of about thirty, slightly balding, and with the easy smile that Jesse lacked. His hands were large and covered with nicks and calluses. I could see Eleanor noticing his hands at the same time I did, and nodding approvingly. This was a man unafraid of hard work, she seemed to be thinking.

When they headed over to the old diner site, Nancy, Jesse, and I followed. Eleanor pointed to where the office and the bathroom should be, where shelves should be hung, and showed him the napkin that had been our original plan. Tom nodded, took notes and walked the space, hitting beams and saying how solid they were.

I looked over at Nancy, who for all her insistence on being included, seemed as distracted as I was.

"I hope he can do this quickly," I whispered to her.

"I'd love to get this over with myself," she whispered back.

Eleanor shot us a look as if we'd been caught passing notes in an exam. We immediately shut up.

"Let's look at the other side," Tom said.

Nancy, Jesse and I held back as my grandmother hobbled toward the door. Tom, being new, offered to help without being asked, and even called her ma'am.

"I'm fine," she shot back, even as she leaned on his arm to get down the one step to the street.

Outside the women completely lost interest in Ryan as they saw us head toward the quilt shop door. This was what they had come to see, and each of them wanted a good look.

"I thought only the killer was supposed to return to the scene of the crime," I said to Jesse as we walked into the quilt shop.

"Maybe they all did it." He smiled as he closed the door on everyone but Tom, Nancy, Eleanor and myself.

Inside the shop seemed cold and full of secrets. Outside I could see the women were openly staring through the large display window, but there wasn't really anything to see. Marc's body was gone, though traces of his blood remained on the floor. Nancy and I stared at them, but Tom merely stepped past as if they weren't even there.

"Is this where you want the cash register?" he asked as he moved in front of the picture window.

"I hadn't thought of moving it there, but I like that idea." Eleanor nodded.

"With the bigger space you can move it. It makes for a better flow of customers," he said.

"I can see that." She smiled brightly at him.

Tom lit up at her response. In only ten minutes of knowing my grandmother, he already sought her approval as much as the rest of us did. He started making other suggestions, changes in the plan on the napkin. He talked about adding whimsical touches, like a crib to hold the baby fabrics. He suggested a stronger wood for the shelves, crown molding at the ceiling and a revarnish of the wood floors.

"I was thinking of replacing this floor," Eleanor said.

"People don't look down when they shop," Tom said. "All you need to do is freshen it up and cover up the . . . stain." He pointed to Marc's blood. "There are better places to spend your money than on a floor."

Eleanor nodded. "Marc was going to do this for very little money. As you can imagine, a quilt shop in a small-town operates on a thin margin of profit. And I'm an old woman. I'm not likely to reap the benefits of a complete overhaul for more than a few years." She was playing him, but he seemed not to notice. "With the added expense of your labor, which is, I'm sure, well worth the cost, I'm don't know that I can afford all these fancy extras."

"I suppose I can cut out some things," Tom replied.

"What things?" I interjected.

"We can do something simpler. Keep as many of the old materials as possible. I can work without an assistant, but it will take longer."

"That won't do," Eleanor said. "This can't take longer than a few weeks or it's not worth doing." She seemed to be genuinely considering just returning the shop to its previous, overcrowded state.

"Oh, Eleanor, we've gone too far to turn back now," Nancy said.

Tom looked as his feet. "I know a young guy who works practically for free just to get some carpentry experience," he said. "And as far as my labor is concerned, I can lower the price a bit, for a trade."

Eleanor smiled just a little. "Trade what?"

"Well, I passed this shop many times when I visited my sister. And someone here made her a quilt when she went to the hospital."

"The quilt club," said Eleanor. "The ladies outside, Nancy and myself."

"Well, it was really nice, and it cheered up my sister throughout that whole ordeal." Tom looked toward Jesse, who nodded slightly and looked away. "It got me to thinking. My wife is home with our twin boys all day, and she's awfully stressed about it. I thought maybe if I . . . if you . . . made her a quilt, she could curl up in it at the end of the day and it would be, you know, something special just for her."

"That's the trade you would like?" Eleanor said.

"If it's not too much trouble."

"What are your wife's interests?"

"Um," said a puzzled Tom, "she likes to garden, or she did before the boys."

Eleanor steadied herself on one crutch and held out her hand. "It's a deal," she said. Tom reached out his, and they shook on it.

"You'll start tomorrow?"

"Yes, ma'am . . . Mrs. Cassidy."

"So will I. On the day I'm done with the quilt, I'd like you to be done with the shop."

"She's fast, by the way," I warned.

Tom just nodded. "First thing we should do is get paper over the picture window. I'll need to leave tools and supplies in here overnight, and people sometimes help themselves to things on a construction site. Especially if they can get a clear view in like this."

I turned bright red, remembering my afternoon with Marc.

"I've got the paper in my truck," Tom said. "I can do it now, if that's all right."

"It's fine," Jesse said. "We've done all the fingerprint and blood work here, but I'm not releasing the scene completely until tomorrow morning. I want to give it one more look."

"We'll stay out of your way until tomorrow," Eleanor said. "In fact, we should all go now."

Eleanor headed for the door, and the others filed behind her, like a rock star's entourage. But my attention had turned to the hole in the wall. I walked over and examined the space.

"What?" Jesse was suddenly behind me.

"The hole . . . it's larger," I said.

"You remember the size?" He looked at me, a bit impressed, maybe, but mostly skeptical.

"Yes," I said. "Marc and I discussed it. I remember it was about the size of an orange. It's bigger now, grapefruit size, maybe."

"Well, you know your fruits," he said lightly, but he bent down and examined the hole more closely.

"Are you coming?" Eleanor called back to me.

"In a second," I said. Then Jesse and I both turned and followed the others out of the shop as Tom came back in with a large roll of brown paper.

CHAPTER 30

Tom felt he would need two weeks, with one helper, to complete work on the shop. I agreed to supervise the work while Nancy helped my grandmother out at the makeshift shop at her house.

"We have some work to do," she said to the ladies as she exited the shop. Then she told them about Tom's extra charge for the work. "Construction on this place starts tomorrow morning, and then it's a race to see if we finish before Tom. I don't want to give him any excuse for delays."

"I say we keep it simple, maybe small squares in color-wash effect, greens, yellows, pinks, purples . . . a kind of Monet's garden," said Nancy, immediately sketching out a quilt on the back of an envelope. "If you all work on that, maybe Eleanor and I can appliqué flowers and vines along the borders."

Everyone had gathered around to see her design, and then just as quickly they dispersed to their cars, ready to get started.

"We should get to Eleanor's and pick the fabrics," said Maggie.

"Natalie," Jesse called out. "Can I speak with you a second?"

Natalie stopped and turned to Jesse. "Sure," she said nervously. "What for?"

"Just a quick question."

"Well, we'll wait," said her mother, Susanne.

"That's not necessary," Jesse said firmly. "I can drop her at Eleanor's."

Susanne took a long look at her daughter, then climbed into her car. Ryan was all but kidnapped by Bernie, who insisted repeatedly that he join her for the ride over. After a few protests, he went along.

Eleanor was taking her time walking toward our car. The hard-nosed businesswoman of a minute before suddenly seemed tired and fragile.

"Just give me a minute, dear," she said. "Maybe this has all been too much for me."

So while Tom took measurements in the shop, Eleanor leaned against the car as if she needed to catch her breath and Barney and I stood by, waiting. I watched as, inches away from me, Jesse moved close to Natalie.

"Where did you go the other night?" Jesse asked.

"Home," she said quickly.

"Not according to your husband. And why didn't you return my calls yesterday?"

"I was busy," she said, even more quickly.

"Try again," Jesse almost snapped, in an uncharacteristic show of emotion.

"After what happened I went for a walk," Natalie said, her voice quivering. "I could hardly go home. I needed time to . . . grieve, I guess."

I watched Jesse blink slowly, deliberately. "Where did you walk?"

"I don't know."

"You don't know where you walked? You've lived in this town your entire life."

"So what?"

"It's not much of an alibi, Natalie," he said coldly.

"Do I need an alibi?"

"Yes, I think you do, considering your history with Marc."

Marc, I suddenly realized, was the man with whom Natalie had had the painful affair my grandmother mentioned—not an old boyfriend from before her marriage but an old boyfriend from a time when she, like me, had been vulnerable. And maybe Marc had been taking advantage of her, as Jesse suggested he was about to do with me. My mind was racing and I leaned toward Jesse and Natalie unconsciously, only to pull back when I saw Jesse look over at me.

"I have to go to Eleanor's now," Natalie said stiffly.

"We'll drive you," I found myself saying, not even pretending I wasn't eavesdropping.

"Thanks," said Natalie, and she hopped into the back of the car.

Jesse paused, then stepped toward my grandmother. "Feeling better, Eleanor?" he said without obvious sarcasm but with a tone that suggested he didn't quite believe her need for rest.

"Yes, thanks," she said, and smiled. With a sudden burst of energy she got herself into the car.

Jesse looked at me, his face slightly flushed.

"Are you okay?" I asked, and then felt intrusive.

He nodded. Then he turned and walked back toward the shop without saying anything else.

✂

In the car on the way back to the house, Natalie burst into tears and sobbed, "He hates me."

"Who hates you?" I asked, but Eleanor touched my hand to quiet me.

"Don't let him get to you, dear," she said to Natalie.

"I'm not a perfect person. I admit that," Natalie said. "But I did my best. I really did."

"Of course you did," Eleanor said soothingly. "Jesse is just very sensitive on the subject."

"It was hard on me too," Natalie said through her tears.

"Of course. It was a terrible thing," Eleanor said. "But you can't take it so personally."

Behind me Natalie sniffed and continued crying, while Barney whimpered and tried to comfort her. With nothing else to go on but the obvious tension between Jesse and Natalie, my mind started to go through the possibilities. Did Natalie have some kind of criminal record? Or maybe there was something about her relationship with Marc that was worth killing over. Or, as unlikely as it seemed, had Jesse, Marc and Natalie been involved in a romantic triangle? Whatever the case, it didn't seem like anyone was anxious to fill me in on the details. If I wanted to know, I would have to fill them in for myself.

CHAPTER 31

All the cars were already parked in the driveway when we pulled up, and everyone was waiting by the front door. Except Ryan. Somehow he must have managed to get away from Bernie's grip, but I wondered where he had gone.

"Everything okay back there?" Susanne called out as we pulled up.

"Fine, just fine," said my grandmother.

Natalie jumped out of the car and she and Susanne huddled just a few feet away from the rest of us. I assumed Natalie was filling her mother in on the details of the conversation, but they were just out of listening range.

While the women went to the dining room to choose fabrics, I went back to the kitchen to make coffee. And to look for Ryan. Mostly to look for Ryan. He wasn't in the kitchen. He wasn't upstairs. I was tempted to ask Bernie where he had gone, but I didn't want to seem interested. So I ended my search, went back to the kitchen and made coffee for the others.

"Look at you, Susie homemaker," came a familiar voice.

I turned to see Amanda standing in the doorway.

"What in the hell are you doing here?" I almost knocked over a chair running to hug her.

She hugged me back and we stayed locked like that until another familiar voice broke the spell.

"I don't remember you ever being that glad to see me," he said. It was Ryan, standing just behind Amanda.

"Did you know Amanda was coming?" I asked.

"No, she just showed up a few minutes ago."

"I took the train up," she said excitedly. "I tried to call you, but I couldn't reach you, so I called Ryan's cell. He picked me up at the train station. I can't believe this house. It's so cool."

"Why did you come?" I said. "Not that I'm not glad to see you."

"You seemed like you needed me," she said as she sat on the kitchen chair. "Is that coffee for anyone?"

"Yeah, sure." I poured a cup, then sat next to her and stared. "I'm so glad you're here."

"I'll bring the coffee in to the ladies," Ryan said. "Don't talk about me while I'm gone."

"You think you're so interesting." Amanda winked at him in that flirtatious way she had with every man, even ones that were taken. Of course Ryan wasn't exactly taken, and getting the story was why, I knew, she had really come to Archers Rest. As soon as Ryan was out of the room, Amanda turned to me and leaned in. "So . . . tell me everything."

"There isn't anything to tell. Not really. I mean there's a million things, but nothing with Ryan."

"Where did he sleep last night?"

"Upstairs in my room," I said.

"Then there's something to tell," she said.

"I slept with my grandmother and her dog."

"That's not some creepy small-town tradition, is it?"

Amanda was anxious to meet my grandmother and the women I'd been talking—and complaining—about since I arrived in Archers Rest, so I led her into the dining room.

There the group was huddled over piles of fabric in every shade of the rainbow. They all seemed like solid colors until I got close and realized they were mottled, with variations of the same color in a cloudlike effect. Others seemed to have been tie-dyed in different shades. It seemed to me they didn't need to be cut up and made into a quilt. They were beautiful just as they were. But the rest of the room's occupants didn't seem to share my view. They were already debating how to cut the fabric, in what order and by whom. And it was a lively debate. My grandmother sat in a chair leaning over so far to examine the fabrics that I thought she would fall out. Maggie and Natalie, the oddest of friends, yet always joining forces, grabbed fabrics and threw them on the floor to where Nancy sat with Bernie and Carrie. The three women would put each one next to fabrics that had already been chosen, while the others shouted out "yeahs" and "nays" to each new selection. Only Susanne didn't seem to be interested in the free-for-all. She sat quietly next to Eleanor, staring into the pile of fabrics, a million miles away from the rest.

"Who's this?" Eleanor suddenly noticed that Amanda and I were in the room.

"This is Amanda, my friend from New York," I said. "This is my grandmother and her Friday Night Quilt Club."

"And Ryan," said Bernie.

Ryan was busy moving coffee cups out of the way of flying fabric and didn't even look up.

"Amanda and Ryan and I work together," I said.

"Well, Amanda," Nancy held up a bolt of mottled light green fabric, "what do you think of this?"

"I think it's lovely," she said, clearly unsure of what answer she was supposed to give.

"I agree." Nancy added it to the quickly growing pile of chosen fabrics.

"Don't you have enough?" I asked as the bolts of fabric teetered over.

All the women laughed. Not just laughed, but laughed as if I had uttered truly the stupidest thing ever said.

"You can't have too many fabrics, dear," Maggie admonished sternly.

"Why not?" Amanda asked with just the right amount of naiveté and interest. They had her.

"This," Nancy explained, pointing to the fabric, "this is our paint box. I use one green for, say, a leaf. But I shade it with a slightly darker green from a different fabric."

"So the more fabric, the more depth," I jumped in.

"Exactly." My grandmother's eyes lit up. "The more fabrics you use, the more you can say in your quilt. You can draw someone in, make it so their eyes move across it. Two fabrics in a quilt is fine, but it has to be a deliberate choice. And it can be tricky to create emotion in a quilt with two fabrics. But you can make even the simplest patterns seem complicated by using lots of different fabrics."

"Oh, cut out the baloney," Bernie interrupted. "I use a lot of fabrics for one reason. Because I love to buy fabric and I need an excuse to buy a lot, and I'm not alone."

"That's okay too," Eleanor laughed. "That's what keeps me in business."

"Well, I guess we should leave you to it, then," I said. I nodded toward Amanda and we made a quick exit before we were drafted to help.

✄

Amanda and I grabbed our coats and were heading out the front door when Ryan caught up with us. "Let's all go out for coffee," he suggested.

"Can Amanda and I have some time alone?" I asked. He looked

toward Amanda. "Why are you looking to her for permission?" I demanded.

Amanda smiled. "Don't worry, Ryan. I won't give her any more ammunition to throw you out on your ass."

I laughed, but Ryan looked back at me worried. "What am I supposed to do while you're gone?"

"You're the one who wanted to be here," I reminded him as I got in the car.

Ryan stepped back, but I could tell he was not pleased, and— this surprised me—I really didn't care.

CHAPTER 32

We parked in front of the bakery, but I'd run out of interest in coffee and pastries, so we walked down the block to
Moran's Pub. Inside it was dark and a little run-down. The sort
of place where three or four rumpled old men sit continuously at
the bar from opening to closing, drinking without getting drunk.
But there were no such men sitting at Moran's, just a cooing young
couple at the bar and two college-age kids playing pool.

We ordered two beers and sat at a corner booth. I hadn't even
had a chance to take a sip before Amanda started.

"Ryan is trying to win you back," she said.

"That's the only thing that makes sense, except he isn't exactly
doing anything to get me back."

"Like what?"

"Like telling me that postponing the wedding was a big mistake. Or telling me that he never wants to be with anyone else." I
took a breath. "And that's just for starters. Where are the flowers,
the candy, you know . . . the stuff?"

"Would that make a difference?"

That stopped me. I didn't know. "It might," I said. "But it
doesn't look like I'm going to find out."

Amanda sat back and took a sip of her beer. Behind her the
door opened, and Jesse walked in. He waved. I waved back, and
Amanda turned around to see who had caught my attention.

"Who's that?" she asked with an exaggerated smile.

"The local police chief."

"He's cute." I could tell she was heading into flirtation mode.

"He's not cute," I protested.

He'd ditched his overcoat and was wearing jeans and a sport coat layered over a navy blue V-neck sweater and T-shirt. Between the clothes, the glasses, and the low light of the pub, he looked like he belonged with the college students playing pool. When he glanced up and saw me watching, I turned back to Amanda, but he was already walking over.

"Hey there," he said and grabbed a nearby chair. "I thought you were all going back to Eleanor's for the great quilt extravaganza."

"We ran from that," Amanda said, smiling. "I'm Nell's friend Amanda. I'm up for the day from New York."

"I'm Jesse."

"Like Jesse James. Are you an outlaw, Jesse?"

It looked like he blushed a little.

"What are you doing in a bar in the middle of the day?" I changed the subject.

"I could ask you the same thing," he said.

"Drinking." I held up the beer bottle as evidence. "But you don't strike me as the kind of man who drinks in daylight or on duty."

He shrugged. "It's a nonalcohol brew."

Amanda lifted her glass. "Well, here's to hanging out in bars in the daytime, whatever you drink." Jesse and I joined her toast, sipped our beers and stared at our glasses.

"Where's your boyfriend?" Jesse cleared his throat and asked. "He hasn't decided to go back to the city, has he?"

"No. We ditched him at the house," Amanda volunteered.

Jesse shot me a surprised look. "I thought you two were back together. Judging by the looks of things in your room the other day."

I was embarrassed that Jesse knew Ryan had spent the night in my room. I was also aware of Amanda's curious eyes boring into me.

"Amanda and I wanted to talk, so we left him at the house where he is probably being fussed over by half a dozen women as we speak," I said quickly, and once again looked for a new topic. "How's the investigation going?"

"We've sorted through the fingerprints on the scissors," he said.

"So do you know who killed Marc?" I was almost afraid to ask.

"No. Unless you, Eleanor, Nancy, Carrie and the others all killed Marc together. There are at least half a dozen partial prints on that thing."

"What about Ryan?" I asked and held my breath.

"Nothing on the scissors, but there were a few prints too smudged to identify."

"But if his prints weren't on the scissors that means...," I started.

"It doesn't mean anything. Nell, it's not that simple. He isn't—"

I stopped him midsentence. "I get it. He's not out of the running."

"No one is yet," he said.

"Not even Nell?" Amanda interrupted.

"Why would you think I killed anyone?" I stammered.

Amanda looked embarrassed. "I just thought if he suspected Ryan, he must suspect you. I'm sorry. I was completely off base."

"No, you weren't," came Jesse's flat reply. "Obviously she was on the short list of suspects right at the beginning. She knew the victim, had something of a relationship with him, and had access to the shop."

"But I didn't do it," I jumped in.

Jesse nodded. "She has a pretty good alibi."

"Thanks to Eleanor." I smiled wryly. I decided to ask about one of my suspects. "Why did you jump all over Natalie today?"

He stared at the table for a moment, then asked, "Want another beer?"

Without answering my question, Jesse was up and headed toward the bar. As he was ordering, Ryan walked in.

"Well, I guess we had the same idea," he said, trying to sound casual.

"Hey," Amanda said. "Why don't you join us?"

"Thanks," I muttered and shot her a look, but she was playing innocent. Ryan took Jesse's chair and looked from me to Amanda. "So what were you guys talking about?"

"Nothing," I said sharply. "I told you I wanted some time alone with Amanda."

"You weren't alone. You were drinking with that cop."

Amanda rolled her eyes. "We were talking about the grisly murder." I wasn't interested in explaining any further, so I went up to help Jesse with the drinks.

Jesse took two beers and left me with two, but I lingered just for a moment. "I'm Nell," I said to the bartender. "Were you working here Friday afternoon?"

"I own the place," he said warmly. "I'm here every night."

"There's a guy sitting at my table . . ."

"You mean the guy who isn't Jesse."

"Yeah. Him. Was he here Friday afternoon?"

The bartender leaned toward me. "Why don't you ask him?"

I could feel myself turning red. "Humor me. It doesn't look like it gets too crowded in the middle of the day, so if he was here, you might remember him."

"I might," he said, looking straight at Ryan. "Yeah, he was here. But if you're going to ask me how long he stayed and what he drank and who he spoke to, I can't tell you." He hesitated for a moment. "But I remember he seemed kind of upset. I do remember he was on his cell, 'cause that irritates me. He kept telling someone he'd made a big mistake."

"Did he say what mistake?"

"Not that I heard."

"Thanks," I sighed. "Sorry to bother you."

The bartender smiled and shrugged and I turned back toward the table. I caught Jesse's eye as I headed back.

"Everything okay there?" he asked.

"Perfect. I just had a question about the history of the bar," I said as innocently as possible.

Ryan had taken Jesse's seat and Jesse was sitting on my side of the booth. Amanda had left plenty of room on her side for me to sit, but that would have put me next to Ryan. So I motioned for Jesse to get up and let me in on his side. Ryan took a long gulp and set his drink loudly on the table.

"So are the three of you having fun?" Ryan asked.

"Yes, actually," I replied, trying to imitate Jesse's flat, indifferent tone, but without much success.

"Jesse has been filling us in on his hunt for the killer," Amanda told him excitedly. "Apparently, everyone in town is a suspect."

"Everyone sure seemed to hate that guy," Ryan said.

"He was hated?" Amanda seemed fascinated by this new piece of information.

Okay, I got it. No one liked him. No one but me. And apparently I was being played. Still, there's a huge difference between wanting to kill someone and actually killing him. And killing him in my grandmother's quilt shop—there was something about the location that seemed especially strange.

"Okay, so he went around making enemies everywhere he went." Amanda's face lit up as she embellished what she knew, as if she were talking through the plot of a new movie, rather than the death of a real person. "So someone goes after him and knifes him?"

"It was scissors," Jesse corrected.

"He was scissored, if that's a word," Ryan added.

"Okay, so someone came into the shop and scissored him?" Amanda was playful now and Ryan seemed to be jumping in.

"It was a real murder." I admonished them both. "Someone is dead. It would be great if you could stop using that fact to entertain yourselves."

Amanda leaned back, looking chastised. Ryan just looked annoyed. But something in what Amanda had said stuck with me. Someone had come into the shop and scissored him. I leaned toward Jesse. "But why that night? Why in the quilt shop?"

"What do you mean?" Jesse asked.

"Why pick that particular night?"

"Because he was in the shop alone?" Jesse suggested.

I turned to face him. "Okay. But let's say someone has had a problem with Marc for weeks, or months or years, or however long they've been building up to this moment. They must have gone to my grandmother's shop to confront him, and things got out of hand and Marc ended up with scissors in his chest."

"So what?" interrupted Ryan. "Things got out of hand. That happens."

"But why that night?" I asked, more emphatically.

"You think something happened that day to cause a confrontation?" Jesse leaned toward me. "That makes sense."

"Are we back to my having killed him?" Ryan demanded. "Is that where you're going with this, Nell?"

I ignored him. "I'm trying to think of anything that was different about Marc that day, and there wasn't anything. He was in a good mood when I left him."

"You put him in a good mood," Ryan snapped.

Jesse turned his body fully toward mine, so we were now facing each other on our side of the booth. Amanda and Ryan were shut out, but I didn't care, and it seemed, Jesse didn't either.

"He didn't mention any plans he had, any meetings, jobs . . . anything that was coming up that day or that week?" Jesse asked me.

"No," I replied. "Except he said something about a doctor's appointment. I don't know what kind of appointment. But it was supposed to be on Thursday."

"Hold that thought." Jesse picked up his cell phone and hit one button. "It's Jesse," he said into the phone. "Call the local doctors and Sacred Heart Hospital. Find out if Marc Reed had a doctor's appointment with any of them for last Thursday. Call me back." He hung up the phone and leaned back. "Let's see if that gets us anywhere."

✂

But when his phone rang five minutes later, it wasn't with news about Marc. Someday Quilts had been broken into, and the officer on the scene was sure that the person was still inside.

CHAPTER 33

When we arrived at the shop all four of us were breathless from having run the two blocks, which didn't say much about our level of fitness. But while Ryan and Amanda caught their breath, I followed Jesse to the door of the shop.

Tom had done an excellent job of covering up the large picture window. I tried, but I couldn't see anything that might be going on inside.

"Nell, stay back," Jesse directed, but I kept following. He grabbed my arm and pulled me away from the door. "I'm not kidding around," he said angrily. "You don't know who's in there. You don't know if they have a weapon."

"I'm not going to get hurt," I snapped, annoyed that he was literally pushing me around.

"Oh, yeah," he snapped back. "If you take one step from here, I'll shoot you myself."

I reluctantly stepped a few feet from the shop. Jesse went back to the officer standing at the door.

"Any movement inside?" Jesse asked him.

"None in the last few minutes," said the young officer, who seemed young enough to have gone straight from a Boy Scout's uniform to a cop's.

What were they waiting for, I wondered. My heart was beating a mile a minute. For the second time in a few days someone had turned my grandmother's shop into a crime scene, and I was ready to kill whoever it was that had violated such a happy place.

Ryan and Amanda walked toward me. While we waited, Ryan put one arm around me and the other around Amanda. She and I exchanged a look that said the same thing. As much as he annoyed me, I had to admit I did feel a little safer in his arms. But I didn't want to feel safe. I wanted in that shop. I pulled away.

Jesse moved for the door slowly, and as he did there was a noise from inside. He drew a gun that had been holstered under his sport coat. The minute I saw how comfortably the metal fit in his hands, I knew he was a real cop. Not a small-town bumbler happy to pick up the occasional drunk, but someone who could handle dangerous situations. Like this one was turning out to be.

Jesse pointed his gun toward the door and signaled the young officer to open it. The cop turned the knob and pushed. The door opened, and for a split second I could see shock on Jesse's face. Then a large hairy creature came running out of the shop and jumped on Jesse, knocking him to his knees. For maybe half a second my brain couldn't process what I was seeing. Then I realized—it was Barney.

The young officer pulled the dog off Jesse, who put away his gun, petted the dog and pointed him in my direction. Barney came running over with a goofy grin and a greeting that suggested he'd never been happier to see me.

But I left him behind and walked over to Jesse, who had already taken a few steps into the shop.

"There's no one in here?" I started.

"What the hell are you doing?" He turned to me. "Didn't I tell you to stay back?"

"Barney's not part of some international crime ring."

"Well, he didn't break into this place on his own," Jesse whispered angrily, pushing me back, "so until I know who else is here, get out."

I moved back. Not out, but out-ish. Jesse started walking toward the stairs. As he did, we both heard footsteps coming up.

Jesse pulled out his gun again just as Nancy came walking up with a large box. She saw Jesse and dropped it.

"Oh, for God's sake," Jesse muttered, lowering his weapon. "What are you doing here?"

"You gave me a horrible fright, Jesse Dewalt! Honestly, I'm not a young woman."

"I'm sorry," he said. "But this place is a crime scene. You aren't supposed to be here until tomorrow afternoon."

Nancy's eyes filled with tears. "We're going to appliqué flowers on the border for the quilt. I had a pattern I'd made here in this box. I hadn't had a chance to clean out the office."

"You had to get it today?" Jesse said through gritted teeth.

"Eleanor wanted me to start on it tonight."

"You should have called me and asked me to let you in," he said gently, though a hint of exasperation just made it into the tone of his voice.

"You try saying no to Eleanor," she sniffed. Then she looked around. "You've let that dog out. He's doesn't have the sense God gave a tree."

"He's okay," I said, stepping forward.

"Please remind Eleanor that no one is allowed in here until I say so," Jesse said. He leaned over, picked up the box Nancy had dropped and handed it to her. "You need a whole box for a quilt pattern?"

"It's not just one. There are lots of patterns, scraps of fabric, I don't know," Nancy stammered. "It seemed easier to take the whole box than search through it here."

"Can I look?"

"If you like," she said with an air of resignation. Then she opened the box for him to see.

I watched Jesse lift out exactly what Nancy had described—bits of fabric, scraps of paper with patterns drawn on them, thread. Nothing suspicious or even interesting. He took out what looked to be a small photo album, and began flipping through it.

"It's a quilt journal," she said. "I take pictures of each of my quilts."

"I didn't realize you had made this many," he commented.

"I don't have much else to do now that the boys are older," she admitted and smiled down at the photos.

"I'm sorry, Mrs. Vanderberg." Jesse closed up the box. "Just stay out of here until tomorrow, so we don't accidentally shoot you."

"You tell Eleanor not to send me here again, and I won't," she said and headed for the door.

Outside I could hear Nancy call for Barney, and I watched them as they passed the door on their way back to Eleanor's house.

"Well, that was, what do you call it, small-town fun," Jesse sighed as he took a deep breath.

"My grandmother doesn't always think the rules apply to her."

"Family trait, I guess."

"I really wish people would stop comparing us," I complained. "We're really nothing alike."

Jesse smiled a very broad and very relaxed smile. "Okay, Eleanor. That's your real name, right?"

Just as I was about to think of something clever to say in return, the young officer came inside.

"Sorry to bother you, sir, but I got a call from the station."

"What now, a domestic disturbance between two squirrels?" he asked, rubbing his eyes.

"No sir, I didn't hear anything about that. It was Betty about Marc Reed. His appointment was with a Dr. Parnell, but he didn't show up for the appointment."

"What kind of doctor is Dr. Parnell?" Jesse asked.

"A gynecologist, sir. He's not in his office until tomorrow, but I can try to find out his home number."

"That's okay. How did Betty find out so quickly on a Sunday afternoon?" Jesse asked.

"Betty's sister-in-law has a neighbor who works over at the medical center."

"Gossip makes detective work so much easier." Jesse smiled a weary smile. "I'm heading home to my daughter."

He walked past me out into the sunshine. "Close up the shop, and put police tape over the lock," he instructed to the young officer. "And write a report that we apprehended a quilter and her canine partner."

"Yes sir," the officer said in a serious tone, as if he hadn't realized Jesse was kidding. Jesse just shook his head.

Ryan and Amanda walked toward us. "So everything's okay in there?" Ryan asked.

"I guess so," I replied. "I guess it was just wishful thinking that Marc's killer would show up and wait to get arrested."

"Ryan," Jesse said. "Can we talk for a second?"

"What about?" I asked.

Jesse ignored me and walked a few feet down the street, with Ryan following. I couldn't hear them talking, but it didn't appear to be confrontational. In fact, it seemed pretty friendly. By their body language, Jesse could have been getting a football score, but I doubted it.

After a minute or two, Jesse waved good-bye to Amanda and me and walked away. Ryan came back and shrugged his shoulders.

"What was that about?" I asked quickly.

"Nothing. He just had some questions about the fight that guy Marc and I got into."

"Like what?"

"Nothing important. He's just hammering out the details."

"And you told him the truth, right?"

A flash of anger crossed Ryan's face. "What else would I have told him?"

CHAPTER 34

We walked away from the store with no particular direction in mind. At first we tried to walk together, with Ryan between Amanda and me, but something kept getting in the way—a tree or a light post. One person would get out of step and awkwardly try to keep up. So we alternated pairs. For a while Amanda and I walked next to each other with Ryan slightly ahead, then Ryan and I walked side by side, then Ryan and Amanda.

"Where do you want to go," I asked, "to the house or back to the bar?"

"I guess I should head back to New York," Amanda said quietly. "I wish I could stay longer, but we can't all abandon the office." She stopped. "When are you guys coming back, by the way?"

"I'm not sure. A few days, maybe. When things are settled here," Ryan said. "I just wouldn't feel good leaving right now."

"And you?" Amanda turned toward me.

"Me? Maybe when my grandmother's feeling better," I shrugged. "I haven't exactly decided what I'm going to do next."

"What does that mean?" Ryan narrowed his eyes at me. "You can't stay here forever. You have to go back to New York. You have to go back to your life."

I didn't want to be told what my future *should* be, so I ignored him and turned toward the train station. Amanda and Ryan stayed several steps behind the rest of the way. We walked up the steps to the platform and sat on a bench to wait for the train. Ryan was quiet and I wasn't feeling very chatty either, so Amanda filled the silence with office gossip.

It had only been a week since I left and yet all of these people had faded from my mind. I no longer cared about the crazy last-minute demands of my boss, or the ongoing affair between the office manager and the vice president of sales. I didn't even care when she told me that our favorite Chinese takeout place had stopped the five-dollar lunch special that sustained us. A couple of weeks ago news like that would have required a long phone call with Amanda and strategic planning to find a replacement. And I would have enjoyed every minute of it. Now it just felt trivial. As Amanda talked, I realized I liked being here in Archers Rest. And it didn't feel like I was running away from my life. It felt a little like I was building a life here.

When the train came, I hugged Amanda a long time and promised to call and let her know how the "cute sheriff" was doing with Marc's murder.

"I'm going to miss you," I said and hugged her.

"I'll visit really soon," Amanda said. "You'll get sick of me."

"Never," I said. "I miss you already."

✂

After the train pulled out of the station, Ryan and I silently walked back to Eleanor's. But it didn't feel as strange between us as it had the last couple of days. Amanda's presence had made Ryan feel more familiar to me, and somehow reminded me that the change in our relationship hadn't killed me. And by the way Ryan looked at me as we walked along the river, it also seemed that he respected me more, even liked me more, because I wasn't so desperate for his approval. Maybe I was imagining it, but it felt good.

As we walked up the driveway, we saw there were cars parked by the house.

"The quilt shop is open for business, I see," I said.

"Guess so." Ryan stopped. "Do you mind if we don't go in right now? It's not my scene."

"Do you think it's mine?"

"I don't know." He smiled. "I wouldn't have thought so, but you're different up here. And you're pretty artistic. Remember those paintings you used to do when we met? They were cool."

"You liked those? You never told me that."

He blushed. "That's because I'm an idiot."

"I'm aware of that." I smiled.

He grabbed my hand and held it. It felt safe, and I found myself letting go a little of my hurt and just enjoying the moment. "Let's not go inside yet," he said.

We went around the house and headed for the river. Trees were dropping their red and orange leaves into the water, and they drifted downstream slowly as sunlight bounced on the river. We walked as close to the edge as we could and sat on a small patch of grass to watch. Ryan absentmindedly played with some small stones, then began tossing them into the river.

"See that leaf?" he asked, pointing toward a mass of leaves in the water.

"The reddish orange one, or the greenish brown one?"

"The red one, in the center." Then he tossed a stone that hit the red leaf and sent it plummeting into the depths of the water. Ryan looked over at me with a goofy grin. "That was good, huh. Did you see how I nailed that leaf?"

"It was great." I smiled. He threw a few more and each time looked back at me for approval. I knew he was trying to impress me. Sure, it wasn't flowers or plane tickets to Paris, but it was something. I put my head on his shoulder.

"If I start saying I'm sorry now, how long will it take until you forgive me?" Ryan said quietly.

"Fifty years."

"Just in time for our golden anniversary."

I had to stop and rewind the moment in my head. He had just said golden anniversary, as in wedding anniversary, as in wedding, hadn't he? I didn't know what to say.

"Nell?"

"I thought you needed time."

"I did. But I don't need it anymore. Maybe with everything that's happened, with your coming up here, then that guy dying . . . I don't know. It made me think how I could lose you so easily."

"A lot has changed," I reminded him.

"Not us. We haven't changed." He leaned over so his eyes met mine. "It's only been a couple of weeks. Can you really say you don't want to marry me?"

I looked away from him and stared at the water. "No," I finally said. "I can't say I don't want to get married. I just can't say . . ."

"Then don't say anything."

Ryan leaned over and rested his head on my lap. I stroked his head and watched the water. I had just gotten used to the idea that we wouldn't get our happy ending. A little part of me was even beginning to enjoy the open, unplanned landscape of my future. And now things had spun 180 degrees again. So how did it feel to be here? I asked myself.

I looked down at Ryan and decided. It felt good.

CHAPTER 35

The sun was beginning to go down and as it faded, the wind picked up. Romantic as it was to sit together and stare at the river, it wasn't worth pneumonia. We headed back to the house, holding hands.

"So when should we get married now?" he asked.

"Ryan," I started, but he looked so happy that I just smiled and kept walking.

"Did you cancel the reception hall and everything?"

"No," I admitted. "I kept planning to, but I just couldn't do it."

Ryan smiled. "Then everything is exactly the way it was. This was just a bump in the road." He leaned down and kissed me, as if everything was now right with the world.

I smiled back at Ryan. "We don't have to talk about any of this with my grandmother."

"She'll be thrilled," he said. "I know it."

I reached out to open the front door to the house just as Carrie came out with a small box overloaded with fabric.

"My assignment," she said, nodding to the box. "We all have to make blocks for the quilt by Friday. I don't know how I'm going to get it all done."

"I'm sure someone will help if you get behind," I said, to be helpful.

"They'll have to," she laughed. "Do you know your grand-mother has been wondering what happened to you?"

"We went for a walk," Ryan volunteered.

Carrie looked from Ryan to me and back again. Then she smiled. "I hope it was a productive one."

She shifted the box to one side to reach into her pocket, and as she did, the box tumbled to the ground. Ryan knelt down to gather up the mess and Carrie stood there, looking a little helpless.

"I was trying to get my keys," she said, and took a large set out of her pocket. It was tangled up with a small set of keys that also fell, hitting Ryan on the head. "I'm so sorry." Carrie leaned over to grab the errant set, but I grabbed them first and handed them back. There were just two keys held by a worn black leather key chain.

"You should put these on the same key chain as the others," I said.

"These," Carrie quickly stuffed them back in her pocket, "they're to my husband's office. I really don't even need to carry them."

Ryan handed back her box.

"Marc had a key chain . . . ," I started, suddenly remembering where I'd seen that black leather before.

"I really need to get home and start dinner," she said quickly and headed for her car. "Ryan, thanks for picking everything up."

"No problem." He smiled and waved as she drove away. "She's a nice lady."

I nodded. "A little frazzled, don't you think?"

Ryan gave me the "you're crazy" look I'd seen a hundred times before, and we headed inside.

✄

"Nell," I heard Eleanor calling me from the moment I opened the door.

"We're back," I said. "Sorry we were gone all day." I rushed to the living room, expecting to see her alone and feeling helpless. Instead Nancy, Bernie, and Susanne were with her eating lasagna.

"There's plenty," Bernie said, gesturing to their plates. "Have some."

"How did your meeting go?" I asked.

"There's lots of work for everyone to do, including you," Nancy said.

"I thought I was supervising at the shop."

"You disappeared, so you got drafted." Eleanor laughed. "Ryan here is lucky we didn't drag him into the cause."

"I have enough on my plate," he said and winked at me. If it was meant to be subtle, it wasn't. All the women looked at us, with the hopeful expectation that gossip was soon to follow. Instead I sat with Nancy to find out what part of the quilt I was going to screw up.

"You ladies enjoy taking over the world. I'm going to heat up a slice of lasagna," Ryan said as he headed out of the room.

He was gone exactly three seconds before Bernie broke the silence. "So, are you going to fill us in?"

"Leave her alone." Eleanor, surprisingly, came to my defense.

But for once I didn't need her help. "He wants to get back together, to get married as planned. He seems to have been really shaken by everything that's happened, and he doesn't want to wait anymore."

"What do you want?" Eleanor asked sharply.

"I want . . . I want what we were . . . what we were supposed to be." I shrugged. "A part of me wants to forget everything that happened and just be what we were, what I thought we were."

"And the other part?" Maggie asked softly.

I sighed. "The other part doesn't think it's possible, or even a good idea."

"Well, whatever happens, you know you can stand on your own two feet, and that's important," Bernie offered.

Had I been standing on my own two feet? I didn't bother to ask.

"It's all going to be okay," I said. "It is okay. We just have to get through this whole Marc thing."

"Jesse doesn't think Ryan had anything to do with it, does he?" asked Susanne.

"No," I said empathically, but I wasn't sure what Jesse thought.

"I think it was a lover, anyway. It seems like a crime of passion," offered Bernie.

"Jealousy is passion," Susanne pointed out.

"Maybe it was someone who was jealous that Marc had taken to Nell," Bernie said. "Maybe Marc had a girlfriend hidden away somewhere."

"Several girlfriends, I'd bet," Susanne sniffed. "God knows what the women saw in him, but he was never short of company."

I could feel Eleanor staring at the back of my head, but I didn't turn around. I ignored the dissection of Marc's character going on around me and sat with Nancy while she explained how I would be responsible for cutting out two dozen fabric flowers using a pattern she had drawn. Seemed simple enough.

"Whoever it was," Eleanor stated as if to end the discussion, "they must have felt very desperate. Whatever anyone thought of Marc, murder is a terrible thing."

Bernie nodded, and looked toward Susanne, who looked toward me. I just was grateful that Nancy was focused on the quilt project.

✂

After I got my instructions on my part of the quilt, I headed to the kitchen in search of Ryan and food. He wasn't there, but the lasagna was on the kitchen table. Susanne appeared as I took the food out of the microwave.

"I'm heating up the lasagna," I said. "It looks good. Who brought it?"

"Bernie. She left you the recipe." Sure enough, on the table was a beautifully handwritten lasagna recipe on pale pink paper.

"That was sweet of her, but I'll never make lasagna. It's too much trouble." I put our plates on the table.

"We all do things we once said we'd never do," Susanne murmured as she made herself a cup of tea.

I grabbed a fork and started eating without looking at her.

✂

An hour later, the women were all out of gossip and food, so they started heading home. I walked Nancy to the door first, promising to be at the shop to keep an eye on "the new one" as she called Jesse's brother-in-law. Then I walked Bernie out, and she gave me a tight hug.

"We're all getting very fond of you, dear," she said.

"It's mutual."

As Bernie walked to her car Susanne said good-bye to my grandmother and came up behind me.

"I think I warned you that if you stuck around, you'd get drafted into the quilt club." She smiled.

"You guys may come to regret that decision."

"No." Susanne reached up and touched my hair lightly, sweeping a loose strand behind my ear. "We love having you here, almost as much as Eleanor does." She stepped through the door into the darkness. "It's nice to see someone coming into her own."

"You mean someone getting into trouble."

"You can't get into too much trouble making a quilt. It's too bad you didn't start making one the moment you arrived."

"Is that your way of saying that I wouldn't have gotten involved with Marc?"

She shook her head. "You dodged a bullet with that one."

I decided to go for broke and ask what had bothered me since I saw Jesse talking to Natalie. "What did Marc do to Natalie?"

"Leave it alone," Susanne almost whispered. "Be grateful that he didn't stick around to destroy what you have."

"But he didn't destroy Natalie either. I keep hearing about her wonderful husband and baby," I protested.

"You're right. I'm very grateful he didn't have his chance."

I hesitated for a second, but I had to say what I was thinking. "Did he get killed before he did?"

Susanne tilted her head slightly, as if wondering whether to answer. "I suppose he did. My guess is that whoever killed him was just trying to protect someone they loved. And can you really find anything wrong in that?"

She looked up at the house as the light in my bedroom went on. I looked up too and saw the shadow of Ryan moving around the room.

CHAPTER 36

The next morning I got up early and took Barney for his walk. Only this time I didn't take him toward the river. I walked into town and let the confused dog follow me.

I stopped in front of the shop and tried the door. It was locked. A strip of police tape covered the lock, brown paper covered the windows. It seemed abandoned and unloved.

I didn't really know what I was looking for, but I couldn't leave. I only knew that Susanne's words echoed in my mind. If someone had killed Marc to protect someone, was that really so bad? What good would it do for anyone to know? But if it was Ryan, was it okay that he might have killed a man to protect our relationship? I knew the answer was no. I knew what the real question was. Could I live with him if I didn't know?

✄

"What are you doing?"

I turned around to see a minivan. Natalie was waving at me from the driver's seat.

"I haven't the vaguest idea," I admitted.

"Then I'll drive you guys home."

I didn't want the company, but I did have a question.

After putting Barney in the back, I jumped in Natalie's car, pushing aside baby toys, pacifiers, a carton of diapers and a CD called *Jammin' with Baby* with a picture of a toddler rocking out on a play guitar. I smiled and said, "How adorable." But as Natalie moved in her seat and sat on a juice box, I had one of those moments that single people have when we feel slightly smarter for not having reproduced.

"He's getting really cute," Natalie told me as she brushed off the juice from her jeans. "My husband says now that he's past the poop and sleep stage, he's getting to be good company."

"Your son, right? Not your husband."

She laughed. "No, my husband is still in the poop and sleep stage."

"Where is your son?"

"At my mom's. She kept him for me last night. I was on my way to pick him up." Natalie was beaming. "Do you mind if I pick him up before I drop you guys off?"

I did mind, but I figured it would give us time to talk, so I shook my head.

Natalie kept talking. But it wasn't so much that she was talking to me, just talking to herself about her good fortune. I recognized it from the way I used to talk about the wedding. Jabbering on and on about details no one but you cares about, expecting the world to be fascinated. Listening to Natalie, I realized how annoying I must have been.

"He's really brought us closer—Jeremy, my son," she continued, as I half-smiled. "He's turned us into grown-ups. We used to have all these stupid fights, and break up and get back together, but now we're solid." She gripped the wheel. "I never want to lose that."

"You won't," I said, with the reassurance only a stranger can give. "Jeremy's not going anywhere."

She looked straight at me for a long second. It made me nervous enough to look toward the road and make sure we weren't headed into oncoming traffic. But just as I was about to say something, Natalie turned her eyes forward.

I wanted to ask her about Jesse, her history with Marc. But I didn't want her driving off the road. So I said, as gingerly as possible, "Marc's death seems to have stirred a lot of emotions in everyone."

She nodded. "Almost there." She ignored my comment, responding with the same cheery tone she'd had at my grandmother's shop.

✄

We pulled into the driveway of a modest frame bungalow, much the same as the others on the block. The only thing that separated the house from its neighbors—and it was a big thing—was the bright purple door.

Susanne walked outside with Jeremy in her arms.

"Hey, sweetie, I brought you this," Natalie said, waving a small green dog. Jeremy's tiny hands reached out for the stuffed animal as if it were a long lost friend. And Natalie reached for her son, grabbing him and holding him tightly as if it had been weeks since they'd been together.

✄

At Susanne's urging, we left Barney in the car and went inside for coffee and freshly made pumpkin doughnuts, which prompted me to say, "Who makes doughnuts from scratch?"

"Not me, honey," Susanne laughed. "I make quilts. Jeremy and I took a walk to the bakery this morning. Your grandmother is the one who tries to do it all. My guess is she's trying to make you over in her image."

"Well then," I laughed, "it will be the first thing she fails at."

"I don't know. You remind me of Eleanor," Natalie said and turned to Susanne, who nodded in agreement. "You have her absolute sense of right and wrong."

"That can get you into trouble." Susanne leaned in to me.

The small dining room we sat in opened onto an equally small living room. Both rooms were as overdone as Susanne's makeup. Gilded mirrors hung on nearly every wall and dozens of family photos filled almost every available shelf. There were several black-and-white photos of Susanne at what must have been beauty pageants many years before, some of Natalie, and what amounted to a shrine of baby Jeremy.

An ornately carved wood coffee table sat in the center of the room. It had been painted gold, with postcards glued to the top and covered by a scratched piece of glass. An old plaid couch next to it was draped with a red, black and white check quilt. Three cats were happily sleeping on the quilt and on the purple throw pillows that dotted the couch.

Across the room a large dog sat chewing a bone next to an elaborately decorated artificial Christmas tree. I kept staring at it, trying to figure out what, aside from the fact that it was September, made the tree seem so odd.

"I leave it up all year long," said Susanne, with pride. "I know people think I'm silly, but it makes me happy, and Jeremy gets a kick out of it too."

"No, I think it's great," I said. "Very festive."

"She changes the decorations for each holiday," said Natalie.

I took this as permission to examine it closer, and realized that little skeletons, witches, and pumpkins—many of them handmade—had been carefully hung from the branches.

"Halloween," I said in an uncomfortable moment of obviousness.

"My favorite holiday," said Susanne.

"They're all her favorite," laughed Natalie.

"Jeremy's going to be a pumpkin," Susanne told me. "I'm making his costume myself."

"He's going to be a bumblebee, Mom," Natalie sighed. "I told you that."

"A pumpkin is so much more in keeping with the theme," Susanne argued, and scooped up Jeremy from his high chair.

"He needs to eat," Natalie objected.

"Oh, he's fine. He's a big strong boy," cooed Susanne.

Since they seemed to forget about me, I stood back and watched the way the two women doted over the little boy. He seemed to take it for granted, the way only children can, that he was the center of the universe.

But there was something odd too. It was almost as if Susanne didn't trust her daughter with Jeremy. Maybe it was something a lot of mothers felt when they saw their own children struggle with parenthood. But it was clearly a source of frustration for Natalie.

"You should get Nell home," Susanne said, just as Natalie had wrested Jeremy from her arms. Susanne kissed the small boy on his head, and lingered close to him for what seemed to be a dramatically long time. Especially since she saw him nearly every day.

"Susanne," I turned as we were leaving, "have you talked to Jesse?"

"About what, dear?" She blinked innocently at me.

I smiled. Were we really going to play a game? "I was just wondering who he'd spoken to about . . . what happened at the shop."

She nodded. "Oh, yes. He did talk to me."

"What did he ask you?"

"Nothing special. I suppose he's talked to everyone in town now."

"But last night you seemed to think it was someone who was trying to protect someone. Did you have someone in mind?"

She laughed and glanced toward an impatient Natalie standing at the door. "Everyone has a theory about this thing. Who wouldn't? It's good gossip." She took my hand. "We talk a good game, but we're all harmless. Don't you know that by now?"

I nodded, and smiled, as if I did know that.

CHAPTER 37

As I walked through the front door of the house, I heard a thud. Barney started barking and ran ahead of me. Another thud.

I ran into the living room.

Eleanor was standing in the middle of the room, balancing on her crutches. A table was knocked over and the lightbulb of a lamp was blinking on and off. Barney jumped around barking excitedly.

"Are you okay?"

"I'm fine. That's enough," Eleanor said repeatedly. "Calm down, you silly dog. You'd think the house was on fire."

"What happened?"

"I knocked over a table with my crutch," she said in frustration. "Honestly, this is so annoying."

I picked up the lamp and the table and grabbed Barney's collar. "Wait for me," I said to my grandmother. I walked the dog to the kitchen door and pushed him out. "I'm sorry, sweetie, you're upsetting Grandma right now." I headed back to the living room, but Eleanor was already hobbling toward the kitchen.

"What a way to start the day," she said brightly. She dropped into a chair and put her injured leg up on another. "So, you're up early. What were you doing?"

"I took Barney for a walk into town."

"Walks are good for thinking."

"I'm not sure how much thinking I did, except about how hungry I was. And with you taking over the diner, there's no place in this town to get a really greasy breakfast." I poured my grandmother a cup of coffee and after making one for myself I sat down at the table with her.

"What are you sitting down for? There's still one place in town to get a good breakfast, but I don't want it greasy."

"Where's that?" I looked at her for several seconds before I realized what her stare meant. I laughed. "What, me? You want my famous muffins again?"

"How about pancakes?"

"I don't know how to make pancakes. I know how to make frozen waffles."

"Well, you'll learn how to make pancakes today."

"Susanne mentioned that you were trying to turn me into a version of you." I laughed. "Well, it won't work."

She rolled her eyes. "You eat, don't you? I don't know why people go around talking about how independent they are and then don't know how to take care of themselves in the most basic way. Get out the griddle."

Then she began pointing to cabinets and drawers, and before I knew it, I was digging out a griddle and mixing pancake batter from scratch. By the time the griddle had heated and the first batch was finished, Ryan was walking in the kitchen.

"First muffins, now this," he said, smiling broadly. "I could get used to all this domesticity."

"Well, don't," I laughed. "Unless you want to make them for yourself."

"How about we switch off? I'll do every other Sunday," he said as he dug into his breakfast. I let the comment pass. No point in continually bringing up my ambivalence.

"Modern marriage," Eleanor said. "Too bad I'm not fifty years younger."

"Well, I could probably fix you up with a couple of guys I know who like a more mature woman," Ryan joked.

"I'm too much trouble for any sane man," she said. "Nell can tell you."

"Yes, I can," I offered.

Eleanor winked at me. "So what's on the agenda for today?"

"I have to go to the shop," I said. "Remember, we're doing construction today."

"I know that," she said. "And Ryan, what are you doing to keep yourself busy?"

"Actually, I was thinking that I might head back to the city today," Ryan said quickly.

"Since when?" I looked at him, but he was looking at his pancakes. "Saturday you said you were going to stick around for a while."

"And you were none too happy about it, if I remember," he said.

"That was different."

"Exactly."

The last of the pancakes were burning on the griddle, but I couldn't take my eyes off Ryan. "I don't get it. Why leave now?"

I could feel Eleanor getting antsy, being in the middle of it, but with her broken leg she wasn't going to get out of the room fast, so she sat there. I knew she was trying her best not to interfere, but it would only be a matter of time. I looked to her for help, but she just shrugged and nodded toward Ryan.

"Don't we have a lot to talk about?" I asked Ryan.

He dug into his pancakes and with his mouth half full answered me. "I was thinking that I'm going to have to take some time off for the honeymoon. So it's better if I don't take days off now."

"Have we decided there's going to be a honeymoon? I thought we were just talking about it."

Barney whimpered at the door and Ryan jumped up to let him in. Eleanor gave me a look that said "Give him a break," and I sighed heavily in response.

"It makes sense that you should go back to work," I said to Ryan, but I looked straight at Eleanor.

"I'll head out as soon as we're done with breakfast," he said. "I'll drop you off at the shop." He kissed me and practically ran from the room.

"What was that about?" I said to my grandmother the minute Ryan was gone.

"Maybe it's exactly what he said. He doesn't want to take too much time off work."

I nodded. "Maybe."

"You know, if you have this much doubt . . . ," she started.

"I know." I was about to say that I should talk to Ryan about my feelings when the pancakes still on the griddle started to smoke.

✄

An hour later, Nancy arrived, exactly on time. She had a package for me—scissors, a pencil, a plastic pattern of a simple flower and scraps of colorful hand-dyed fabrics.

"It shouldn't take long," she said, "but it's a tremendous help if we're going to meet Eleanor's deadline."

"I hope I do this right," I said, staring at the package.

"Whatever you do, it will be exactly right," Nancy said with a smile. "You have no idea the joy it gives your grandmother and me to pass this tradition on to you." She gave me a quick hug and with it the confidence to make my small contribution to the quilt.

"I'll find a quiet space at the shop to cut these," I promised, as Ryan and I left.

CHAPTER 38

On the drive to the shop, Ryan and I held hands and smiled a lot, but we talked little. When we pulled in front of Someday Quilts, he leaned over and kissed me passionately. I kissed back, but with less enthusiasm than I'd ever kissed him before. I got out of the car. Leaving felt like another decision he'd made without consulting me, but rather than being angry, I felt a little relieved. There was something that I really needed to do and I realized it would be better if Ryan wasn't around to get in my way.

I headed over to the shop as Tom was loading in.

"You don't need me babysitting you?" I asked.

"Not really, but you're welcome to stay if that's what your grandmother wants."

"Let's just say I did."

"Keeping secrets from your grandmother?" he said. "That seems risky." He smiled and went back to getting his tools from the truck.

I walked up the street until I was sure I was alone. I dialed information on my cell phone.

"I'm looking for a Dr. Parnell in Archers Rest, New York."

The computer on the other end connected me to a doctor's office, and a receptionist gave me a quick appointment when I implied I might be pregnant and was concerned about some heavy cramping.

I walked straight over to the medical center, about a half mile from the center of town. I was reading a year-old *Good Housekeeping* when I heard a concerned voice say my name.

I looked up to see Jesse standing in front of me.

"Are you okay?" he asked.

"I'm fine. I just have a doctor's appointment."

"When did you make it?" He looked at me suspiciously.

"Recently."

A nurse walked into the waiting room. "Nell Fitzgerald."

"That's me," I said, and got up. Jesse grabbed my arm.

"How recently?"

I took a deep breath. "This morning."

He let go of my arm. "What are you doing?"

The nurse came over. "Are you ready, miss?"

"Yes," I said.

"We're going in together," Jesse said.

"Are you the husband?"

He looked at the nurse. "Let's just say we want to do this together."

Dr. Parnell was a man in his early sixties, with a thick head of snow-white hair and silver-rimmed glasses. His office had a full wall of baby pictures, as well as charts on the female reproductive system.

"What week are you in?" Parnell said to me.

"What week of what?" Jesse interrupted impatiently.

"Pregnancy." Parnell looked at me. "Do I have the wrong chart?"

"No," I said weakly. I moved slightly down my chair in the hopes of disappearing.

Jesse seemed on the verge of saying something, but instead sat in stunned silence. I thought briefly about keeping up the charade, but I knew it wouldn't last through an examination. And, quite frankly, I wasn't prepared for that level of undercover work.

"I'm not, actually," I stammered. "I just wanted to talk to you about Marc Reed. Do you know who he is?"

"Yes, I know who he is. Or was. The young man who was killed over the weekend." The doctor leaned back in his chair.

"Look, she doesn't belong here." Jesse gave me a long hard look. "But I don't want to waste time arresting her for impeding a police investigation right now. She's here, and I'm here, because Marc Reed had an appointment with you on Thursday."

"I remember. Quite unusual, as you can imagine."

"What did he want?"

The doctor sighed. "Despite the appointment, he wasn't a patient, so I suppose there is no doctor-patient confidentiality." He leaned forward. "I know Marc's father, Dr. Michael Reed. He's a good man who has suffered a terrible loss. I don't want to hurt him by helping you."

"If you help me find Marc's killer, then you're helping his father," Jesse said.

Dr. Parnell looked at Jesse and sighed. "I agreed to see Marc when he called. I suppose I was curious to find out what he wanted. He was here asking about paternity. He wanted me to check the records of a patient of mine. Obviously, I turned him down."

"He thought he was the father of Natalie's baby," I blurted out. It made sense. He glared at Natalie, had mentioned something about building a business for his son, and Susanne seemed to see Marc as a threat. I looked at the doctor and knew I was right.

"That's not something I can discuss further," the doctor said sternly. "I can tell you what I told Marc. If he had a question about the paternity of a child, then he should approach the mother for a DNA sample. Lacking her permission, he should seek remedy from the courts."

"Did Natalie know he was here?" I asked. Jesse put his hand up to signal me to stop talking, but that wasn't going to happen.

"No. I didn't mention it," Parnell told me, "but I believe my nurse, Angela, mentioned something to Maggie Sweeney. She's Mrs. Sweeney's daughter-in-law. It was inappropriate, I suppose, but it's a small-town and they are related. I didn't make an issue out of it because frankly I was a bit concerned for Natalie."

"Concerned about what? Did Marc make threats?" I asked.

Jesse stared at me. "Excuse me, Doctor. Please don't answer her." He turned back to the doctor. "Did he make threats?"

"Marc was a very smart young man. Such a disappointment to his father when he dropped out of school and . . . drifted. He was unfocused, a little headstrong, and perhaps a bit mean. If he did make threats, and that is possible, he didn't make them in front of me."

"What's your opinion of Natalie's husband?" I asked and met with the same icy stare from Jesse.

"I don't know him. I believe he and Natalie were having some marital difficulties during her pregnancy, so he didn't come to any of the prenatal visits. He was at the birth, but I certainly didn't speak to him enough to form an opinion.

"Thank you for your time," Jesse said as he rose. I got up and was about to follow him out of the office when Dr. Parnell called us back.

"By the way, Marc offered me five thousand dollars for a look at my patient's file. It was a ridiculous offer. If for no other reason than I can't imagine where he would get five thousand dollars. His father was paying his rent half the time."

Jesse nodded and pushed me ahead of him down the hall. I

waited by the entrance while Jesse chatted with Dr. Parnell's nurse, confirming, I suppose, that she had talked with Maggie. Then he came walking toward me. Though his face was devoid of emotion, I knew he was just waiting for the moment when it was safe to yell at me.

It came in the parking lot.

"What are you doing here?" he asked.

"I want to know who killed Marc."

Jesse's head tilted slightly, like a confused puppy. "Why? Did you care about him that much?"

"Do you have to care about someone to want justice for them?"

"That's bull. That's not why you're here." He started pacing. "And just for your information, it's my job to get justice for people."

Instantly I was twelve years old and getting a talking-to from my father for skipping math class. What I had done, as far as he was concerned, was indefensible. And yet I was required to stand there and defend myself.

"If you felt that way, why did you let me go into the doctor's office with you?"

"Because if I hadn't, then you would have gone in alone and told me that you had an appointment. I wouldn't have been able to prove otherwise." Jesse looked at his feet and then at me. "I will arrest you," he said. There was no anger in his voice, but it was serious in tone. I was meant to be scared. But I wasn't.

"No you won't."

"Because you will not do this again. Do you understand?"

Without meaning to, I laughed. This did not go over well.

"Nell," he said as he fingered the handcuffs that were attached at the side of his belt. "If Ryan did it, I will find out."

"He didn't do it," I said.

"If you really believed that one hundred percent, you wouldn't be here."

"I just don't want this hanging over us. He wants . . ." I hesitated. I wasn't sure if I should say it. "He wants to get married."

Jesse's face changed into a sympathetic half smile. "Congratulations," he said softly. "As of when?"

"Yesterday."

He stood silent for a minute, then lowered his eyes. "Get in the car," he said.

CHAPTER 39

"Where are we going?" I asked for the second time, but Jesse was ignoring me. "Shouldn't you obey the speed limit?" I asked as he flew down Main Street.

"I'm going like twenty-five miles an hour." I looked at the speedometer. He was going closer to forty, but it wasn't as if anyone would pull him over.

"Are you going to tell me or not?"

Jesse glanced over. "Let me ask you something," Jesse said. "When Ryan came to the shop on Friday to see you, did he come inside?"

"I think so," I said, but I was lying.

Jesse looked over at me. "Okay."

"Why?"

"His fingerprints."

"You said they weren't on the scissors."

"They weren't," he said. "But they were on a number of items in the box that contained the scissors. Did he have any reason to touch that box?"

"He helped me move some things . . . in the shop." Another lie.

A moment passed, then, "Okay."

Jesse slowed the car down and made a turn, and I instantly knew where he was taking me. In another few seconds we pulled up in front of my grandmother's house.

"Enjoy the rest of your day," Jesse said as he stopped the car.

"Jesse . . . ," I started.

"Nell, I know you mean well. But you can't prove Ryan is innocent and you can get yourself in a lot of trouble. I don't want to see that happen, so this ends here. Okay?"

I gritted my teeth and nodded. "It ends here," I agreed and got out of the car.

✂

Inside, Nancy and Eleanor were busy helping customers. I thought for a second I might be able to slip by without being noticed, but no luck.

"Things okay at the shop?" Eleanor called out.

I walked into the dining room and nearly tripped on one of the bolts of fabric that now had taken over the room. "Everything's great. I'm taking a break. I thought I would call Natalie and see if she wanted to get together for lunch, actually," I said. "Do you have her number?"

"Oh, how lovely." Nancy smiled. "Hold on a second." Nancy went to a pile of papers and began sorting through them, finally stopping on one. She handed it to me. "The quilt club phone list. You should have a copy anyway."

I was about to protest that I wasn't really a part of the quilt club, but I had the list with the names, numbers and addresses of the entire club, so I just smiled. I was almost out of the room when Eleanor spoke again.

"Have you cut the flowers for the quilt?"

I stopped. "Almost done," I said quickly and headed for the kitchen.

In the kitchen I grabbed the car keys and headed back out of the house, in the car and back on the main road.

Natalie lived in a two-bedroom apartment just a few blocks from her mother's house. I expected the place to have the same eccentric flare as her mother's, but the living room was almost completely beige. Not "haven't gotten around to decorating" beige, but beige as a design choice. All shades and all textures of one color scheme in what seemed almost a deliberate break from her mother's view of the world. The only exception was a six-foot square quilt hanging on the wall behind her couch. The quilt was an abstract design of circles and half circles appliquéd on squares. It seemed to be made from dozens of fabrics in the deepest shades of red and purple. Against the monochromatic background, it was startling and beautiful.

"We made it together, my mom and I," Natalie said when she caught me studying it. "It was my first quilt."

"If I could make something like that my first time out, I might take up quilting myself," I said. For the first time, I was a little envious of the artistry that each of these woman could access. They seemed to take it for granted that anyone with a few bits of fabric and some time could create an object that would not only keep you warm but also be an object of beauty.

"You should do it," she said. "If you don't want Eleanor to teach you, I can. I think it's really the absolute best way to deal with a problem."

"What do you mean?"

"Nancy says it's a right brain, left brain activity." Natalie settled into a beige leather chair, while I sat at the corner of the couch. "There's a lot of math and figuring out patterns and amounts of fabrics, so that's one side, then the other is taken up with the whole creative process. So when you're quilting, you are completely involved in it. There's no space in your brain left over for worrying about your problems." She pointed to a pile of about ten quilts neatly folded on top of an armoire. "I made most of those when my husband and I were separated. It kept me from going crazy."

"Well, then, I should take it up," I laughed. "And quickly."

"Let me get you some soda," Natalie said. "Diet or regular?"

"Regular," I said. "The more fattening the better."

Natalie left the room and returned with two Cokes and some store-bought cookies. "It's so great to have someone come to hang out," she said. "I'm so glad you dropped by."

I took a deep breath. "I was at Dr. Parnell's office today, asking him some questions about Marc."

Natalie blushed. "Why would Dr. Parnell know anything about Marc?"

"Apparently," I said as gently as I could, "Marc went to see him about you and your son."

"Did Dr. Parnell tell you that?"

"Not exactly, but that was what we figured he meant."

"We?"

"I was with Jesse. I just happened to be there when Jesse was questioning the doctor," I said, lying for the fourth time today. I wasn't fond of my new habit, or the fact that it was getting easier each time.

Natalie blinked at me several times, clearly trying to take it in. I wasn't sure for a moment whether she was going to throw me out, but instead she started to tear up. "So why do you think Marc wanted to see Dr. Parnell?" Natalie stuttered.

"He was trying to find out if he fathered your son," I said matter-of-factly. I took a breath. "Did he?"

Natalie's eyes narrowed, and it was clear she didn't appreciate my directness. "No, he did not." Then her gaze waned. She swallowed and looked away. "I don't think so."

"You're not sure?" I asked.

"Look, things were difficult enough then. Larry and I were on and off the whole time I was pregnant." She sat quietly for a moment, looking small and tired. When she spoke again, the defensiveness had left her voice. "Marc and I had a brief affair. You obviously know how charming he can be. How he can make you feel wanted at exactly the time when you feel completely unwanted. It wasn't right, though, so I broke things off and a few weeks later Larry and I started to reconcile. When my son was born, he was early, and Marc was absolutely convinced I'd lied about the date of conception."

"Did Marc threaten you?" I asked quietly.

"Not threaten, exactly. He wanted to see my son. He wanted to visit with him. If Larry found out, that would have ended everything." Natalie suddenly realized what she had said. "But I didn't kill him, if that's what you think. And that's obviously what you think. I just want to protect my son."

As if on cue, a loud cry came from the baby in another room. Natalie jumped up and went to him.

Natalie came back in the room with baby Jeremy in her arms. She set him down on the floor in front of me and he smiled and handed me a small teddy bear, then gestured to have it back. When I gave it back he giggled with delight and handed it to me again. He was a handsome little boy with a chubby face and sweet soft brown eyes. For the first time I really looked at the little boy, who smiled back at me.

"Marc wasn't the father," I said suddenly.

"Excuse me?" Natalie said.

"He has brown eyes. You have blue eyes. Marc had blue eyes. Two people with blue eyes can only have a child with blue eyes. It's genetics 101."

Natalie grabbed her son and stared at him. Then she started to cry. "I can't believe it's that simple." She smiled. "I knew he wasn't the father. In my heart. But he was so sure."

"But he studied biology in college, didn't he?" I asked.

"I think so," she said. "He went to school in New York for a while."

"Did he ever see Jeremy?" I asked.

"Once. A few months ago he came to the house with a stuffed toy. He wanted his son to have it," she said, a touch of anger in her voice. "He made a big point of saying that. Jeremy and I were on our way to the park, and Marc took him out of my arms. He wouldn't give him back for, like, ten minutes. It was really terrifying."

"He had a good look at Jeremy," I confirmed.

"So he would have known that Jeremy wasn't his son. He would have seen the brown eyes. Is that what you're saying?" Natalie looked at me, a little surprised.

"Yeah, I think he knew. I think he was just torturing you," I said. "Did he ask you for money to keep his mouth shut?"

"I don't have any money. We're just getting by as it is. Marc knew that. He had to have known that. Besides, I wouldn't have stood for having that hanging over my head the rest of my life." As the words came out of her mouth, she turned pale.

The baby handed me his teddy bear and we handed it back and forth. To give Natalie some time to compose herself I played with her son. After a few minutes, I patted the child on his head and got up to leave. "Do you know where Marc would have gotten a lot of money?" I asked.

"He gambled at an off-track betting place about twenty miles south of here. Charley's, I think it was called. I don't think he won all that often, but that's the only place I can think of where he could have gotten money."

"Not his father?"

She shook her head. "His dad paid his rent sometimes, I know that. But he would never just give Marc a check. In fact, Marc once broke into his dad's house looking for cash." Natalie scooped up the baby and walked toward the front door. "I have to get his lunch."

I followed her. "I may take you up on teaching me to quilt," I said.

"I wish you would," she said. "It would take your mind off your broken engagement."

"Actually," I smiled slightly, "I think Ryan and I are getting back together."

"Really," she laughed. "Why didn't you tell me this morning?" I shrugged. Why didn't I tell her?

"Too busy butting in where I don't belong, I guess." She smiled, but her lips were tight and tense. "Eleanor will want you to start making some baby quilts." I rolled my eyes, which made Natalie's face relax. "I want to hear everything," she said, "if you want to talk about it."

I nodded. Natalie kissed her smiling son and held his small hand up to wave good-bye to me.

CHAPTER 40

Information listed one place named Charley's on the main road leading south. I pulled up outside a run-down frame building with a small sign that read OTB. The neighborhood looked a little shaky, just two boarded-up buildings, an empty lot and a closed tire store. I was completely out of my element and I realized I had no idea who to talk to or what to ask.

"I live in New York," I said to myself. "That has to count for something." I took a deep breath and headed in.

✂

Inside I wasn't so sure of my street cred. The place was about half full, mostly with tired, blank-looking men, their eyes glued to small television sets bolted to shelves. It had a dark, dirty, stale feeling to it that made me cough as I walked in. I was just about to turn around and leave when I saw a familiar face. Jesse was standing just a few feet ahead of me, talking with an older man. Before Jesse could see me, I darted behind him and pretended to study a discarded newspaper.

"It's a sad thing about poor Marc, such a young guy," the man was saying to Jesse. He was either in his late sixties and had lived well, or in his early fifties and had thrown away every chance at health. He was smoking right below the NO SMOKING sign, but no one seemed to care.

"When's the last time you saw Marc?"

The man lowered his eyes. "Tuesday, I think. Yes. Tuesday. He came in here with a wad of money. I'd say close to seven thousand dollars. And he kept betting." He laughed. "Man, he was on a streak. He won over and over. Must have walked out of here with close to fifteen grand. He even gave me a C-note. Said I should treat the missus to a nice dinner." He looked at Jesse. "Lost it on the next race, or I would have."

"So he had fifteen thousand dollars?" Jesse asked.

"Something like that. Why? Does that have something to do with his dying?"

"I don't know," Jesse said. "It answers one question, but it doesn't make a lot of sense."

At just that moment, Jesse turned and bumped right into me. I tried, ridiculously, to ignore him, but he grabbed my arm.

"Nell, what are you doing here?"

"Nell?" The man Jesse had been questioning smiled at me. "You aren't Eleanor's granddaughter, are you?"

"Yes," I said, stunned. I studied the man to see if I knew him, but he didn't look familiar.

"Well, my wife says the nicest things about you. The nicest things." He smiled and his eyes focused in on me. There was a twinkle that made it immediately clear he was, or had been, quite charming.

"Your wife?"

"Nancy. She works for your grandmother."

"Oh, hi, Mr. Vanderberg. It's really nice to meet you." I could feel Jesse's eyes boring into me, but I decided to pretend otherwise.

"Are you a quilter too?" Mr. Vanderberg asked.

"No, though Nancy and the others keep mistaking me for one," I said and smiled a little at him.

"Well, you take it up. It has given Nancy years of joy. And she deserves it too," he sighed. Behind the ashen face and deep wrinkles was a kindness that I quite liked. "Better her hobby than mine."

"Speaking of hobbies," Jesse interrupted. "Nell has one that keeps getting her into trouble." He led me out the door.

✂

When we walked out, the strength of the sunlight hit me and it took a moment just to readjust.

"Okay, Nancy Drew, I thought we had a deal."

"I was just . . ." I started to say that I was just here to make a bet, but I knew that wouldn't fly.

"Get in the car and drive back to your grandmother's house and stay there."

"You're not actually allowed to tell me where I can spend my time."

He almost smiled. "I am allowed to arrest you."

"Not here, we're not in Archers Rest."

Jesse opened his mouth to speak, then closed it and headed toward a blue sedan parked up the street. I followed him.

"So we know where he got the money he was going to pay the doctor," I called after him.

"No we don't. We know he walked into the place with seven grand. We don't know where he got that."

"Blackmail?"

Jesse shrugged. "Maybe."

"But not Natalie."

Jesse stopped and turned toward me. "Why not Natalie?"

I told him about my visit with Natalie and though he was clearly upset with me for going to her apartment, he listened.

"So Marc knew he wasn't the father" was all he said when I finished.

"I think so." I was excited now to have someone to talk to about the case. "One thing bothers me, though. He had nearly three times the amount he offered the doctor."

"Why does that bother you?" Jesse asked. "He was keeping the rest for himself."

"Yeah, but this was so important to him. You would think he would have put everything he had in the pot. He was a gambler, after all. It's not like he was putting money toward his retirement. What do you think?"

Jesse unlocked his car. "Go home, Nell."

"Did you find the rest of the money?" I asked as Jesse got in his car.

"Go home, Nell," he said. "This isn't the kind of neighborhood you want be in."

Jesse closed his door and started the car, but he didn't go anywhere. I realized he was waiting for me, so I got back in my grandmother's car and pulled out of the spot. He pulled out after me and followed me the entire way back to Archers Rest.

When I stopped in front of the quilt shop, Jesse waved and drove past. I sat in the car for a minute before getting out. I was about to walk into the shop when I got another idea Jesse wouldn't like. I turned and walked up the street.

CHAPTER 41

Marc's apartment was above the pharmacy, in the center of town. I walked up the steps and tried the door. Locked. I knew it couldn't be that easy. I went back down the stairs and into the pharmacy.

"Hi," I said to the pharmacist. "I'm Nell Fitzgerald. Eleanor Cassidy's granddaughter. Is Mrs. Avallone around?"

"Bernie," the pharmacist called out. Bernie walked out of the back room. "Hi dear, what can I do for you?"

"Do you own this building?" I said. "I mean I know you own the pharmacy, but do you own the whole building?"

"That's an odd question," she said. "Yes, dear, I own the whole building."

"So you have a key to the apartment upstairs."

"Why, are you looking for an apartment?"

"I'm just . . ." I tried to think of a lie, but I'd run out of them. "I'm just snooping. Is Marc's stuff still in there?"

Bernie walked into the back room, leaving me standing by the counter feeling confused and stupid. But only a moment later she was back out holding a key. "Jesse asked me to keep things the way Marc left them until he was done with the investigation. But he's been through the place three times, so I assume he's done." She handed me the key. "Trying to get Ryan off the hook, I assume."

"Is that what your psychic intuition is telling you?"

"Maybe."

I ran up the stairs to Marc's apartment and opened the door. The apartment was small and messy. There was only one room with a large unmade bed, dirty white walls and a microwave on a small countertop. Paper was everywhere. There were travel magazines, car brochures and half a dozen credit card bills with PAST DUE stamped on them spread across the bed.

I stood in the room looking at the mess. I pressed the message button on Marc's machine and listened to a woman thanking Marc for the lovely night they'd spent together. The night she was referring to was the night before he'd been killed—the night he told me he had spent alone. Susanne had said it perfectly—I had dodged a bullet.

"What should I be looking for?" I asked myself. "Where would someone hide fifteen thousand dollars?"

There was a small painted bookcase in the corner of the room that seemed as good a place to start as any. There were at least a dozen books on architecture, a couple of dog-eared paperbacks and a stack of paper. I took each book out one by one and flipped through them. There was nothing. I went through each slip of paper. It was an odd collection of receipts, women's phone numbers and assorted jewelry—mostly single earrings. There was a note on pink paper: "Please come tonight. I'm desperate," but no indication who had written it or when.

"Find anything?"

I jumped. Jesse was standing in the doorway.

"How did you find me here?" I was a little annoyed, even though I had no right to be.

"When I followed you back to town I parked down the street and waited for you to go into the shop. When you didn't, I followed you."

"I didn't see you," I said.

"You weren't supposed to."

I could feel my face turning red, so I decided to change the subject. "Is this anything?" I showed the paper to Jesse.

He examined it. "It's something, but it's not enough of something to matter."

"You don't think it's a clue?"

He smiled. "We like to call it evidence. But I don't think this qualifies." He sighed. "I'll put it in an evidence bag, just in case."

I started to move toward the door, knowing I was going to be thrown out anyway. "I'm sorry, Jesse. I just thought I would look to see what was here."

Jesse came toward me, so I stepped back. I moved toward the wall near the door and he stood only an inch from me. "We're in Archers Rest now, Nell," he whispered, his warm breath hitting my cheek. "Do you know what that means?"

"You can arrest me."

"Don't make me do that. Please, just go home."

I paused for a moment, enjoying the way his aftershave smelled. Jesse had a strong presence, and standing this close to me, I felt protected and excited at the same time. It seemed to me that Jesse's breathing had sped up slightly, but I couldn't be sure. I was about to lean in and press my head against his chest when I realized just how stupid I was being. Jesse was on the verge of hauling me off to jail, not asking me on a date. I took one more step back, and as I did my foot caught on something. I bent over and picked up a key. I held it up.

"It's probably his apartment key," he said.

"He would have had that with him," I said. Jesse opened the door and tried the key in the lock. It didn't fit.

"Would it be the key to the shop?" he asked.

"Wouldn't he have had that with him too?" I said, but I took the key and compared it to my shop key. It wasn't a match.

"It's seems like that one," Jesse said as he pointed to another key on my chain. I compared the two keys. It was a perfect match.

"What does that open?"

"My grandmother's house."

"So Eleanor gave him a key to the house."

"I don't think so." I grabbed my cell phone and dialed the house. "Hi. It's me. Did you give Marc a key to your house?" It took nearly five minutes to find out that all of my grandmother's keys were accounted for, and to explain that nothing was wrong. But I was a little creeped out by the fact that Marc had a key to someplace he didn't belong. When I hung up I looked to Jesse, who seemed as confused as I was.

"So how did Marc get the key?" Jesse asked.

"Why did Marc get the key? That's what I want to know."

Jesse dropped the key in an evidence bag. "I'll find out. And for the last time, I'll drop you home and you'll stay out of this investigation."

I nodded. "No. Back at the shop."

"Good. And from now on when you have an idea, or a clue or a hunch, or anything involved with this case, you can call me at the sheriff's office. I'm always happy to listen to a concerned citizen."

"Message received," I said. "I'll just be at the shop checking on Tom's progress."

"He's a good guy, and a hard worker. Eleanor is better off having him do the shop than depending on Marc."

"I don't understand something. Why would my grandmother have hired Marc if he wasn't up for the task? She's not a fool."

Jesse shrugged. "Marc was good to her. He helped keep that old house of hers from falling in." Jesse turned off the lights in Marc's apartment, and I felt the darkness around me. "And he needed someone to believe in him. Your grandmother is a sucker for that kind of thing."

"Isn't that a good thing?"

"It is, most of the time. But sometimes it gets you into trouble."

"Is that another way Eleanor and I are alike?" I asked. I looked up at him and we locked eyes. I was looking for something personal in his eyes, but all I got was the solid, emotionless stare of a cop. Jesse walked out of the apartment.

I stood for a second in the dark and then followed Jesse out.

CHAPTER 42

Jesse dropped me off in front of Someday Quilts just as Tom and his helper were coming back from lunch.

It was clear that a lot of work had been done in just a few hours, but the place looked a mess.

"We framed the entryway between the two spaces," Tom pointed out with a shy pride that I found endearing. "We have to do some patchwork, of course, and clean up, but we should be ready to paint Wednesday."

"That fast?"

"We're in a race, aren't we?" He smiled. "I'm determined to be done with the remodel before your grandmother is finished with the quilt."

The quilt. I'd completely forgotten to cut out the little flowers Nancy had given me, and I knew that I could not go home without them.

"I'm going to be downstairs if you need me," I said as I grabbed the bits of fabric from my purse.

Downstairs Nancy had done a good job of cleaning out the office. All the boxes that had cluttered it were gone and it was a perfect empty space for my assigned task. I sat on the floor and set out my tools in a row: the template, the fabric, a pencil and scissors. Nancy had told me to draw the flowers on the wrong side of the fabric and cut them out on the line. Easy. So I laid the fabric down on the floor and drew around the plastic template of a flower. Then I cut exactly along the pencil marks. It was simple, and by the sixth flower it was really boring as well.

I lay on the floor with the pile of fabric under my head and listened to the work upstairs. I could hear a power saw cutting wood for something, then lots of clanging and moving about. Jesse had been right to recommend his former brother-in-law for the job. He was serious and committed and really knew what he was doing.

It made me wonder what noises Marc would have been making had he been up there doing the work. It was obvious to me now that he was all enthusiasm and ambition but he probably didn't have the skills to do a good job. I thought about what Jesse had said, that Eleanor had given him the chance because she liked the idea of someone rising to the meet the challenge, as she had done. She must have wanted Marc to feel pride in having accomplished a difficult task. Maybe then he would have moved beyond his reputation as town womanizer.

But someone else didn't see such possibilities in Marc. To that person he was dangerous and expendable. I stared at the ceiling and listened to the noise so I didn't have to think about who that person might be. But out of the corner of my eye, I saw something. I turned my head toward the doorway of the office and realized what it was.

I reached out and grabbed the piece of green paper. It was a twenty dollar bill. It seemed careless of Eleanor and Nancy to have money lying on the floor near the back wall, but with the chaos that once ruled this room, I guess it was possible.

I sat up and started on my fabric flowers again. However these turned out, at least I wouldn't get in trouble for not having held up my end of the bargain.

I had to admit that the flowers were quite pretty, even if my edges weren't cut as precisely as Nancy or Eleanor would have done them. I laid each one out to make a kind of bouquet. Natalie was right. The entire time I was working on my flowers I hadn't thought about my on-again, off-again fiancé, the murder of the town gigolo or any of the dozen or so secret spats and sad stories I'd encountered in Archers Rest. I just thought about the flowers. Eleanor and the other quilters in her group were constantly praised for industriousness. But all the time they were secretly using quilting to take a break from life. Well, I wasn't going to tell anyone.

I was on my last flower when I heard Tom closing up the shop, so I headed upstairs and home to Eleanor. I dropped my finished flowers on the kitchen table where she was sitting having tea and going over the day's receipts. I sat at the table while she looked through my work.

"These aren't half bad," she said. "Though I think the shape may be a tad traditional for the kind of quilt we're making."

"These are the shapes Nancy told me to cut," I protested. "I just spent the better part of the day cutting those."

"Well, that's the artistic process isn't it?" She smiled. "We started off with a traditional look, but it's moving in a different direction." When she saw my disappointed face, she added, "I'm sure we'll find a use for them."

"If you don't, I'll make my own quilt with them." The words came out of my mouth quickly, and to my surprise I even meant them. I liked my flowers too much to let them end up on a scrap heap.

I could see Eleanor smiling, but she only said, "How were things at the shop?"

"Good. But I found this," I said as I held up the twenty dollar bill. "It was on the floor in the office."

"Well, it didn't come from the shop's deposits." She pushed the large binder containing the shop's balances toward the middle of the table. "Every penny accounted for since we opened the shop."

It was a neatly organized system, with debts in red ink and income in black, both printed in the neatest of handwriting. "This is kind of old-fashioned. You should do this on a computer. It would be so much easier."

Eleanor leaned over the notebook. "It's worked for me for years." She looked up at me and smiled. "But I suppose we could use some updating. We'll have more inventory now."

It was an unexpected concession, but it also felt like she was beginning to see me as more than a granddaughter. Maybe I was becoming an ally, a partner. Eleanor peered into her empty cup.

"More tea?" I asked. She nodded. Okay, maybe she didn't see me as a partner, maybe she saw me as the help, but at least she saw me as capable of something. That had to be an improvement. I got up and put her kettle on.

"I ran into Bernie," I said tentatively, figuring she'd find out anyway. "I wanted to take a peek into Marc's apartment."

I waited for a scolding, but none came. Instead she sat up and gave me a curious stare. "Find anything?"

"A note asking to see Marc. Jesse said it didn't mean anything."

"You were there with Jesse?" The curious stare had turned into astonishment.

"More like he found me there," I admitted. "He thinks I'm interfering with his investigation."

"You are."

I waved my hand dismissively, filled my grandmother's teacup and sat down again. "I also went over to Natalie's place to talk to her."

Eleanor's mouth dropped open. "About what?"

"Marc. What else?" I told her what I'd realized about Natalie's baby. Eleanor shook her head and listened. "So, what's the Jesse-Natalie story? Another love triangle?"

"Heavens, no," Eleanor said. "When Jesse moved back to town, his wife had just gotten diagnosed with cancer. She was new to the area, didn't know anyone. Natalie was about her age and they became friends. Good friends, I understand. But Natalie was young and I think she got a bit spooked by the enormity of the illness. I believe she just backed off, stopped returning calls, that sort of thing. It really hurt Jesse's wife. And anything that hurt her hurt Jesse."

"Still, that's hardly a reason to be so hard on her about Marc."

Eleanor shook her head. "You weren't here to see how he loved her. Even in her situation, it was impossible not to envy what they felt for each other." She smiled a half smile at me.

And even though I knew almost nothing about Jesse and his wife, I did feel a shudder of envy. "I suppose tragic circumstances make people closer," I said.

"I don't know. I think they just bring out what you really feel for each other. If you are close, you'll become closer. If you're not, then a difficult time may well pull you apart." She sipped her tea. "Did you talk with Ryan this afternoon?"

I shook my head. Eleanor nodded at me, picked up my flowers and examined them again. "You did a lovely job with these. Did you enjoy making them?"

"Yes. But don't get any ideas."

"I think quilting is a lot safer than being an amateur detective, Nell," she said, with a worried tone in her voice that made me feel a bit guilty for running around. "As much as you want to clear Ryan, you shouldn't interfere anymore. Promise me."

I nodded. I didn't want to tell her that there was now another reason why I was looking for Marc's killer—a reason I'd only just realized. It was fun. And now that I knew that, I wasn't sure I could stop.

CHAPTER 43

I knew it was better if I appeared to stay out of the investigation for a while, just in case Jesse made good on his threat to arrest me, so for the next week I immersed myself in the renovations at the shop and helping my grandmother. I drove to the mall a few towns over and bought a computer program for finances. By Friday morning I had a newly purchased laptop on the dining room table. Though I wasn't much of a computer wiz and Eleanor was sitting beside me the entire time asking questions about how to copy or delete things, I still managed to put her store's books and inventory onto the program.

"It's a pity they didn't have these years ago," she said.

"They did have these years ago, Grandma. And now that you have this one, you should update the cash register at the store to one that's computerized. That way you will always be able to keep track of the money and the inventory."

She eyed me with a flicker of suspicion that quickly disappeared. "I never lost a penny or so much as a spool of thread. But if you are so convinced this is the right thing, you have a new project to research," she said. "Leave me alone with this thing while I play with it. You can't understand things unless you fiddle around yourself. You learned that with the muffins."

So I left her in the dining room and headed out for a walk. Nancy was running the shop that had now spilled out from the dining room to the front hallway. Tom was working hard at the store. I knew that Eleanor, Nancy, Maggie and Susanne had finished their parts of the quilt, and only Carrie and Natalie had outstanding blocks. Everything seemed to be moving along quickly. All except for Marc's murder.

I wandered around town for about twenty minutes, passing the police station three times. I hoped to run into Jesse, but I wasn't having any luck, so I headed inside. The young uniformed officer from the day of the accidental break-in was sitting at a desk. He smiled as I walked in.

"How's it going?" he asked. "The renovation going okay? I hear Tom might be finished before your grandmother and the other ladies are done with the quilt."

"Maybe." Everyone in town knew everything and felt everything was their business. I was still getting used to it, but for once maybe it would work to my advantage. "How's the investigation going?"

"Not good. We're stuck. I'll tell you, absolutely stuck." He shook his head to emphasize his point.

"There was a note on pink paper. Did you find anything on that?"

He shook his head again. "It had only smudged fingerprints on it. It's a dead end so far."

I knew I would be pushing my luck if I kept asking questions, but I had one more. "Is Jesse, Chief Dewalt around?"

"No. He went out to get some lunch at Marabelle's over by the highway. Want me to give him a message?"

"No. In fact, don't bother telling him I was here."

✂

Marabelle's was a sandwich shop I'd been to several times in the years I'd been coming to visit my grandmother. When I arrived,

I saw Jesse's car parked on the street in front and I pulled in right behind it.

I had rushed over so that I wouldn't miss Jesse, but now I had to make it look casual, so I strolled into the shop and tried not to look around. The place was small, with a few tables near the window, but I kept my eyes on the counter.

"Chicken salad on wheat," I said to the woman behind the counter. I spoke a little loudly with the hope that Jesse might look up. It worked.

"Nell," I heard Jesse call out.

I turned and tried to look surprised. "What are you doing here?"

Jesse pointed to his half-finished sandwich. "Same thing as you, I guess."

I picked up my sandwich and joined Jesse without his asking. "How are things?"

"Good. And you?"

"Good."

"The fiancé?"

"Good, I suppose."

"Things not going well?"

I sighed. "So much has happened."

Jesse leaned back in his seat and nodded. "It's got to be hard, not being sure."

I looked into his eyes and for a moment saw a sweetness in them. "I still love him; I just don't know if I want what he wants anymore," I admitted.

"People think that the moment a relationship is over you need to have one good cry and move on," Jesse said. "It's not that simple. Sometimes those old feelings linger, even when you start to have new feelings."

I looked up at him, but he suddenly looked down at his plate. "I don't know that it's over," I said. "I just don't know if I'm ready."

"You think he might have killed a guy. How do you get past that?" I looked at Jesse a long time without any idea how to answer him. Finally he said, "So are you going to ask me?"

"About what?"

He shook his head. "Okay, I'll go back to small talk," he said. "This weather is sure turning cold."

"Okay. How is the investigation going? If you don't mind sharing details of an open investigation with me."

"I do mind sharing details, but I will tell you that I'm a bit stuck. I've checked with girlfriends, gambling buddies, anyone I can think of. It's gone nowhere."

"So where does that leave you?" Jesse took a sip of his Coke. I waited for an answer, then realized none was coming. "It leads you back to the quilt shop," I said.

"So what have you come up with?" he asked. I was surprised by the question, and it must have shown. "You're telling me you haven't been looking for, what did you call them, clues?"

"I haven't, actually. You told me to stay out of it."

"And that worked?"

"Yes," I said a little indignant. Then I leaned in. "But that doesn't mean it has to do with the quilt shop. You're leaving out the possibility that it could have been a robbery or something. Some stranger came into the shop and killed Marc."

"Yes, I am. I'm leaving out the possibility that a robber came into an empty quilt shop and Marc let him in. And then, with nothing to gain, the guy stabbed him with a pair of scissors he found at the shop."

"Marc had fifteen thousand dollars. Maybe the robber killed him for that."

"How would a robber know that? And that's assuming that Marc still had the cash on Friday. For all we know he went back to the OTB and lost it the next day." Jesse stopped talking and finished his sandwich, but I'd lost my appetite.

"If your suspects are now my grandmother and her friends, you're crazy. It can't be anyone connected to the quilt shop," I said.

"It doesn't have to be."

"It can't be Ryan either."

We sat at the table quietly staring out the window.

"How's the quilt coming?" Jesse finally broke the silence.

Glad of the change in subject, I said proudly, "I cut out a bunch of flowers."

Jesse smiled. "Well, that calls for a celebration. They have a really good chocolate cake here."

"You don't have to ask me twice."

Jesse jumped up, a wide grin across his face, and brought over chocolate cake and coffee. For the next half hour we sat and talked about quilting, his daughter, Allison, and the way the last of the autumn leaves were already falling.

Ryan, Marc, and the identity of a murderer were far away and forgotten subjects, and it seemed that Jesse was as glad of that as I was.

CHAPTER 44

By the time I got home all the members of the quilt club had already arrived. Nancy was pouring M&M's into a bowl while Carrie set out coffee for everyone. Bernie sat with my grandmother looking over a new quilting book that had arrived that morning. Maggie and Susanne leaned over a vibrant quilt top Natalie had made.

"I still have to quilt it," she was saying, "and I just can't figure out the best design."

"Since it's strips, I would do circles," Susanne suggested. "You want to do something simple, so as not to interfere with the design of the top, but you also want to play against the strong rectangles the strips make."

I walked closer to see the quilt they were studying. When Natalie saw me, she held up the top she called a Bargello, and I was stunned. The quilt was made of two-inch strips of about forty fabrics that were then cross-cut into strips that varied in width from a half inch to three inches. Then these strips were sewn together to make a kind of wave effect. The quilt pattern was, according to Maggie, named after a needlepoint stitch and replicated the look. It looked like about the most complicated pattern I'd seen so far, but everyone loudly assured me it wasn't.

"The hardest thing for this quilt is choosing the right fabrics," Bernie told me.

"And putting them together in the right order," Susanne added.

"Still," I hesitated. "It looks like you have to be precise."

"That just comes from experience."

I walked over and took the quilt top in my hand. A red square caught my eye. In the first strip it was near the middle but its position moved up and down on each succeeding strip across the quilt. It was quite a beautiful effect until I got to the last three strips. There two red squares were next to each other.

"Is this on purpose?" I asked, as I pointed to the red squares.

Natalie grabbed the quilt. "Damn," she said. "I can't believe I missed that."

The other women circled around. "You can fix that easily," Maggie reassured her. "You just have to unsew the last bit."

"Unsew?" I asked.

"That's our way of saying rip up the part you got wrong and sew it back together," my grandmother told me. Natalie grunted at the thought.

"I thought if something didn't work, you threw it out," I said. "UFOs, you called them, right?"

"That's only if you don't like it," Carrie spoke up. "If you make something and realize that the design isn't working or the fabrics are wrong, something that can't be fixed."

"If you like it, if you just made a mistake, then you do whatever it takes to fix it," Natalie sighed. "No matter how depressing that is." She looked down at her quilt, fingering the mistake in her sewing that put the two red squares next to each other.

"But how do you know when to give up and when to repair?" I asked. "It seems like a lot of work when you could just move on to something else."

"It is a lot of work," Natalie said. Maggie put an arm around her.

"That's the tricky part," Bernie acknowledged. "When you put a lot of work into something and then realize that you've made a mistake, or something isn't working, you can get so frustrated that you want to throw it away. What I do is give myself some time."

"That's right," Nancy agreed. "I put it away for a little while, maybe a few days or a week, then I look at it with fresh eyes."

My grandmother shifted on her chair. "The thing is, Nell, if you decide that something isn't worth the effort, then you have to let it go. But if you decide that it is, then you have to do whatever is necessary to make it work."

I nodded. The metaphor wasn't lost on me.

✂

An hour later, as the discussion turned to the quilt we were making for Tom, I left the room for the kitchen. My grandmother had asked me to put together gift bags of fat quarters of fabric as a thank-you for all the pies, cakes, casseroles, and brownies the quilt club had been bringing us.

"Well, hello there," Susanne said cheerily as she walked into the kitchen with an empty coffee mug.

"We're out of coffee," I said. "It will take a minute for me to make some more."

"How about tea?" I put the kettle on and Susanne leaned against the kitchen counter, watching me fill the bags. "How are things going at the shop?"

"Tom's doing a great job. He may be finished before you're done with the quilt."

"Not a chance." She held up several finished blocks. They were shades of purples, blues and reds. They looked pretty, but I couldn't figure out what they would look like once they were sewn together. "Natalie told me about what you said. About the baby. It's a big relief."

"I'm glad."

"And it means that Jesse can leave Natalie alone about this Marc thing."

"Yes, hopefully." I didn't want to say anything about a possible new motive, so instead I was a little out of line. "But Marc was still harassing Natalie. She still had a motive." I swallowed hard. "So did you."

Susanne smiled widely and warmly. "I certainly did. I would have happily killed that SOB if I'd had the courage."

I nodded. "Look, for what it's worth, I don't think Jesse would try to railroad Natalie into a murder charge just because she bailed on a friendship with his wife."

"Is that what he's telling you?"

"He isn't telling me anything."

"Well, then, you should ask him," she said.

"I find that he's better at listening than talking."

She laughed. "He is a man with many secrets," she said.

CHAPTER 45

I had talked with Ryan every night, but the conversations were short and, for the most part, perfunctory. Work was fine, he said. He was getting a cold. I was busy with the shop. Things were going well and my grandmother was healing nicely. Had we really gotten this dull?

I'd started dreading the calls, but after Jesse's and my grandmother's veiled advice, I needed to hear Ryan's voice, so as soon as the quilters left, I went upstairs. He sounded tired from a long day at work but otherwise the same. It was getting confusing—liking Ryan's familiarity, but also Jesse's new stories and way of looking at the world. Love in the fairy tales wasn't like this. You met, fell in love, and lived happily ever after. You didn't kiss the local bad boy or share chocolate cake with the soft-spoken widower. I wished I could just say all of this to Ryan, but I knew any attempt would be met with the same anger and pain that Ryan had encountered when he tried to talk to me the night he broke the engagement. Instead I chatted about the quilt and he talked about the office. We were on the phone for about ten minutes of dull, everyday talk when Ryan brought up the subject we'd been avoiding.

"We need to talk about the wedding," he said.

"What about it?"

"If we're going to keep the same date, then you have to send out the invitations."

"I can't remember where I packed them," I told him.

"Well, look."

"What's the rush?"

"Are you kidding me?" an exasperated Ryan practically shouted into the phone. "What is with you? You want to get married, don't you?"

I hesitated. "Yes," I said. I didn't know what I wanted. I just knew I didn't want to fight about it.

I could hear Ryan's voice soften. "I know things are hard for you right now, but I'm really proud of you for doing this," he said, changing the subject, "helping your grandmother this way."

"Thanks."

"It's hard for me too, you know."

"I know."

"I walked past the skating rink in Central Park yesterday. Do you remember?" I did remember. On our third date Ryan had taken me there and we spent an hour skating and falling before giving up and taking a hansom cab ride through the park.

"It was pretty hokey," I laughed.

He laughed too. "You loved it." I did love it. "I was trying to impress you with how romantic I could be."

"You were?" I thought about how I felt with him that night, nervous and excited and almost in love. "I thought you were so smooth you didn't need to impress me."

"I want to keep impressing you, and I feel like I've fallen down on the job lately."

"It's okay," I said softly. "We can't spend our lives on a third date."

"But you still love me?" he asked.

"I still love you," I said. I did love him, and maybe that was reason enough not to just throw things away, not if they could be repaired.

"Well, then, look for the invitations."

"I will. First thing tomorrow."

✂

By four the next afternoon I hadn't looked, so after spending the day at the shop, I dragged myself to the bedroom and began opening the boxes from my apartment.

I found a CD I'd been looking for and my favorite pair of socks, but I almost missed the invitations until I opened the last box. The one containing summer clothes and other items I didn't think I'd need for a while.

I pulled out the dark blue box of invitations and opened it. Inside were dozens of beautifully printed cards waiting to be addressed and stamped. I stared at them for a long while, unsure of what to do. But I had been right when I spoke to Ryan, you can't live your life on a third date. Maybe the excitement of standing near Jesse or kissing Marc was just the thrill you have at the start of something, whether it's a quilt or a relationship. But excitement has to give way to work, and if I wasn't willing to give up on Ryan, and I wasn't, then I had to be willing to try.

I took the invitations downstairs, intent on spreading them out on the dining room table to work. But downstairs was still quilt central. Nancy was showing a new line of Indian-inspired fabrics to Eleanor and they were debating which of the fabrics to order. One woman was pulling out bolt after bolt of fabric while two other women were choosing fat quarters from a large basket.

"Shop still open?" I asked. "I thought you closed at four."

"We are." Eleanor looked up. "What's that in your hands?"

"The wedding invitations. I promised Ryan I'd get them in the mail by Monday." I plopped down next to my grandmother at the dining room table.

Just as Eleanor opened her mouth to speak, a woman walked

over. "Excuse me," said the woman with half a dozen bolts under arm, "I'm having a little trouble here."

The woman dropped the bolts on the dining room table and held up a quilting magazine. Nancy walked up behind the woman and offered her assistance, I assume to give Eleanor and me a chance to talk. But I wasn't interested. I preferred to watch Nancy and the customer than talk about the sudden appearance of wedding invitations. It seemed that the woman wanted to make the quilt in the magazine, but only if she could find the exact fabrics that were in the picture. Nancy patiently explained that this wasn't likely, but something very similar was sure to be here. I watched her maneuver through the room, pulling fabric after fabric for a full twenty minutes until the woman was satisfied. All the while Nancy smiled.

But as soon as she left, Nancy shook her head. "I wish people had a little more faith in their imaginations," she sighed. "It's a beautiful quilt in that magazine, but instead of duplicating it, she could have chosen her own colors. People are so afraid of making their own choices that they end up with something that isn't really theirs. I'm not putting it down, mind you," Nancy said to me, "I've done it myself. But there is something to blazing your own trail." She smiled a little and moved over to help the women picking fat quarters.

I looked down at my box of invitations. The pretty, simple lettering that looked like a thousand other wedding invitations. "Better get to it," I said to no one in particular, as Eleanor was playing with the computer and Nancy was busy with customers. "I can't believe these will be in the mail."

"Neither can I." Eleanor gave me a slightly confused smile and I left the room to look for a quiet place to work.

✂

I sat in the kitchen and placed envelopes, invitations and RSVP cards in separate piles. I took each envelope and wrote the name and address of each friend or family member invited. It didn't take long before I got to the end of the list, but I realized there were a few people missing. I wrote the names of each of the women from the quilt club on an envelope to be hand-delivered. Then I stared at a blank envelope. "What the hell?" I said to myself. I wrote Jesse Dewalt on it.

CHAPTER 46

On Monday I took my pile of invitations with me to the shop. Tom had the place freshly painted in a soft white that made it look very clean but a little sterile.

"Strict instructions from your grandmother," he said when I commented on the color. "She doesn't want anything to interfere with the colors of the fabrics and the quilts."

"What if we just did one wall? Something in a really neutral tone. Maybe behind the cash register. With the window there, there's hardly any wall anyway. She can't object."

"Your funeral," he said. "Pick up the paint and I'll do it."

So I headed out to the hardware store down the street and picked out a soft, creamy beige that would have looked dull in any other room. But when Tom put it on the wall it gave the place a nice crisp pop. Hopefully Eleanor would agree.

Then I headed over to the police station to see Jesse.

"Want to have lunch?" I asked.

"Sure," he said, pushing aside a pile of papers on his desk. "What's under your arm?"

"Invitations."

He eyed the box. "To what? The reopening of the shop?"

"No," I said, then wished I'd lied. "Ryan asked me to address them and put them in the mail."

Jesse sat back. "Wedding invitations. I guess you figured out what you wanted."

"I guess. He is a good guy. And sometimes it's better to fix something than to just throw it away."

"Absolutely." The flat cop tone was in his voice.

"I have something for you," I said, and reached into the box, pulling out an envelope. "It's for you, and a guest, if you want to bring somebody."

"Thank you," he said, eyeing the invitation as if it were a piece of evidence. "I'd be very honored." He dropped it on his desk.

"There's a catch."

"Solve Marc's murder first?" He smiled. "I might be able to do that." He dumped a plastic bag on his desk. "What do you see?"

There wasn't much to see. A wallet, a car key, a handful of change. "What are you showing me?"

"It's what I'm not showing you."

"Are you the riddler now? Because we could be here all day if I have to list all the things you're not showing me."

"When we were at Marc's apartment, we found that key to your grandmother's house. At first we thought it might be his apartment key, but you said that he probably would have had that with him."

I looked at the items again. "He didn't, though." I looked up at Jesse. "And if he didn't . . ."

"Somebody else does." Jesse leaned back in his chair. "But who that is . . ."

"Carrie."

"Carrie? Why would . . . ?"

"I saw her the day after the murder with the same key chain that Marc had. She said it was the key to her husband's office."

"You are sure it was the same key?"

"I am absolutely certain." I looked at the pile of Marc's things on Jesse's desk. Was it the same key? "I'm positive," I said. "I think."

Jesse smiled. "As long as you're sure."

"We should talk to Carrie."

He nodded. "I think I can handle that on my own. Give me about a half an hour and I'll be ready for lunch. Is that okay?'

"Perfect," I said. I dropped the box of invitations on Jesse's desk and left his office.

"I barely knew him," Carrie said. I was standing at the front door of her sprawling two-story home. It was getting a little cold outside, but she wasn't letting us in.

"When we first met you said Marc was really talented." I stepped into the hall as Carrie unhappily moved back to make room. "You practically gushed."

"I did no such thing. I thought he was a talented carpenter. So, obviously, did Eleanor since she hired him to redo the shop. And what business is it of yours anyway?"

It wasn't, of course. "Do you have a key to your husband's office?" I asked.

"Of course I have a key."

"Can I see it?"

Carrie stared at me for several seconds, then walked away. I stood in the hallway, listening to the sounds of some children's movie playing in the family room. When she came back she handed me a small set of keys on a gold chain.

"That's not it," I said.

"Of course it is. These are the keys to my husband's office. You can drive over there yourself and try them."

I put them in my pocket, ignoring Carrie's surprised expression. "I'll do that, thanks for your help." Then I moved outside.

"Are we still expected to bring our blocks for the quilt on Friday?" Carrie said, in a slightly higher pitch than normal.

"I think so," I said.

"I guess I'll see you then." She closed the door.

><

Carrie's husband, a pediatrician in a larger town near Archers Rest, was with a patient when we arrived. He stepped out only long enough to say that his wife had called and explained why I was there.

"You can leave the keys with me when you're finished," he said. He was, it seemed, close to fifty, with softly graying hair and warm hazel eyes. He was friendly and open and asked about Jesse's daughter, who was also a patient. He even offered his own keys for us to try, saying that he often took Carrie's set when he couldn't easily find his own. "Here you go," he said as he took them from his pocket. "They might be the ones you saw."

It was a set of keys on a leather chain, but it was a larger set than I remembered and the leather was brown, not black. "I don't think that's the same set," I said to myself. But my half hour was up and I knew Jesse would be wondering where I was, so I headed back to his office.

><

Jesse took me to a Chinese restaurant in the next town over and we shared plates of beef with broccoli and kung pao chicken. I felt he was studying me the entire time and it made me incredibly self-conscious, especially since I couldn't figure out why.

"How's Ryan?"

"Fine. He's getting a cold."

"You must miss him."

"How long were you married?" I don't know why I changed the subject, but I'd been curious and if Ryan was fair game then so was Jesse's wife.

"Just over five years."

"When did she get sick?"

"She had cancer before I met her. She thought it was all in the past, but just after Allie was born Liz got sick again. She died almost two years ago."

"That must have been hard. Not just losing your wife but suddenly being a single parent."

"I have a lot of help."

"But don't you miss being with someone?"

"Sometimes. But you can't get into a new relationship until you're over the things that happened in the old one."

"My grandmother says the two of you had the kind of love even she envied."

He stared out the window for what seemed like several minutes. Finally he leaned back in his seat. "So they weren't the right keys."

I nearly choked on a piece of beef. "What?"

"I called Carrie to ask her about the keys and she told me you had stopped by for a visit."

I couldn't tell if he was angry or amused, and there was no point in denying it, so I told him about my frustrating visit to Carrie and then her husband.

"You might be wrong about the color of the leather. Witnesses often get small details wrong," he said. "At the time the keys weren't important, so why would you remember?"

"I had seen Marc's keys," I argued. "If they're not with Carrie and they're not with his stuff at the apartment or in the evidence bag, where are they?"

Jesse stared at me for a while, then said quietly, "The shop."

✄

After lunch Jesse dropped me at the shop, and while he was there he searched outside, just in case. Then we went inside, where Jesse stood for a minute taking in the changes to the once crowded quilt shop.

"This place is going to be beautiful," he said. Tom and I both smiled proudly. We looked around. Tom was already building the new table for cutting fabric, and his assistant was attaching shelving at the far end of the shop.

"At least things aren't going to be falling all over each other anymore," I said.

Jesse smiled at me. "I'll bet Eleanor will be thrilled with what you've done." I blushed. I hoped so.

"The keys," I reminded Jesse.

"Tom," he said to his former brother-in-law. "Did you find a set of keys on a leather key chain?"

Tom shook his head. "The ladies had the place cleaned out before we started to work."

"It could have gotten into a box and taken to Eleanor's. If Marc put them on a shelf or left them on a table . . . ," I offered.

"I thought of that. But we took crime scene photos. I looked at them this morning. No keys."

"Carrie could be lying."

"She could," he said. "So could you." I wasn't sure if he was kidding or not. His voice was so steady and lacked intonation that I didn't know how to react.

"So could you," I said, a little cocky.

"What's my motive?"

"Bored police chief. Looking for something to do. You killed Marc so you could spend a few weeks solving the crime."

He smiled. "I'll take my statement and fingerprints later. Right now you need to tell me if there's anywhere in here a set of keys could have gotten hidden?"

"What about in that pile of quilts that was sitting on the countertop?"

"We opened each one before we released them to Eleanor. Of course we kept the one next to Marc's body."

"I wonder why he grabbed it."

"Probably to steady himself. It seems to me that after he was stabbed he must have turned around and grabbed the counter, holding on to that quilt." Jesse took a few steps toward the door. "Then he must have walked over to the door . . ."

"Maybe tried to grab his killer as he fled."

Jesse nodded. "But instead he fell by the door. Losing his keys and fifteen thousand dollars in the process."

"I thought you weren't convinced he still had the money."

"I'm keeping my options open. You can't pick a theory and try to prove it. You just have to follow the facts wherever they lead you."

"All right," I said. I decided to ignore what I assumed was his dig at my insistence that Ryan was innocent. "If we are following the keys, then everything that was in the shop is now at my grandmother's."

CHAPTER 47

"What is he looking for?" Eleanor asked me as Jesse methodically examined each basket, box, and bin that had come from the shop.

"Let's go in the kitchen," I said. "I'm starving."

Though I was a long way from becoming the kind of cook my grandmother was, I was getting comfortable in the kitchen. I boiled some pasta and made a rosemary butter sauce. I followed Eleanor's recipe but threw in a few ingredients of my own.

"Not bad," Eleanor said. "It has a bit of spice to it." She leaned in. "Did you get your invitations mailed?"

"Oh, God. I left them somewhere."

"You lost them?"

"No. I didn't lose my wedding invitations. I just put them down somewhere." Eleanor rolled her eyes just slightly, but it was enough. "I did not do it on purpose."

"Am I interrupting?" Jesse stood in the doorway.

"Did you find what you were looking for?" Eleanor turned to him.

"No. I didn't."

"Well, then sit and have some dinner. Some good might as well have come of the trip."

So Jesse sat and ate some pasta and had a slice of cake from one of Eleanor's regular customers. We talked about the shop and the town and everything we could think of except the murder.

"How bad is the quilt?" Eleanor asked with a serious, quiet tone. "The quilt found near poor Marc's body."

"How bad? You mean is there blood on it?" Jesse asked. She nodded. "There isn't much, actually. Marc had blood on his hand and it got on some of the fabric near the corner."

"I could probably get it out. Or I could repair it," she said. "If I can get it back soon, I probably can fix it. I've had that quilt in the shop since day one. It would feel very strange not to have it hanging there when we reopen."

"I wish I could guarantee that."

She nodded, a sadness across her face. "I'm off to bed then. You young people have yourselves more cake and coffee."

Alone in the kitchen, Jesse finished the last of his coffee and looked out at the darkened hallway beyond the kitchen. "I think it's pretty amazing that your grandmother lives here all alone. This place has to get a little spooky at night."

I smiled. "It does. Especially when you're here by yourself. The night Eleanor went into the hospital, I could have sworn someone was trying to break in. It freaked me out."

He sat up. "Why didn't you call?"

"Yeah. I was going to call the police to tell them I was scared."

"That's what we're here for."

"It was nothing. I came downstairs and looked around. There wasn't anybody here. The door was open, but it was a really windy night. And it's an old door." Jesse got up and checked the door. It was locked securely. I smiled at how protective he suddenly was, and then I looked to his left at the small shelf near the door. "The key."

"The key?" he looked at me.

"When my grandmother went into the hospital, I couldn't find the key to the car. Marc drove me to the shop. Then later that night the door is somehow open, and the next morning, I found the key. It had to be Marc."

"You think he made a duplicate?" Jesse's eyes darted around the kitchen. "What would he want to take?"

"There isn't anything here. I told him, too, but he didn't seem to believe me."

"So he's not trying to take anything."

I shook my head. "Maybe he wanted to leave something here."

Jesse looked at me as if he were taking it all in. "You think the fifteen grand is here?"

I jumped up. "Oh, God. Do you think it could be?"

"I went through all the stuff taken from the shop when I was looking for his key."

"So it wasn't hidden with that stuff. It's somewhere else."

"You don't think Eleanor would have found it?" Jesse was whispering now and I started to lower my voice in response.

"No. She can barely get around. And if she had . . ."

"Yeah, she would have said something."

"Okay," I said, my heart beating louder than my voice. "It can't be upstairs because I would have heard someone coming up the steps."

"It isn't in the dining room, because I've searched that." Jesse was looking around. "Plus, he didn't have that much time. You said you got up and started to come downstairs."

"I did—I listened for a minute or so, then I got up."

"So, maybe the kitchen." Jesse got up and started walking around the room. He opened cabinets and starting emptying shelves. "Look in the jars," he said.

I opened the flour and sugar canisters. I went through the tea bags, the coffee beans, the baking soda—anything that was open. There was no money.

Eventually most of the kitchen cabinets were on the counter. Jesse had spent an hour looking through the entryway and came up equally empty-handed.

"Well, it was an idea," he said as he came back to find me putting things away in the kitchen.

"You don't think he would have hid anything in the living room?"

"That would be something. Right under Eleanor's nose." He smiled. "I'll talk to her tomorrow about going through the living room."

"I can look," I said, but Jesse was already shaking his head.

"I've got all the deputies I need, thanks."

✂

When Jesse left, I sat in the kitchen and listened to the silence. He was right. The house did feel spooky. The idea that Marc had—possibly—come into the house to hide something left me a little unnerved. But if he had, there was a bigger question. Why hide it here? Was Marc afraid of someone, someone who knew he had come into a large amount of money? That thought was comforting to me because it meant that the killer could have been one of Marc's gambling buddies. The other, more frightening, thought sat at the back of my mind. Susanne's theory that someone had killed Marc to protect a loved one. A loved one like Natalie and baby Jeremy. Or a loved one like me.

CHAPTER 48

The next morning Eleanor was up early and hobbling around in the kitchen, so I figured it was safe to search her room. I tried to get Barney to be my watchdog and sit at the door to the living room, but he interpreted my hand gestures as an invitation to play, so I wasted five valuable minutes roughhousing with him in the hallway.

When he was finally tired he plopped down in the doorway. I just looked at him for a moment. Poor old thing. It must be tough to have the enthusiasm of a puppy in the body of a deaf old dog. But he seemed happy enough, savoring the joys of a few pats on the head or a few minutes of play. Maybe Barney knew what I was only beginning to see. That you have to make a little happiness for yourself wherever you can, rather than dream about what may be down the road.

As I stood in the doorway changing my life philosophy once again, I heard noises from the kitchen. I could either stand there or do what I came to do. I moved slowly into the room.

Where to start? When Marc broke into the house the night Eleanor was in the hospital—if Marc broke into the house—then none of the bedroom furniture or television would have been here. There weren't a lot of hiding places. The room, like all of Eleanor's rooms, was sparsely furnished. I looked behind the curtains. Nothing. Under the rug. Nothing. I stuck my hand up the fireplace.

Eleanor never used the fireplace. "Waste of good wood and good central heating," she said at least a hundred times. I felt around. There was . . . something. A piece of tape. I inched my fingers up a little higher and felt a bulge against the wall of the fireplace. It was paper, taped to the wall. But I could only touch the corner of it.

"Nell," Eleanor was calling from the other room. I ignored her. "Nell, are you awake?"

"I'll be right there," I yelled back. "Are you okay?"

"Coffee's ready. And it's hot."

I strained my arm as high as it could go and felt a slight cramping in my shoulder. I had promised myself a dozen times that I was going to spend twenty minutes every day stretching. If I had known it would have such a practical use I would have done it. Oh, well, tomorrow, I thought in another likely to be broken promise.

I reached in and pulled. As I did I fell against the fireplace. "Damn it."

"What did you say?" I heard Eleanor. "What are you doing?"

"Nothing." I glanced at the envelope in my hand. My fingers were trembling slightly as I opened it. It was filled with cash.

"Nell, what are you up to?"

"I'm coming," I said as I left the living room, nearly tripping over Barney as I did. My coat was hanging in the hall closet, so I stuffed the envelope into a pocket and headed into the kitchen for coffee.

✂

"Well, you were slow to start your day this morning." Eleanor greeted me with a suspicious eye.

"I know. I'm sorry," I said as I gulped down the piping hot coffee and nearly burned off my tongue. "I have to head into town and check on the shop."

"That's a good idea. And when you go to the police station ask

Jesse to see the quilt Marc had in his hands. See how damaged it is."

"What makes you think I'm going . . . ," I started, but what was the point of protesting? The woman had spies everywhere. "I'll ask to see the quilt."

✂

"I told you I was going to search the living room," Jesse said as I handed him the envelope.

"I was cleaning."

"The fireplace?"

"Yes." I stubbornly stuck to a story that he clearly he didn't believe. "Besides, you said that I could bring you anything I found, any clues, any hunches, just as any concerned citizen would."

Jesse grunted but put on a pair of gloves, opened the envelope and began counting the cash.

"How much is it?" I sat impatiently. I knew he would probably prefer I left the office, but I was going nowhere, and since, technically, the cash was not part of any crime, at least not yet, he didn't throw me out.

"Just over six thousand," he said. He spread the dollars over his desk.

"So Marc was hiding the cash at my grandmother's."

"Maybe. Half the cash, anyway."

"Well, the other half was for the doctor."

"But he never gave it to the doctor." Jesse looked at me. "So that money is somewhere."

"You said he might have gambled it away. So maybe he didn't have time to get back to Eleanor's to get the rest."

"How do you know it's not Eleanor's?" he asked.

"We just put her books on computer. I saw. She's got every penny accounted for. Besides, my grandmother doesn't like leaving twenty bucks in the register overnight. There's no way she'd store this kind of cash in her house."

"Okay. If someone knew Marc had this money, then they may have come to the shop looking for it. When Marc didn't have it, he was killed so the killer could look for it."

"If Marc told the doctor he had money, he could have told other people. He could have flashed it around." I could hear the excitement in my voice as it felt like we were getting close to the answer. "Have you gone through his phone records, seen who his friends are?"

Jesse leaned back in his chair and hesitated. Then he leaned forward. "I'm only telling you this to stop you from running around town interviewing suspects. There's nothing unusual." He reached into a file and took out a list of numbers from Marc's cell phone.

"He called this 212 number a lot, including Friday," I said. "He told me he never went into the city anymore, so who would he call there?"

"Maggie's daughter. That's her cell number," Jesse said flatly.

"Why would he call Maggie's daughter? You don't think that's odd?"

He shook his head. "Not really. She's his cousin. He's Maggie's nephew." Jesse put the list back in its folder and looked at me for a long time. "Assuming this is Marc's money and assuming that someone knew about it and was after it, that's good news for you. It pretty much leaves your fiancé off the hook."

With all the fun I was having being a junior detective, I'd forgotten the whole reason I wanted to find Marc's killer. I nodded but didn't say anything.

Jesse leaned over and put the blue box of invitations on his desk. "So you can mail these out. You left them here."

I touched the box lightly. "I will," I said. "I just have somewhere I have to go first."

"Where?" Jesse asked as I walked out of his office empty-handed.

CHAPTER 49

Maggie answered the door before I had a chance to ring. "There's coffee in the kitchen," she said.

Maggie's home was large and traditional, with classic quilts hanging on many of the walls from the living room to the kitchen. Some were muted, others bright and playful. It was the sort of contradiction that mirrored Maggie's personality exactly.

"My blue period," Maggie said as we noticed two blue and white quilts hanging side by side above the kitchen table. "So you want to find out why Marc called my Sheila."

"Yes." I always felt intimidated in her presence. "I was also curious why you didn't mention Marc was your nephew."

"He was my husband's nephew actually," she said gruffly. "I don't like to take credit for how that boy turned out."

"Still," I said, "you made it clear you didn't think much of him and you never said . . ."

"Didn't see much of him." She poured more coffee into my almost full cup. "He ingratiated himself to my daughter, though, and she has more tolerance for his kind."

"What kind?"

"Well, she has that art gallery of hers in New York . . ."

"So, she has a tolerance for artists." I was confused and a little annoyed, and I knew both were showing.

Maggie leaned in. "I have no issue with artists, young lady.

Sometimes creative people live a little outside the lines, but it's necessary. It's good. You have to take a step back from accepted society
if you are going to comment on it." Beneath the print dress and
tight bun was a bohemian. Who knew?

"So what kind was Marc?"

"A petty con. A drifter. He had no direction. He was always
looking for the easy way. If he spent his days building furniture,
like he always said he wanted to, I would have respected that boy.
I would have encouraged him. But he spent his days *talking* about
building furniture. And there is a difference."

I nodded. You can't argue with that. Not that I would have argued with Maggie. I doubt anyone would have.

"I'd love to see her gallery sometime," I said. "I think I told you,
I've always wanted to be an artist, or at least be around art. Maybe
your daughter can give me some guidance."

Maggie got up from the table and rummaged around in a
drawer. She handed me a card. "This is her business," she said, and
then she smiled at me. "I'm proud of you for moving forward like
this. It's important to go after your dreams."

✂

The gallery was a long, narrow space on Manhattan's west side. It
had only twenty or so objects in it, but everything looked ridiculously expensive. A woman who could have been a supermodel
in a previous life walked over to me and glanced up and down.
Though her facial expression never changed from an insincere
smile, it was clear what she was thinking—I did not belong in
such a fine place.

"Sheila?" I asked.

"Yes."

"I'm a friend of your mom's. A friend of Marc's."

Suddenly the look of bored superiority melted away and an

actual smile took its place. "I'm sorry. I didn't realize. How are you?"

"Can we talk somewhere?" I said as I nodded toward the single customer looking at a painting near the front.

"Are you looking into what happened to Marc?"

"Yes," I said, "in an unofficial kind of way." She nodded, as if she suddenly figured something out. Then she looked me over. It took me a moment, but I realized what she was thinking. "I wasn't a girlfriend," I explained. "More of a friend." I was digging a hole for myself, so I stopped talking and let her take the lead.

Sheila motioned me toward the cash register and away from the customer at the front. "Marc called me a few times, including the day he died," she said. "I couldn't believe it when Mom called. She was so upset."

"She was upset?" I repeated. "I got the impression she didn't like Marc."

"She didn't. She liked him as a kid, he was really fun and creative, but he . . . I don't know, he didn't live up to expectations, I guess." She stared off for a moment. "Still, she was crying when she called. And my mother doesn't cry often."

"I can imagine."

"Why did Marc call you?"

Sheila shook her head. "He said he was going to make boxes. Carved boxes. And he wanted to know if I would sell them in my shop."

"Would you have?" I asked. Looking around, the gallery had a fairly eclectic mix of objects. It was more of a fine craft than traditional art gallery. There were ceramic bowls and blown glass pieces as well as paintings, sculptures and textiles.

"Sure," she said. "Marc was actually very talented. Not disciplined, but talented. He said he had a little money and he was going to use it to start his furniture business. But he was going to start small—with the boxes. If that went well, he'd make bigger pieces. He was quite excited about it."

"But you must have thought that was just talk," I said.

"I suppose I should have, given Marc's track record." Sheila smiled. "But he said he had been inspired by someone to turn over a new leaf, and I believed him. He'd even picked out a display area for the boxes." She pointed to the center of the room. "I'd asked him to make me five, and we would see what happened."

The display case was filled with glass vases that had the texture of sand, as if they were unearthed from some archeological site. But a tag on the table explained that the pieces had been made by an artist in New Jersey. I could picture Marc's boxes sitting there instead, even though I really had no idea what they would have looked like. Still, it was nice to think of Marc as happy, excited, focused—the man I knew—instead of the person I'd been hearing about for days. And strange to think I might have been the inspiration.

The customer at the front of the shop waved toward Sheila. "Excuse me," Sheila said. "I hope you find what happened to Marc. He really was a wonderful guy in so many ways."

I took one more look around the little shop. It was pretty. A place for up-and-coming artists to show their work. But it was something at the back of the shop that caught my eye. The quilts were small, but even from a distance they looked quite beautiful and remarkably familiar.

I should have left, but I walked to the back wall of the gallery. Three two-foot square quilts hung on the wall, each with tiny appliquéd flowers, machine embroidered details, and intricate quilting.

"They're Nancy's," I accidentally said out loud. "They have to be."

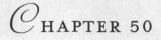

CHAPTER 50

I knew it would probably get me into trouble, but I had to call Jesse anyway and tell him what I'd learned at the gallery. I dialed his number as soon as the train back to Archers Rest had pulled out of Grand Central. It's generally frowned on to make calls on the train, since tired commuters aren't that interested in listening to the details of someone else's day, but I didn't care.

Only it wasn't working out as I had planned. Jesse wasn't at the police station. I had to call Bernie to get Jesse's mother's number, who gave me Jesse's. I could hear his daughter playing in the background, and I immediately felt guilty for interrupting their time together.

"How did you get my number?" he asked me as soon as I identified myself.

"What difference does it make?" I said. "I got it. I butted in. I snooped. Yell at me later."

As my voice got more exasperated, I could hear his voice relax. "What did you do?" he asked.

I told him about my visit to Maggie and to her daughter's gallery. Jesse didn't seem too surprised by the idea that Marc was trying to sell carved boxes to an expensive gallery. "Except he didn't actually make the boxes," he pointed out. "He just talked about making them."

"But he would have needed money to do that. Maybe that's why he only offered the doctor five thousand dollars."

"You don't need ten thousand dollars to make boxes," Jesse countered. I could hear Allie calling for him. "Look, Nell, I don't know how many ways I can say this. You need to stay out of this. I can't keep you from talking to Maggie or her daughter, any more than I can keep anyone in town from gossiping about this, but . . ." He stopped. "I'll be in the office tomorrow. You should come by."

✀

That evening I sat in the kitchen with a little notebook, writing out every clue and every suspect. If Jesse was going to let me be a part of the investigation, I wanted to have something to say.

When Eleanor and Nancy finally closed up shop and Nancy left for the night, I stopped my work and made my grandmother dinner. While I cooked, she sat at the table looking over my notebook.

"What is this?"

I turned red. "It's my list of suspects," I admitted.

"Carrie, Natalie . . . these aren't suspects. These are my friends. Your friends," she said.

I put a plate of chicken tacos and rice in front of Eleanor and a second plate at my place. I sat down but was too excited with my theories to actually eat. I told my grandmother about my weeks of detective work.

"Carrie needed money to open her own business. She said so," I said. "Plus she was having an affair with Marc, then he started going after me, so she was upset and jealous and she killed him," I said as we headed back to town.

"Based on the fact that she gushed about him."

"And she had his keys."

"Why did he give her his keys?" Eleanor asked.

"So they could meet at his place. They couldn't exactly go to her house. They couldn't get a hotel room in town. It makes perfect sense."

"*If* Carrie knew about the money. *If* she was having an affair with him. *If* she had his keys," my grandmother reminded me.

"Okay. Natalie. She had tons of motive."

"Yes, she did."

I looked at her. "You don't think it was Natalie."

"She doesn't have the stomach for that kind of thing." I realized Eleanor was considering each suspect as carefully as I was. "Susanne had the same motive."

"I don't think so. For all her faded glamour girl stuff, she's a pretty smart person. If she were going to kill Marc, I think it would have been planned out," I said.

Eleanor smiled. "So we're ruling Susanne out because she's more of a premeditated killer and we've got a spur-of-the-moment murder on our hands."

"Do you think she did it?"

"Not really. I think you're right on that one."

"Ha." I smiled. "Okay, who's left?" Eleanor glanced over at me. "You said he didn't do it," I said.

I didn't feel like playing this game anymore, and I wasn't hungry either.

The next morning I went to Jesse's office early. Maybe it was better leaving the investigation to the experts. As an amateur I kept coming back to the same suspect. I was anxious to hear what Jesse had come up with, especially if he finally was willing to be open with me about the investigation. The problem was, Ryan was the only suspect Jesse wanted to talk about.

"We have to consider it so we can rule him out," he said. "Ryan punched Marc on two occasions on the day he was killed. Plus he admits that he saw you and Marc kissing in the shop, so he knew where Marc was."

"He was at Moran's Pub when Marc was killed."

"So he says."

"No. I checked with the bartender."

"You checked your fiancé's alibi?"

"Yes." I didn't want to say any more, but Jesse would find out anyway. "The bartender remembers him, but he can't be specific about the time, and Moran's is only a few blocks away. Besides, Ryan was on the phone saying he'd made a big mistake."

"About calling off the wedding?" Jesse asked. "Who was he talking to?"

"A friend. I don't know. What difference does that make?"

"Did he tell you calling off the wedding was a big mistake?"

"Yes."

"When?"

"Later."

"Nell." I looked away from him. I knew his next question, and I didn't want to answer it. "When did he tell you that calling off the wedding was a mistake?"

"After the murder."

"After you expressed doubts about his innocence."

"I was mad at him about the wedding. I felt like he wasn't being honest. But I never . . ." Jesse looked over at me.

"What are you holding back?" he asked flatly.

"Nothing." I bit my lip but said it anyway. "He didn't come into the shop."

"What?"

"You asked me if Ryan came into the shop with me on the day Marc was killed. He didn't. The only way he could have gotten his fingerprints on the stuff in that box is if he . . ."

"Was in the shop after you left." Jesse stared straight ahead.

"Say something," I prompted.

"You should have told me when I asked."

"I was trying to protect him."

"And now?"

I didn't have an answer. Jesse waited for a moment, then opened a drawer in his desk.

"I wasn't sure whether I should play this for you, but I think I probably should," he said.

Jesse put a small tape recorder on his desk and popped in a tape. I sat down, with my wedding invitations still on his desk where I'd left them days before. They blocked my view and made me feel uncomfortable, so I put them on the floor.

Jesse pressed play, and I heard his voice, "So if the wedding was off, why did you come up here?"

"I felt like I owed Nell a better explanation," I heard Ryan say. "She left her apartment, her job, her friends. I felt bad."

"You didn't come to win her back?"

"No."

"So why did you punch Marc?"

"He said some really crass things about her. It made me mad."

"How mad?"

"Look," I heard Ryan say, "it wasn't like he was taking my girlfriend. She wasn't my girlfriend anymore. And that was my choice."

Jesse stopped the tape. "I'm sorry. But you seemed to want to know the truth."

I felt a ball form in the center of my stomach and tears well up behind my eyes. I wanted to run into the bathroom and cry, but I didn't want Jesse to see me fall apart. "He didn't want you to think he had a motive," I said.

"That's possible. He could have lied about why he came up here. Just liked he lied about being with you in the store."

I nodded. "I think he was nervous. And maybe he didn't know at that moment that he wanted me back."

"You're playing one hell of a tennis game with yourself," he said. Jesse pointed to the blue box at my feet. "Do you still want those?"

I picked them up and started to walk toward the door, hoping I'd get out before I burst into tears.

"If you need to talk . . . ," he said quietly as I opened the door. I nodded, but I didn't answer him.

CHAPTER 51

Though it was a Wednesday, the entire Friday Night Quilt Club was at Eleanor's house when I got home. I was in no mood for quilt wisdom or the kind words of women I had pretty much accused of murder, so I walked past the activity and headed upstairs. I dumped the invitations on my bed and was about to lie down when Barney came in the room.

"Hey there, fellow." I patted his head lightly. I could hear the activity in full swing down below and I knew he had come to me for an escape, but he wasn't going to get it. I suddenly realized I didn't feel like examining my conflicted feelings for Ryan. I'd spent enough time doing that already, and it was getting a little old. "Sorry, boy. We have a quilt to make."

Barney reluctantly followed me out the door and down the stairs, and when we walked into the dining room, I could see why he needed a break. There were three sewing machines set up, with Carrie, Eleanor and Natalie each manning one. The rest of the women were furiously cutting fabrics. Nancy was in the middle of it all, arranging sewn blocks on a long piece of white flannel that looked as if it had been stapled to the wall.

"The fabric sticks to the flannel without having to pin," she said when I went over to check out the progress.

"Everything looks great," I offered. "Is there anything I can do?"

"Ladies, we have a volunteer," shouted Susanne.

"I'll put you to work right here," Maggie said. "Each of these blocks needs to be pressed very carefully before you give them to Nancy. And watch out, the iron is hot."

"Sounds easy enough." I picked up a block and ran the iron across it, nearly giving Maggie a stroke.

"No, dear," she said. "We don't iron a block. We press it." She held the iron and moved it onto a spot on the block, held it there for a moment, then picked it up and placed it on another spot. "It's simple."

"I know there's a difference," I said, choosing my words carefully. "But what is it?"

"If you iron back and forth, you might distort the block, stretch out the fibers," Maggie said, sounding patient and soft toward me for the first time. "It's a mistake we all make, dear."

I took the second block and carefully placed the iron on it for a few seconds. Maggie nodded her approval and left me alone to the task.

"How's the progress at the shop?" Bernie asked me. "Are we ahead or is he?"

"It's hard to say. He's got the place painted and the shelves are up. He still needs to put in the countertop and a few other things."

"It'll be a tight race," said Eleanor.

"Then we need reinforcements." Bernie smiled and walked out of the room, returning a few minutes later with a plastic container full of fudge.

I grabbed a piece, even though I wasn't sure if Maggie would approve of my eating and ironing. "This is amazing."

"I'll give you the recipe."

"Hand it here, Bernie," Maggie said with a smile. Apparently quilting and chocolate did mix. Maggie grabbed herself several hunks of fudge and tossed a piece to Natalie, who barely caught it, making both women laugh.

After I finished with the pressing, I was put on one of the machines. I think it was more to amuse the rest of the group than to teach me sewing, but I did a pretty good job sewing a straight line. As it turned out, it wasn't that hard. It just took a little coordination.

"Piecing a top," Bernie said, referring to sewing the top of the quilt, I had figured out, "can be pretty easy if you choose a simple pattern."

I took a deep breath and kept sewing. I felt an odd satisfaction in taking the separate pieces of fabric and making them one. After twenty minutes of steadily sewing block after block, I looked up for my next piece.

"Let me see," Maggie said. "Not bad," she said as she examined my work. "Let's look at it." She handed the quilt top to Nancy, who put it on the wall. Then Nancy placed long pieces of mottled purple fabric on each side of the quilt.

We all stepped back and took a first look at what the quilt would look like. The effect was mesmerizing. Alone the blocks had seemed like a jumble of multicolored squares, but put together it was like an impressionist garden.

"I hope the shop is as nice as this quilt," Natalie said, and we all agreed. Bottles of wine were opened, toasts were made and everyone sat around feeling pretty good—and a little high on the strangely satisfying combination of white wine and fudge.

"Well, you're not a virgin anymore." Bernie poured me a second glass of wine.

"Honestly, Bernadette," Maggie said, "you have the oddest way of putting things."

"It's okay," I laughed. "I guess I'm a quilter now."

"Well, you hang out with the wrong crowd and you're going to pick up some bad habits." Nancy patted me on the shoulder.

I looked over at my grandmother sitting on a chair, her broken leg propped up. She smiled at me and I smiled back. I could finally see what had brought her to quilting. It was creative, it was practical and it was tradition. Passed down from one generation of women to the next going back hundreds of years, no matter the circumstance. From the slaves in the pre–Civil War South, who sewed scraps to warm themselves and celebrate their individuality . . . to Victorian-day women who showed off their high social station by making elaborate embroidered pieces on silks and satins to display both their wealth and the amount of leisure time they had . . . to the Amish women who even today use bright colors and elaborate stitching to showcase their abilities, while still remaining humble . . . to the women in this room with their unique styles, often strange personalities and strong friendships. I was proud to be considered one of them, even if only for one night.

✄

"Isn't there still a lot of work to do?" I finally asked.

"Tomorrow," Nancy laughed. "Unless you can figure out a way to stall Tom."

"I guess I should get home to the baby," Natalie sighed.

"Oh, yeah. Children," Carrie said. "I should go too."

Nancy and Bernie agreed to stay behind and clean up the dining room so it would be ready for customers in the morning. I walked Barney, who had spent most of the evening in the kitchen.

"What is his problem?" I asked Eleanor, who was making herself tea when I got back to the house.

"He's not used to so many people, all day long," she said as Barney dropped into his dog bed. "I think the poor thing is petted out."

I petted him anyway, and he did his best to ignore me. And then I did the dishes.

"Well, you've put that one to work, haven't you," Bernie said to Eleanor as she walked in the kitchen.

"She has," I admitted. "And I've got the dishpan hands to prove it." I held up my dry hands in kind of show-and-tell.

Bernie reached into her purse and took out a small jar. "Try this," she said, and tossed it to me. "It's quilter's hand wax."

"What makes it for quilters?"

"It's not specifically," Eleanor said. "It's just a great waxy moisturizer that softens hands but won't get greasy and ruin fabric, so you can use it while you're sewing."

I opened the jar and smelled it. It didn't smell like anything. I dipped in. It was, as described, waxy. I spread a little on my hands and rubbed it in. My hands felt softer, but she was right—there was no greasiness. I put my finger back in the jar and took a little more. It seemed familiar. It seemed like the same stuff that had been on the stairs in the shop—the stairs Eleanor and I had both slipped on.

"Where did you get this, Bernie?" I asked.

"At the shop. Your grandmother sells it by the truckload." Eleanor nodded.

I turned the jar upside down. "What are you doing?" Eleanor asked.

"I'm just trying to see if it spills. If it could have been accidentally spilled on the steps."

"Doesn't budge."

"No, Grandma, it doesn't."

"Well, it's a lovely science experiment, dear, but I should be going." Bernie patted Eleanor's arm. "Good work today, I think."

"It was."

Bernie walked over to me. "I almost forgot. I wrote down my fudge recipe for you." She pulled out a piece of pink paper from her purse and handed it to me, smiling. "Maybe you'll make it for a future meeting."

I looked at the pink paper for a long second. That didn't make sense. But when I looked up, Bernie was gone and Nancy had entered the kitchen to say good night.

CHAPTER 52

"Please don't say it." Jesse was laughing the next morning when I called him about the pink paper and the hand wax.

"It's not impossible. Bernie told me herself that she had more lovers than she can remember."

"Stop. Now."

"She could have been having an affair with Marc."

"Mrs. Avallone is a friend of my mother's."

"Then explain the pink paper. Explain the hand wax."

"Okay," Jesse said. "The stationery store said that at least a dozen pads of the same paper have been sold in the last six months. And the wax comes from the quilt shop. All of those women probably have some."

"I don't think the paper is a coincidence."

"I tell you what—you follow up on that lead and I'll work on figuring out where Marc could have gotten the money. Last night I was thinking that maybe he was blackmailing someone and when the person came to pay, he or she instead decided to kill him."

"You think he was blackmailing Bernie about their secret affair?" I said, only half kidding.

"I don't want to have that image in my head. Mrs. Avallone plays cards with my mother every Tuesday." I could hear the smile in his voice, and it felt nice. "But the wax is another story. Who went up and down those stairs?"

"Everyone. The bathroom was downstairs and all the regulars at the shop had access to it."

"So it could have been meant for someone else. Someone like you."

"Why would anyone want to hurt me?"

"Why would anyone want to hurt Eleanor?"

I didn't know the answer, but I promised to be careful as we hung up. My cell phone rang again and I was sure it was Jesse calling back, but when I looked at the caller ID, I saw it was Ryan. I just kept looking at the number as the phone rang until it went silent.

I went downstairs where Nancy and Eleanor were already set up for another day of quilting. Nancy was positioning and repositioning the flowers I had so carefully cut out. She tried them on the long plain strips of purple fabric that made up the borders of the quilt, but they didn't work. Then she tried to place them in the blocks.

"No," I said. "That's too busy."

"Any suggestions?" She turned to me.

"The whole quilt feels like a painting, and then when you put the flowers on it, it sort of takes away from it." I touched the soft fabric of the quilt. "I wish you could paint flowers on the borders. That would be cool."

"You can," Eleanor said. "They make paints that you can put on fabric."

"Well, I can't," Nancy protested. "I'm not much of a painter."

"Nell can." Eleanor sat up in her chair. "She used to paint all the time."

"I don't know if I was any good," I protested.

Eleanor dismissed me with a wave. "Nancy, we have some fabric paints, don't we?"

Nancy sorted through several boxes until she found what she was looking for. "I don't know how to paint on fabric," I said. "And I'm certainly not going to ruin this."

"Paint flowers on the borders. That's just plain fabric," Nancy said. "If we hate it, we'll just cut more fabric."

I laid some paper on the ironing board, then put a long strip of the purple border fabric on the board and pinned it down. I was nervous enough without having the fabric move around as I painted. I ordered Nancy and Eleanor out of the room and arranged the paints. Then I stared at the fabric. I had an image in my head of how it should look, but I couldn't figure out where to start.

"Nature isn't perfect, you know," Nancy said from the hallway.

"Better than me," I sighed.

"The Amish have a tradition. They make a deliberate mistake in every quilt as a way of acknowledging that only God makes things perfect." Nancy walked in and pushed me slightly toward the strip of fabric.

"So I'm the deliberate mistake."

Nancy laughed. "I think it's kind of nice. Every time I screw up, I say I did it for God. Makes me feel better."

"Fair enough. But you have to leave the room and stay out until I'm ready." Nancy did as she was told and I turned back to the border.

Using Nancy's flower template as a guide, I lightly painted flowers on one of the border sides. I made dark purple, pink, and yellow flowers, with light and dark green leaves and stems, holding my breath the entire time. When I was done, I called Nancy and Eleanor back into the room. Together we put the painted border next to the quilt.

"That was it," Nancy said. "That was exactly what it needed."

So I painted the other three sides while Nancy and Eleanor cleared back out of the room so, as they put it, they wouldn't disturb an artist at work. As I finished each side of the border, I put it back on the flannel wall next to the interior of the quilt. Stepping back, I had to admit it was beautiful. The painting echoed the garden feel of the blocks without taking away from their impact.

"I'm done," I called out.

Nancy and Eleanor came back in. Nancy praised me repeatedly, but Eleanor just leaned on her crutch and stared.

"What do you think, Grandma?"

She shook her head. "It works."

✄

The doorbell rang, and I knew it was time to open the makeshift quilt shop for the day. Eleanor sat in her chair and rested her leg on a small footstool while Nancy went out to great the customers.

"I should check on the shop," I said.

Eleanor nodded; she was still staring at the quilt. "You'll have to do something like that for the shop wall."

"One of these days," I said, and headed for the hallway before I got too caught up in the moment. Nancy headed me off as I reached for my coat near the front door. "I'm going to check on the shop," I told her.

"I'm sure you like your job in the city, Nell," Nancy said, suddenly serious. "But you have real talent. I know your grandmother said that you dabble in painting, but you should really think about getting some training. I wanted to when I was your age, but . . . well, I got a little caught up in getting married, having kids. I just didn't get around to it. I always thought there would be time."

I nodded. "Thanks. It's really sweet, especially from you, with all your quilts and everything." I hesitated because I knew it wasn't really my business, but she had sort of opened the subject matter. "I was in New York the other day, at a gallery, and I saw your quilts."

Nancy took my arm and led me outside. It was a cold morning and she was shivering in her turtleneck sweater. "I haven't told Eleanor yet," she said quietly. "I haven't told anyone."

"Maggie knows."

Nancy nodded. "It's her daughter's shop. It doesn't matter that you know. Everybody's been telling me to sell my quilts, so I thought I'd give it a go."

"I'll bet you're doing well."

Nancy took a deep breath. "I haven't sold any yet, so who knows if anything will come of it."

"Are you kidding? Those quilts were amazing."

She blushed. "Please don't say anything. I want to keep it to myself for now, in case nothing happens with them. I don't want people being disappointed for me."

I hugged her. "Not a word."

"Art school." She wagged her finger at me. "There's one in Nyack and one in Peekskill. I'll get you brochures."

I'd like that, I thought. Then my phone rang, and it was Ryan again. I put the phone in my pocket and headed into town.

CHAPTER 53

I stopped by the bakery for coffee and a muffin on my way to the shop. As I was walking out, I saw Carrie up the street heading toward the pharmacy. I was about to say hello when I noticed she wasn't going into the pharmacy. She was hovering by the door that led to the apartments above it. She took a key out of her purse and unlocked the door. As she entered the building, I ran to catch her and put my foot in the door just as it was about to close. I waited for about a minute. I wanted her to be in Marc's apartment when I walked in and caught her doing . . . I wasn't really sure what she might be doing, but it was clear she had lied earlier.

I thought, just briefly, about calling Jesse, but I knew he would ask me to wait outside, and I was way too curious to do that. I walked up the stairs to Marc's apartment. The door was slightly opened.

"Hi," I said. Carrie spun around and went white.

"What are you doing here?"

I laughed. "I think I'm supposed to ask you that."

Carrie grabbed my arm and pulled me into the apartment, slamming the door behind me. "Please don't tell anyone you saw me here."

"You lied to me."

"I know." She sat on Marc's unmade bed. "I don't know what's gotten into me lately."

"You were having an affair with Marc."

She looked confused for a moment, then lowered her eyes to the floor. "No, I wasn't. I actually wasn't."

"Then why do you have his key? And what are you looking for in his apartment?"

"I left an earring here."

I walked over close to her. It felt like she might bolt at any minute and I wanted the whole story. "You left an earring in his apartment, but you weren't having an affair with him?"

"I know how that sounds, but it's true. I just didn't want to say anything before because I don't want my husband misunderstanding what happened."

I sat next to her on the bed. "You weren't having an affair, but you wanted to have one."

"No." She teared up. "I love my husband. He works twenty-hour days and I feel like a single mom, but I love my husband. I didn't want to have an affair with Marc." She shuddered. "The guy was a little sleazy, don't you think?"

That was a bit of a slam, intended or not. "I'm not the person who left an earring here."

Carrie nodded. "Do you think it might be here?"

"Carrie, focus. You want me to believe that you came to a man's apartment and left your earring behind, but you weren't romantically involved. So, how exactly did you leave your earring?"

"I gave it to him." She got up and started looking around the room.

"What did it look like?"

"Diamond, a half carat."

"Jesse was here the other day. He took things like that as evidence," I lied.

She sat down again, defeated. "I wanted to open my own business. My husband thinks I'm overwhelmed with the kids and shouldn't take on anything else. I didn't want to get into another argument about what a waste of money it was, so I figured I'd just go through with it and tell him later. Your grandmother once said to me that sometimes it's better to apologize than get permission."

"It sounds like something she'd say."

Carrie smiled a little. "I wanted to take over the diner, turn it into a coffee shop, but you got there first."

"I'm sorry."

"No, it's fine. But there was this place for lease down the street. Marc said he'd help me fix it up, he said he'd make it look like the kind of coffee shop I used to hang out in in Greenwich Village." She laughed. "In another life."

"How does the earring figure in?"

"I didn't want to dip into our savings to put down a deposit, so Marc said I could sell some jewelry. It's stuff I bought myself years ago. Marc said he knew where I could get good money for it, very quietly. I wanted to go into the city myself and sell it, but when would I have the time?"

"So you gave Marc one earring? How much would that have been worth?"

"Maybe a thousand, fifteen hundred. I just wanted him to get me a price. Then I was going to give him the other and a bracelet I had. I was trying to figure out if I should go through with it."

"So you're here to get it back?"

She nodded and took a deep breath. "I changed my mind. Maybe I don't have what it takes to be in business anymore. I don't know. I knew I didn't want to start a business by lying to my husband. I went to Someday Quilts the day he was killed and asked Marc for the jewelry back. He told me he was keeping it as his fee. I saw his keys on the checkout counter, so I took them. I was going to run down here and get the earring, and then I ran into you and got all freaked out, and then . . . Did Marc tell you about our arrangement?"

"Why would he?"

"You were getting . . . close," she stammered. "Maybe you were just as fooled as I was."

Another slam, unintentional or not, but this time I hit back. "You didn't go back to the shop later, maybe when you couldn't find the earring, and kill Marc?"

"If I'd already searched his place, why would I be here now?"

She had a point. I got up, knowing that Jesse would kill me for this, and walked over to the box of jewelry on his bookcase. I handed it to Carrie, who riffled through the mostly cheap earrings. In the middle was a beautiful diamond.

"I don't think he really knew where to sell it," she said. "I don't think Marc was that worldly. He was just really good at fooling people."

"We should go," I said, and we headed for the door. Just as we locked Marc's apartment behind us, I heard steps coming up the stairs.

"I got a report that someone was breaking into Marc's apartment." I turned to see Jesse on the bottom stair.

"I can explain," I said.

"I'm almost certain you can."

✂

Carrie and I sat in Jesse's office for nearly an hour. For ten minutes we explained why we were there, and for fifty we listened to Jesse tell us why we were in big trouble.

"I could charge you with half a dozen things," he said to Carrie.

"What if Marc gave her the key?" I asked. "Then she would have had his permission to be in his apartment. It's not a crime scene. You don't have police tape across it, do you?" Jesse just glared at me. "The earring belongs to her, so really what crime could you charge her with?"

"Tampering with a police investigation, for starters. I could charge you with the same thing." He sighed heavily. "Carrie, go home. I'm keeping your earring for now. I'll get it back to you when we're done with the investigation."

Carrie squeezed my hand. "Thanks," she said meekly and left.

I got up. "Don't move," Jesse said. "I like you, Nell. And I realize that this is my fault. I guess I liked having you around. And I'm the first to admit that you have been helpful. But this is the end of the line, do you understand? You are not a police officer."

"I wasn't being a police officer . . ."

"You followed a potential murder suspect into the apartment of a victim and then aided her in recovering property that could be evidence of her guilt."

"I don't think Carrie killed him."

"You did before."

"I don't now."

"Well, then. You tell me who did, Sherlock, and I can take the rest of the afternoon off."

"I don't like your tone," I said, my voice quivering just a little.

"I don't care what you think of my tone. I'm not going to be responsible for something happening to you, or this murder investigation, because you've gotten a little caught up in playing detective."

"Am I charged with anything?" I asked with as much iciness as I could muster. He was right, and that made me feel all the more angry and defensive.

"No. I'm just going to ask you to stay out of it. Maybe you should be spending your time figuring out why you're planning to marry a man you think could have committed murder. A guy who uses you for an alibi and tells me that you didn't mean anything to him."

"I realize he isn't likely to be the perfect, faultless husband you were." I surprised myself with my sarcasm. "I guess I'm just choosing from what's out there."

"Get out of my office," he said without looking at me.

"My pleasure." I got up and walked out as quickly as I could.

CHAPTER 54

I rushed out of the police station so fast I nearly walked straight into oncoming traffic. It took the sound of brakes screeching and someone yelling "Nell" before I paid attention. I looked around and saw Natalie coming out of the post office with little Jeremy.

"Are you okay?" she shouted.

I nodded. "I'm fine. Just mad."

"You want to get some coffee and tell me about it?"

We headed over to the bakery, where I got coffee, a chocolate-covered doughnut, and an éclair.

"You are upset." Natalie sat at the bakery's one small table. "Who are you mad at?" she asked as I swallowed the donut. "Sure hope it's not me."

"Jesse."

She blinked slowly. "What did he do?"

"Put me in my place, that's what he did. I understand that he's the cop. And I was wrong. I'm willing to admit that."

"You made a mistake and you told him you were wrong and he got mad at you?"

"I didn't tell him I was wrong. I would have, but he was so busy telling me all the ways I've screwed up that I just couldn't."

"What exactly happened?"

"I've been helping him. He's wanted my help. Now, all of the sudden, he's telling me to stay out of it. And he just said the meanest thing to me about Ryan."

"He has that way about him sometimes," she agreed.

"Everybody has to be perfect like him," I said, still exasperated.

Natalie sipped at her coffee and dusted some nonexistent dirt off Jeremy's bib. "He's not perfect."

"I know about you and his wife."

"Who told you?"

"Eleanor."

She nodded and looked away. "Then you don't know, not really."

Out the window I could see Jesse walk out of the police station and stand talking to another officer. "What don't I know?" I asked Natalie.

"When Lizzie, his wife, was really sick, I used to come by and visit. A lot of times, though, she would fall asleep and I would stay to keep Jesse company. It was hard for him, trying to look after his daughter. She was just a baby. I didn't realize at the time how hard that could be." She swallowed. "One night we sat outside, Jesse and me, and talked. He was so scared. So lonely. I don't think he'd admitted that to anyone before."

I could see that Jesse was slowly walking up the street toward the bakery. "Did something happen?" I asked, watching Jesse with one eye.

"It was stupid. One night we were having some wine and talking. Me about my bad marriage, him about his dying wife. I guess we both felt a little sorry for ourselves. He leaned over and kissed me," she said, blushing. "I let him because I was a little shocked, a little sorry for him. It wasn't a big deal, and that's all that happened, but to Jesse it was a huge betrayal. Whenever he saw me, he was ice-cold. He doesn't allow himself much in the way of failure."

"That's why he's mad at you—because you represent his failure to be a perfect husband."

"I guess." She leaned back. "He had also made me promise it wouldn't change my friendship with Liz, but it did. I felt uncomfortable, and I just stopped visiting her."

"And then he felt you had abandoned his wife."

"I guess, and if it made him feel better to be mad at me, then I was okay with it. Maybe I could have handled it better, for Lizzie's sake. But I didn't, and enough is enough. He's human too. He makes mistakes. And I'd tell him that if I saw him. I really would."

"You may have your chance, because he's walking up to the store right now."

Natalie's head spun around, just as Jesse reached the window. But he didn't stop. He just kept walking as if he didn't know we were there. Maybe he didn't. Or maybe I'd gotten on his bad side, just like Natalie, and now I was going to be ignored.

✂

The whole way back to my grandmother's I replayed our conversation. I wanted to be angry at Jesse, but I just felt sorry for him. Not dead wife sorry, but sorry that he was so hard on himself, and by extension everyone else. Namely me. And that thought made me mad at him again. By the time I reached the front door, I was completely confused about everything, except that I was definitely not staying out of the investigation.

✂

"Nell," Eleanor called out as I walked in the door. "Nell, is that you?"

I wanted to go upstairs, but I knew I couldn't. "Yes, I'm home."

"Come into the kitchen."

She was sitting at the kitchen table, rubbing the cast on her leg. "I can't wait to get this thing off," she said. She looked at me. "What's wrong?"

I shook my head. "Nothing."

"I know what it is," she said quietly. "Ryan called here. He's frantic. He said he called you half a dozen times today and you're not picking up your phone."

Ryan. I had forgotten about him. "I'll call him back right now." I took out my cell phone. There were five missed calls from Ryan and three from Amanda. Poor Amanda—he was enlisting her to bug me.

"Nell," my grandmother said softly. "This isn't any of my business, but if you're having doubts . . ."

"Are you telling me that no one has ever had doubts before they walked down the aisle?"

I sat next to her. She laid her hand on mine. "No."

"Did you have doubts when you married Grandpa?"

She smiled a little. "No. But it was a different time. He was heading to Korea. We wanted to have sex."

"Grandma!"

She shrugged. "So tell me about the help you've been giving Jesse."

"I don't want to talk about that."

"You think Ryan might have killed Marc, and you're trying to prove that he didn't."

I shook my head. "I don't know what I'm trying to prove anymore. I really don't. I just have to know the answer."

"Do you love Ryan?"

I looked into her gray-blue eyes. "Why are you asking me that?"

"You've been leaving your wedding invitations all over the place and following Jesse around."

"I left them one place, in Jesse's office. And I haven't been following Jesse around. I've been helping him."

"He doesn't seem to think so, at the moment, anyway."

"I admit we had a fight." I stopped and looked at her. "How do you know about that, anyway?" She smiled. I knew I was turning a little red. "Can I get anything past you?"

"I have spies," she laughed, waking up Barney, who had been sleeping in the corner.

"Barney?" I asked, only half kidding. I wasn't sure how she knew the things she knew anymore.

"Heavens, no. He's dumb as a post, poor handsome thing."

✂

Upstairs I pushed my quilt off the bed and lay under a dark blue blanket. My cell phone rang. It was Ryan again. This time I picked up.

"Finally." His voice seemed far away. "Where have you been all day?"

"Why did you come up here the day Marc was killed?"

"What?"

"Just tell me?"

"I thought we should talk."

"You didn't come up here to get back together, then get spooked when you saw Marc? Because that's what I thought happened."

There was silence for a minute. "I meant what I said that day by the river. I realized what a stupid mistake I was making by letting you go."

"You told someone that at Moran's Pub."

"No, I didn't. What are you talking about?"

"You were on the phone at Moran's Pub the day of the murder. Who were you talking to?"

"How do you know that?" His voice was getting angry. I heard him take a breath. "I was talking to Amanda."

"What did she tell you?"

"She told me that I needed to decide what I wanted. And that once I knew I should go for it. So I decided to fight for you." He stopped. "Not like that. Not like that."

I stared at the ceiling, my mind blank. "You told Jesse that you went into the shop when I was there. That isn't true."

"I panicked. I knew it would look bad."

"Didn't you think Jesse would ask me the same question?"

"I knew you would back me up." I smiled a little at that. He was so sure of me. "It's not a big deal."

I sat up. "Why were you in the shop?"

"To talk to him. He kicked me out. I hit him," he said. "What does it matter? You need to put this behind you. We have to put the past behind us and just move on. You hear me?"

"Yes," I said, but my voice had gone dull.

"You love me, Nell."

"Can I call you tomorrow?"

"Jesus. Yeah, I guess. What's going on?"

"I'll call you tomorrow."

I clicked the end button on my cell phone and closed my eyes. Was he right? Should I just put the past behind me? And if I did, how much of the past should I let go of?

CHAPTER 55

The next morning I walked down to the river and sat on a rock near the spot where Ryan had reproposed to me. I looked out at the icy water. It was only early October, but the air was biting. My cheeks were numb and my eyes were starting to tear, but I couldn't leave that spot. I didn't spend fifty years with Ryan. I didn't have his children or watch his hair turn gray. And yet sitting here, I felt the loss of all of it. It had been hard when I felt he'd taken it away from me. Choosing to leave, which should have been easier, left me feeling sick.

I took my cell phone out of my pocket and dialed Ryan's number.

"Hey," came the voice on the other end. "What's wrong? Have you been crying?"

"I was thinking we should talk."

"About what? Us or the murder?" His voice had a hardness to it.

"Us."

"I'll get on the next train. I'll meet you at your grandmother's house," he said.

"You don't have to come up. I can come to the city. Amanda wants to get together for lunch, anyway."

"You can see her another time," he said softly. "I want to be alone with you."

It made me uncomfortable to hear the tenderness in his voice. As the morning wore on, my nerves got the better of me. I didn't think sitting around my grandmother's kitchen table would make the conversation any easier, so I decided to meet him at the station.

The train was pulling up as I turned the corner. I could barely catch my breath, so I stopped and leaned against the station's small ticket booth. I knew I was doing the right thing, but I still hadn't found the right way to do it. Ryan would be off that train any minute. I swallowed hard as the train stopped. The doors opened and an older man got off at the door nearest me. Down the platform, I saw Ryan step off the train into the sunlight. I could see the cold air from his breath as he stood and put his gloves on. I didn't want to step out from behind the building. I wasn't ready for him to see me. I knew the minute he looked into my eyes, he would know it was over.

Then someone got off the train behind him. A woman. She was wearing a hat, scarf, long red coat, and tall black boots. There was almost no skin showing, but I knew who it was—Amanda. I didn't know if her presence would make things easier or harder, but this wasn't a conversation for three.

I stepped out from behind the building and started walking toward them when I saw Amanda grab Ryan's arm. He pulled away from her in an almost violent motion.

"Get away from me," he yelled. It stopped me in my tracks. "I'm not going to say it again."

"Ryan," she said meekly. She was crying.

"Hi," I said. They both turned to me and stared.

"I thought I was meeting you at your grandmother's," Ryan finally said.

"I decided to surprise you, but I guess you beat me to it." I could hear the flatness, the lack of emotion in my voice. I looked at

Amanda, who was wiping the tears from her eyes. It was clear that she did not start crying as she stepped off the train. Her eyes were red and her face was swollen and flushed.

"I'm sorry," Amanda blurted out as though she had been holding it back with all her strength. Then she started crying again and walked down the platform toward the ticket booth.

"I was supposed to meet you at your grandmother's," Ryan said again.

I paused. I was watching Amanda sobbing and Ryan stammer. Then it hit me. "How long have you and Amanda . . ." I couldn't get the last word out.

"It's not like that."

"What's it like?"

Ryan looked at his feet and shook his head slowly. "I don't want to talk about this here."

"Is that why you postponed the wedding?" I tried to meet his eyes, but he avoided looking at me. "I knew you were lying to me about something. I guess it was easier to imagine you would kill someone, than . . . this. Isn't that sick?"

I smiled, but I felt like throwing up. I had spent the whole morning working on a speech explaining why I couldn't go through with the wedding—a speech that was both caring and clear. I hadn't even had a chance to say it and there was nothing else to say. I walked away.

"Nell," Amanda called out. "I know you hate me." She walked after me as I passed her by. "I didn't mean for it to happen. Ryan didn't either. It just did. We were both really torn about it. Really we were. He came up here to tell you and then that guy was killed and it seemed . . . I've felt just . . . you're my friend."

I wanted to be angry, but mostly I was numb. "Your friend?"

She started crying again. "I've always told you everything.

And I've been hiding this away in some secret place, and it's felt so wrong. Not being able to talk to you."

"That's what felt wrong?" I walked away and she followed. I stopped. "You should be running after him. Not me." I turned away and walked as quickly as I could.

CHAPTER 56

I stopped twice on the way to the quilt shop to find some private place to cry. I kept thinking I would get sick, but it didn't happen. That was probably for the best, but it left a brick in my stomach that I had to get rid of before I faced Eleanor and the rest of them. I stood on the sidewalk, closed my eyes, and took deep breaths.

"You okay? You look like you've been hit with a two-by-four."

I opened my eyes. Bernie was leaning into me, smiling worriedly the way people do around the insane.

"I'm fine." She reached out and touched my shoulder.

"Is it over?" she asked. I nodded. "Was it someone else?" I nodded again.

"How did you know?"

She shrugged. "I'd like to credit my psychic gifts, but I think I've just known too many men not to recognize a man with a secret when I see one."

"Why didn't you tell me?"

Bernie smiled sadly. "I wanted to be wrong." We sat on the curb and watched Archers Rest at rush hour. Three cars drove by in five minutes.

"Why did you write Marc a note to see him later?"

Bernie looked a little confused, and then a smile took over her face. "Jesse asked me the same thing." She relaxed her shoulders.

"Marc was going to fix some stuff at the house. I left him a key and a note."

"And he kept the note?"

"He kept the note and the key. I had to change the locks before that little bugger robbed me blind. He would have, you know. He's stolen from several people."

"So I've learned."

"Did you think Marc and I were having a torrid affair and I killed him in the heat of passion?"

I shrugged.

"Well, I hope you did. I like to think I still inspire that kind of gossip." She laughed to herself. "Are you going to the shop?"

"I'm on my way. Want to go together?"

She held up two deposit bags. "I have to go to the bank first, deposit one into my personal account and one into the business account." She got up. "You have more than a few wonderful moments in your future, Nell."

"Psychic gifts tell you that?"

"No. I've just lived enough to know." Bernie hesitated, then crossed the street and headed for the bank. I watched her for a moment, trying to believe her, trying not to think about the scene at the train station.

As I watched her walk away, there was a feeling that came over me. What I was beginning to think about Marc's murder didn't make any sense, and I did my best to ignore it. It would have been possible, except I turned my head and saw Barney walking up the street, sniffing at every flower and fire hydrant he found. I was about to call out to him, but I knew he wouldn't hear, so I just waited for him to get close enough to see me. I admired dear old Barney. I wouldn't have taken the loss of something so important as easily as he had.

As Barney walked over to me wagging his tail, I felt my face turn hot. The brick in my stomach was jumping around. I wanted to pass out. I knew. I didn't know, and then a second later I did. And I didn't want to know. I took my cell phone from my pocket.

"Chief Dewalt," I heard Jesse say on the other end.

"Can you meet me at the shop?"

"Now?" I couldn't answer. "Is everything okay?" he asked.

"Can you meet me there?"

Silence. And then, "Do you remember when you asked me if anyone else's fingerprints were on the money?" he asked.

"Yeah."

"It annoys me to admit this, but what you said nagged at me, so I checked it against the prints I took after the murder."

"So you know," I said, my throat closing.

"I guess we both do."

✂

I walked with Barney as slowly as I could to the shop, but it still took me less than a minute to arrive at the door. Nancy, holding a large box, was standing with Eleanor.

"Now I see who you went after." Eleanor patted the dog's head. "I used to be your favorite. Guess I have competition."

Natalie and Susanne arrived just moments before Carrie. All three were talking about the huge bag Susanne had in her arms.

"I have the quilt," Susanne said to me. "Finished it last night."

The women gathered around the large shopping bag, but Natalie looked up at me.

"Are you okay?" she mouthed. I nodded.

"Let's see the quilt," I said.

Maggie arrived on the scene. "Not without all of us here."

"Bernie had to go to the bank. She'll be here in a minute," I said.

For the first time since I arrived, Eleanor looked up at me. She gave me a sympathetic smile that made me wonder how bad I looked. "We should go inside," Eleanor said. "I'm willing to wait for Bernie, but not if it means getting pneumonia."

When we opened the door to the shop, we saw Tom and his assistant were putting up the last of the shelves. The place looked huge and new, and not quite finished.

"We beat you," beamed Eleanor.

Tom looked up, a little surprised. "Another few hours and I would have done it."

"Well, we cheated," Maggie huffed. "We do our group projects by hand, but we had Susanne machine quilt this one. But you'll have to wait to see until Bernie gets here."

I took a deep breath. "Can you guys give me a minute. I need to . . . I'll be right back."

✂

I headed into the basement and went straight to the office. I walked toward the back wall. I wasn't sure exactly what I was looking for, or even if I would find it, but I moved my hand across the smooth wall. I kept moving my hand back and forth, getting closer and closer to the ground until I was on my knees. I ran my fingers along the baseboard. It was loose. I pulled at a section until I'd removed the whole piece.

Behind the baseboard was a small hole, and in it an envelope. I could hear the women upstairs talking about the quilt and the construction on the shop. They seemed so happy, and I was about to ruin it. I opened the envelope and found what I'd been expecting. Thousands of dollars in cash.

✂

When I got upstairs, Susanne was pulling the finished quilt out of the bag. Tom, his assistant, and the rest of us rushed over. Nancy took one of the sides so she and Susanne could show off the work.

And it was some work. The squares of purples, blues, reds, and pinks that each of the women had made separately had come together to form an impressionist garden. My painted borders and Susanne's quilted leaves set it off beautifully. We all stood and stared.

"Why didn't you wait for me?" Bernie said as she came into the shop. She walked over to the quilt and joined the rest of us as we stared at it.

"Here to see the shop?" Eleanor turned toward the door. I looked in the same direction and saw Jesse.

"No, ma'am. I'm here about the other matter."

"No more questions today, son. We're unveiling the quilt," Maggie shouted from the other side of the room.

✂

I turned to the women. "You kept money here," I said. "You kept it in the hole in the wall and in the downstairs office. My friend Amanda said something to me about a secret hiding place, and I guess when I ran into Bernie . . ."

Everyone was looking at me. Only Jesse moved to see where I was looking.

CHAPTER 57

"Yes," Nancy said as casually as possible.

"You said you hadn't sold any of your quilts," I said.

Maggie's head jerked toward Nancy. "That isn't true. I send at least ten of your quilts to my daughter a month. She says they sell . . ."

"You send Nancy's quilts to your daughter?" Eleanor looked toward Maggie.

"Nancy asked me so it wouldn't stir up any gossip at the post office—her sending packages to my daughter. But she asked me not to say anything."

Nancy interrupted. "I didn't want anyone to know. I did sell some of my quilts in New York. And I did keep the money here. If I'd put it in the bank or brought it home, my husband would have found it and gambled it away. That money was for my sons' education."

"It was safer here," I continued. "Until the remodel. Until I suggested tearing down the wall. And you tried to stop it."

"I didn't care about the remodel."

"Yes you did," Carrie started then stopped. She turned to me. "Nancy is just very careful, conservative. That's why she cared about the remodel. She didn't do anything."

"That's not why," I said, so quietly I doubted anyone heard me.

Nancy and I locked eyes. There was a steel reserve in them that came from years of struggle. But after a few seconds it melted away into a soft regret. She blinked. "I didn't mean to hurt you Eleanor," Nancy said as she looked at Eleanor's injured leg. "It's just that you always say leaving money in the shop overnight makes us a target for thieves. I thought if you found out, you might make me take the money somewhere else, and I didn't have anywhere else to take it.

"I know, dear." Eleanor patted Nancy's hand.

"You could have killed her," my voice quivered. "She could have broken her neck on those stairs." Nancy nodded meekly. "And then you killed Marc."

"That's enough," Susanne broke in. "I think we should stop now before anyone says something they'll regret." Natalie reached over for her mother's hand and both women looked down.

"I didn't mean for it to happen," Nancy said as tears rolled down her eyes. "Marc found the money. My money. The money that was paying for my children's education."

"In the wall," Jesse said.

Nancy nodded. "Yes, and in the office downstairs. He took everything and didn't want to give it back to me. He said it was his."

"He didn't have the money from the basement." I took the envelope from my back pocket. "I just found it a minute ago."

Nancy stared at me. "That's not possible. He had almost fifteen thousand dollars. Just about a thousand less than I had in the shop. When I came in he was taking money out of the bank bag I had hidden in the wall. I saw him."

"You came into the shop and saw Marc taking money from the bank bag," Jesse repeated. "And you asked for it back."

"Yes," said Nancy, her eyes darting from one person to another. "The money was still in the bag and he had more money, thousands more. The money from downstairs."

"He won that money gambling on some horse races," Jesse said calmly, with a sadness on the edge of his voice.

"No, he didn't. He stole it from me. He was stealing it from me, and I caught him. I asked him for the money back. I begged him." Nancy was frantic now. "And he laughed. He said I could have the money in the bag but the rest was his. He said he was doing his good deed for the day. Can you imagine?" She turned to a sympathetic quilt club, who were crowding around her in support. Even Barney sat at her side.

"I never liked that boy," Maggie said quietly.

"And then he said he had a lot of work to do, so I should get out of his way. He picked up a hammer and started working with his back to me, ignoring me. I kept begging him, and then he turned around and came at me." She stopped and took a deep breath. "I thought he was going to kill me. I just wanted my money."

"Of course you did," Bernie said.

Jesse moved toward Nancy. "So you stabbed him."

She closed her eyes. "I thought he was going to kill me."

"Nancy." I looked to Jesse, who turned up the sides of his mouth, into what might have been a smile under happier circumstances. "I think you caught Marc putting the money back. I think he knew through his cousin that you were selling quilts in the city, and he knew your husband. Since he wasn't gambling it away, Marc must have figured you were hiding it somewhere. And what better place than in the shop."

"That's why he wanted to do the remodel so badly," Eleanor gasped. "I thought he was changing, I really did."

"I think he was," I said. "I think he found the money in the wall and gambled with it. If he had lost, who knows what would have happened. But he won. And I guess he decided to put your money back."

"But he had almost as much money as I hid here," Nancy protested.

"Most of it was his winnings," I said quietly. I could see Nancy was about to fall apart. "The rest was still safely tucked in the basement. When Bernie mentioned something about keeping her money in different accounts, I don't know, it reminded me of a twenty dollar bill in the office. Money that Eleanor couldn't account for. I thought if you were hiding money it might be safer to hide it in a couple of places."

"We found six thousand dollars hidden inside Eleanor's fireplace," Jesse said.

"You found that?" Nancy looked at me. "It's my money. I put it there. Where is it?"

"I have it," Jesse said. "Where's the rest? Where's the money Marc won?"

Nancy pointed to a box on the floor. It was addressed to her youngest son at college. Jesse opened the box. Inside was a large simple quilt that crinkled when he picked it up. He hesitated a moment and then tore at the seam. With some effort, he'd pulled a block apart and inside was a wad of cash.

"I couldn't risk getting money orders, or someone would have mentioned it to my husband," Nancy said. "He's a good man. He can't help himself. But that money is for my kids."

"Of course it is, and they'll get it too," Susanne said. She wrapped her arm around Nancy.

"Marc was doing the right thing?" Maggie's face was frozen, but tears were rolling down her cheeks.

"He came toward me with a hammer," Nancy said almost to herself.

"Did he have it raised up?" Jesse asked, raising his arm to show her what he meant.

Nancy shook her head. "No, but I thought . . ." Her voice trailed off.

"He had such a terrible reputation," Bernie offered quietly. "Any one of us would have been afraid of him."

But Nancy didn't seem interested in any comforting words. "I'm so sorry. I guess I robbed him. I didn't mean . . ." She grabbed the quilt tighter around her, and then just let it drop to the floor.

"I think," I said softly, wanting not to speak but too caught up to stop. "I think Marc grabbed Grace's quilt thinking he was leaving us a message."

Eleanor looked at me. "What message?"

"I kept telling him that if those quilts got dusty, Nancy would kill him." I stopped, looked down. I didn't mean to use those words. "I just kept telling him that Nancy would be upset if those quilts got dirty. He must have thought they were all her quilts. When he grabbed one, he must have thought . . ."

I was looking at the floor, but out of the corner of my eye I could see Eleanor nodding. Nancy had her face in her hands and everyone else was stunned into silence.

"I guess I can get that quilt back to you pretty soon, Mrs. Cassidy." Jesse's voice was low and it seemed almost as if he would cry.

Eleanor was already crying. "It's not important."

Jesse took Nancy's arm. "I'm going to take you down to the police station now, Mrs. Vanderberg. Someone here should call you a lawyer."

I looked at Jesse. "Isn't it kind of self-defense?"

"Maybe. Just get her a lawyer."

Maggie took Natalie's cell phone and called one of her sons. "He'll do it for free, or he'll regret it," she said as Nancy and Jesse walked out of the shop.

✄

I'd gotten so caught up in following clues that I hadn't thought about where it might lead. I walked out of the shop and stopped Jesse and Nancy.

"I'm sorry," I said to Nancy. Jesse let go of her arm and she gave me a long hug.

"If you can get my quilt bag for me and bring it over to the jail, I'd like to do some hand sewing tonight." She smiled weakly and I nodded.

Jesse and Nancy walked across the street and turned a corner toward the police station. Inside the shop, I could hear the women creating a plan of action to help Nancy. I didn't think they would want me there, so I started to walk to the river.

✂

"It's over with me and Amanda." I saw Ryan walking toward me and I stopped.

"I don't care," I said wearily. I really didn't care, and that saddened me. "What was wrong had nothing to do with you or Amanda."

"Then let's fix it."

I shook my head slowly as if it weighed fifty pounds. "The women here, they have these things they call UFOs. Unfinished projects. Sometimes you start something and in the middle decide it isn't worth finishing. The trick is not to get stubborn about it. If it doesn't work, you have to let it go."

"I don't know what that means," Ryan stammered.

"I do."

I took one last look at the face I had loved for so long, then turned and walked away.

CHAPTER 58

"Unlock the door," Eleanor directed me from her spot at the register.

"It's not seven o'clock yet."

"Are the girls out there?"

I lifted up one of the quilts that blocked the picture window. Outside I could see Maggie, Natalie and Susanne. Bernie was holding a plate and chatting with someone I couldn't see.

"They're out there."

"Then open up the door." I did as I was told, opening the door of the new Someday Quilts for the first time.

"Finally," I heard Maggie say.

Each woman walked into the shop in single file. After they had all entered, Jesse walked through the door. He smiled shyly at me and I smiled back, just as shyly. Then he looked around the room, just as the others were doing. After the initial wows, everyone turned in a complete circle to take in all the changes. Gone were the overstuffed shelves and baskets of quilt tools. There were now three aisles of fabric, arranged by color, that made a sort of rainbow effect. On the back wall books, tools and threads were organized and hung securely.

I led them through the opening into what had once been the run-down diner. Now it had specialty fabrics, an office, a bathroom and classroom with a large rectangular table. On the wall above the table were three quilts—one made by Eleanor, one by Nancy, and the repaired quilt made by Grace, the woman who had taught my grandmother to quilt.

"Just as it should be," Susanne said, almost in a hushed tone.

"This is where you can have your meetings," I said, waiting for the applause.

"But we won't be in a circle," Bernie frowned. "Why can't we meet in the other room like we always did?"

Each woman mumbled something in agreement and then dragged a chair from the classroom into the original quilt shop. After they had arranged the chairs in the same circle as they had in the old shop, everyone sat down. Barney took his place in the middle, going from woman to woman for a pat on the head.

"Change is good," Maggie said sternly. "But tradition is good too."

"Well, you'll have plenty of both with Nell helping to run things." Carrie smiled at me.

Jesse looked at me and I shrugged. "She's signed up for art school over in Peekskill," Eleanor explained.

"Part time," I explained. "I'll help out at the shop the rest of the time."

"Well, it's cause for celebration." Bernie unwrapped a plateful of pecan squares and set them on the counter. "God knows we need a little something to celebrate."

Eleanor looked at Jesse. "We're having the meeting for the Friday Night Quilt Club," she said. "Are you staying?"

"No ma'am," he said. "I'll leave you to it." He grabbed a pecan square and nodded toward me. "Can we talk a minute?"

✂

Outside the shop Jesse stared at his feet. "I'm sorry about, you know . . ."

"Our fight? Me too. I was out of line," I acknowledged. "I just was having so much fun working with you."

He looked into my eyes. They were warm and kind, and a little unsure. They were nice eyes. "I was too," he said. He took a few steps away from me. "If you'd like to get dinner sometime, when you're ready . . ."

"I'd like that." I smiled. "I just can't get into a new relationship until I'm over the things that happened in the last one."

He nodded. "You let me know." Then he turned and walked away and I headed back into the shop.

✂

Inside the ladies were sitting in their circle, with Barney in the middle wagging his tail.

"Are you staying?" Eleanor turned her eyes on me.

"I'm staying."

"Well, then, sit down."

So I sat, pulled out the small squares of fabric I'd painted and started my first quilt.